# Cheating the Hog

## *A Sawmill. A Tragedy.*
## *A Few Gutsy Women.*

A novel

by Rae Ellen Lee

**This book is respectfully dedicated
to all women who work in the trades.**

E-book ISNB:  978-0-9619328-8-6
P-book ISBN:  978-0-9619328-9-3

GREAT BLUE GRAPHICS
Book cover design by Kate Weisel, weiselcreative.com

## Also by Rae Ellen Lee

*I Only Cuss When I'm Sailing* — A memoir
(First published as *If* The Shoe *Fits*)

*My Next Husband Will Be Normal*
*– A St. John Adventure*
Sequel to *I Only Cuss When I'm Sailing*

*The Bluebird House – A Brothel. A Diary. A Murder*
A novel set in Montana

*Powder Monkey Tales* — *A Portrait in Stories*
(As told by Wesley Moore alias Post Hole Augerson)

*A Field Guide to Geezers -*
*An Illustrated Look at a Curious Branch of Hominids*
An affectionate humor book

# ACKNOWLEDGMENTS

Many thanks to the Brush Creek Artist Residency Program near Saratoga, Wyoming, for the lovely writing residency in the spring of 2012. I cavorted with fellow residents on horseback, hiked through the sagebrush, heard sandhill cranes, and worked on *Cheating the Hog*. Bobbie Ryder Johansen and Karl Johansen kindly shared their cottage near Sandpoint, ID, for a couple months. In Bellingham, WA, I'm honored to belong to a fine writing critique group. I'm grateful for the attention and thoughtful suggestions made by Sue Erickson, Nancy Canyon, Carol Austin, and C.J.Prince. Thanks to others who offered valuable help and inspiration. They include Tina Pettito, Rebekah Jane Lee, Pam Beason and Mary Lu Perham. As always, I owe a great deal to my dear friends Sherry Gohr, Kathryn Hamshar, and Penny Bews, of Priest River, Idaho, for their readings of all my manuscripts, and for their love and encouragement. Ornithologist, David Drummond, performed the call of the spotted owl at a reading one night. This was a *hoo, hoo-hoot*.

I'd also like to thank Wayne Ude and Marian Blue for critical feedback early on. Both Carol Oberton and Don George offered astute feedback on the final draft. My beautiful tech-savvy daughter-in-law, Lee Suttorp, saved my bacon many times with her knowledge of Word. Lastly (but in no way leastly), I couldn't have described the unique setting of the sawmill without the background, lifestyle, and technical information provided by Sam Irvine, Tom Moore, and especially Patsy Lee Moore. I do take full credit, however, for any mistakes, technical or otherwise, that you might find in this book.

# FROM LOGS TO LUMBER
## The operation of the sawmill in
### *CHEATING THE HOG*

Logging trucks bring logs directly from the woods to the log yard at the sawmill, where they are stacked by species. Front end loaders carry the logs to a debarker. After the bark is removed, the logs are conveyed (on beds of chains and rollers) to a saw that cuts them to the desired length. Next the scragg saw cuts the sides off the logs leaving a square, bark-free log called a *cant*. At a station immediately after the scragg, workers at the tail saw, manually remove the log edgings or odd pieces of wood, and send them down a hole into the basement. They position the cants for the edger. The edger has multiple blades that cut the cants into rough green studs of 2 x 4 or 2 x 6 (inches), or sometimes into railroad ties. Workers at the edger separate the lumber and pick out edgings or cull lumber before the studs are conveyed to the automatic stackers. There, workers place thin strips of lumber called stickers between the wood as it is stacked into units and banded. Fork lift drivers move the units of lumber to the dry kiln to be dried to the desired moisture content.

After the lumber is dried, the units are set aside in the dry sheds until they're delivered by forklift to the planer (in a building that is separate from the mill). There the lumber is surfaced smooth on four sides. At the cull chain, lumber with serious defects or warping is pulled and placed on carts to be sold as farmer lumber, for sheds, etc. Workers at a grading table sort the remaining lumber for quality, and stamp the end of each stud for size and grade. The lumber then travels through the trim saws and on to the automatic stackers, where stickers are again placed between rows of studs before they are re-banded into units and moved by forklift to a storage area. From there, trucks arrive and haul the lumber to market.

The sawmill in Hatfield, WA, where Echo Spangler worked has three shifts a day in both the mill building and the planer. Day shift operates from 5:30 a.m. to 2:30 p.m. and swing shift operates from 3:30 to 11:30 p.m. Graveyard shift is from 8:30 p.m. to 4:30 a.m. The mill and planer only operate on day shift and swing. On graveyard, there is sometimes a cleanup person, a boiler room attendant or two, a person doing security checks, and a millwright, if a piece of equipment needs to be repaired.

# CHAPTER 1

All I wanted was a job, and now I'm gonna die. A freaky, huffing sasquatch with a pony tail is charging toward me and he's gripping a weapon. Looks like a shovel. It's clear he's on a rampage, and I'm his next victim. Frantic, I crank my car window and raise my arm to shield my face, expecting broken glass. But the creature jerks up my car's hood, yells, "God *damn*, lady!" and heaves a forceful shovel of snow onto the engine of my '68 Ford Galaxie, Rooster. My car shakes his faded red feathers, backfires, and gasps one last breath.

I crank my window back down. Over the hiss of cold snow on hot engine I holler, "What the hell you doin' to my car?"

"Christ, didn't ya see the flames?" he snarls, and spits on the ground. "I'm surprised you got here in this piece of junk."

"Now lookie here, mister. I got some tappets out of whack, the carburetor needs an overhaul, and the fan belt's loose, but we ain't *never* caught fire before."

He rests on his shovel handle, spits again, and snarls, "Don't tell me you're the new recruit?" He tosses the shovel over toward a rusty metal shed next to a hand-lettered sign that says, Old Plantation Tree Farm, and leans into my window way too close. "The one with no previous experience on a Christmas tree farm?"

I pull away from his dog-shit breath. "That's right. I'm Echo. You Craig?"

He scratches his straggly beard, sighs like a radiator, and stands to stare at the rows of trees marching off in every direction.

"Mind advancing me some gas from that pump over there?"

He looks at me, finally. "Yeah, I'm Craig. Just back your Caddy up to the pump. That's if it'll start." Moving around to the front of my car, he slaps a fender like it's the rump of a horse. Arthritic hinges shriek as he slams down the hood.

This is gonna take a miracle. Before turning the key in the ignition I whisper, "Rooster, *please*. If you'll start one more time I'll buy you a new set of retreads. And this time I mean it." The old boy screams to life with his usual ticking sound, like a bomb about to go off. I pat the dash and back up toward the gas pump. "What do you say to *that*, Roost? That knuckle-dragger hippie thinks you're a Caddy."

"Appreciate it," I tell Craig, leaning out my window, watching to make sure he's putting gas, not diesel, in my car. "Just deduct it from my first paycheck. Hell, charge me some interest, if you want to."

"Oh, that's okay," he says, removing his filthy once-yellow work gloves to light a cigarette next to the NO SMOKING sign. "Before the season's up I'm gonna be in your pants. You owe me for more than gas. I probably saved your life, putting out that fire."

"Think so, huh?" I remember what Mom said, more than once—*Men, they fool you by walking upright.* Then, too, I am pushing fifty. Haven't been with a man for a while, so I've probably got my own set of mechanical issues. Take Liquid Wrench to get into *my* pants.

"Know so," he says, exhaling slow and easy from his cigarette. He lifts the nozzle from my gas tank and remembers to screw the cap back on. Leaning into my window again he says, "You'll be starting out as a shaker with Yates over there." He stands, points his cigarette in the direction of a woman with long dishwater blond hair climbing up onto a scratched and dented John Deere tractor. "She'll teach you all you need to know. Yates," he yells. "Here's your new helper."

The woman, sitting tall in the saddle of the tractor now, looks at me and slumps. She hollers, "Well, haul your ass on over here and let's get going."

"Park the Caddy next to that truck over there," Craig says.

I park old Rooster and head toward the tractor. Yates looks like another holdover from the hippie generation—out of style everywhere but up here in this sorry north woods corner of Washington. Or maybe I'm jealous of her long, flowing tresses. My own brown hair is naturally curly and from a distance it looks like the nest of a large, roosting shore bird. One of the meaner boys in high school said, "Anyone ever tell you that you have underwear hair?" Someone else once said, "You have trailer park hair," and I said, "They're called mobile homes."

I climb aboard the tractor, brush snow off the fender, and sink down on the cold green metal. *This is the first day of the rest of my life.*

"Hang on," she yells, and drives the tractor between two rows of trees. "Scotch pines," she hollers over the roar of the engine.

"I know," I yell back. "I'm from a long line of timber beasts. We know our trees." I notice that in addition to her long hair she's wearing dangly earrings that look like fishing lures. Seems like a person with any brains around machinery would hide all that hair up under their hat and ditch the earrings. Probably one of them Californians, migrated here on a lark.

We stop not far from where we started, next to a decrepit piece of equipment on wheels. Looks like the base of a blender on steroids. Yates climbs down off the tractor. "Meet your new friend, the shaker."

The thing sits in a clearing the size of the dance floor at The Tool Shed back in Hatfield. Chain saws whine off in the distance. She tells me, "Ten of us work more or less together, counting Craig. The crew out there with the chainsaws cuts the trees off at the ground and saws the bottom branches off so people can stick them in tree holders. Then they measure and tag the trees for height. That is when they aren't drinking beer. Shaking the trees is a one-person job, but we work in pairs around equipment. Owner requires it. Something about insurance."

Yates starts the shaker by pulling a throttle, as if it's an outboard motor, and it roars to life. I've had some noisy temp jobs so I always carry ear plugs, and now I poke them in my ears.

A guy delivers cut trees to us on a flatbed trailer, pulled by a tractor in somewhat better condition than ours. When he pulls up, I have to jump back to keep my feet out from under the tires. Yates yells, "Mickey, meet Echo." He kills the engine, climbs down to meet me, and smiles a goofy grin while he pumps my hand.

We help Mickey unload the trees, and he leaves for more. Yates and I take turns holding each tree on the shaker, which shakes any old, dead needles from the tree onto us and the ground. Every now and then an empty beer can bounces off one of us. We can't talk because of all the noise, but when she shuts off the shaker I say, "This place is great. Cans of beer grow on trees here."

No reply. Just a smirk.

Yates might be forty. Her face looks weathered, either from working outdoors or from a hard life or both. She's tall and skinny and her eyes are green, about the same color as the Scotch pines. My eyes are hazel, like the color of Hat River during spring runoff. Yates and I are the same height, but I have big bones and I like to think of myself as well-rounded. Her voice is deep and a little hoarse, and she speaks right up. No need to strain yourself to hear what she says, even while wearing ear plugs.

At the end of the day we hook the shaker up to the tractor and drive to the metal shed to park it. As we head to our cars. Yates nudges me with her elbow and points at Craig. "He's the best hunk of man you could ever get your hands on. You should give him a try."

"No thanks." No need to mention that we born-again virgins do have our standards. I mean, sex with a Neanderthal? Yates must be hard up.

The next day while waiting for a load of trees to shake, she tells me, "My first name is LuAnn, but years ago someone called me LuLu, as in *Boy, that one sure is a lulu*. From then on I went by my last name."

"Lulu," I say. "Now there's a name with personality. When I asked Mom why she named me Echo, I mean, it *is* different for this neck of the woods, she said, 'I liked the sound of it, and how echoes always come back to you.' Now I live with her and she jokes that maybe she should have named me something else." What I don't tell

Yates or anyone else is that my name reminds me of echoes in a canyon, or maybe a country & western song
written just for me. Gives me hope that I'm not so ordinary after all.

"I like your name," Yates says. "It's so odd it's almost
sophisticated, like a porn star's name."

"Yeah, thanks," I say, thinking *she* should talk with a
name like Lulu. "Yeah, I'm sure when people look at me
they wonder how many X-rated movies I've been in."

"Hey, I meant it as a compliment."

"I know. When I see kids I went to school with, they
like to say 'Hello, Echo . . . Echo . . . Echo . . .?'"

She smiles. "That reminds me of the best job I ever
had. Remember that spotted owl business over in Oregon
a few years back?"

"Oh, yeah," I say, wondering how my name relates to
owls, but what the hell.

"Well, someone thought spotted owls were going ex-
tinct, so every damn national forest had to inventory the
woods to see if they had any."

"I remember. We were all afraid they'd turn up in our
little corner of the world. You've seen the bumper sticker,
SAVE A TREE, WIPE YOUR ASS WITH A SPOTTED
OWL?"

She smirks again, something she's good at. "I helped
with the inventory and loved it," she says. "A wildlife bi-
ologist taught us to call for spotted owls. And talk about
an echo. She told us if there was one out there, it couldn't
help but answer the call." Yates takes a deep breath and
hollers, *"Hoo, hoo-hoo, hoo-ah . . . yeeyowuhhh. . hoo,
hoo-hoo, hoo-ah yee-owuhhh!*

The hairs rise up on my neck. She takes another deep breath and repeats the otherworldly call for the spotted owl. Sounds a little like opera. And what do you know? Here comes our next load of trees to shake.

"Mickey!" Yates yells. He climbs down off the tractor, unaware that the sky has just split apart thanks to Yates' owl calls.

We unload the trees and Mickey leaves to get more. Yates and I take turns holding the trees on the shaker, and then flip the switch on the noisy machine to the OFF position. In the quiet, we smoke while we wait for more trees, stomping our feet to keep from getting frostbite. We make small talk. To make a point about what she's saying, she likes to swing her elbow against my arm.

"You ever think about a career?" she asks. "I mean at your age and all? Something besides these temporary shit jobs?" She whomps me with her elbow. I brace myself so I don't tip over.

"I've tried about everything," I sigh. 'Course, it would be my luck to have a sister who's perfect. Delight—yeah, that's really her name—sewed at the ski jacket factory for years. I lasted there about a month. On my first day it took me all day to sew in one zipper. One day, one zipper, while Delight sat at her sewing machine and sewed forty zippers in forty coats that day. She didn't talk and she didn't smile. She broke records. The boss had the nerve to say to me, 'We thought you'd be more like *her*.'"

"So, what's she doing now, this person named Delight?"

"Calls herself a Life Coach. She actually tells people, including me, how to live a better life." I mimic Delight. *You should quit cussing, you should quit drinking, you should quit smoking. I can help you.* "But you see those are all my favorite things. So I tell her I'll think about it. 'Course, she doesn't even know half my faults. And in a couple weeks Mom and I are going to her house for Thanksgiving. We'll cook a wild turkey Mom shot, and Delight will spout lots of duckie feel-good quotations instead of saying grace."

Yates is either a good listener or she's tuned into the spotted-owl channel, so I keep talking. "Delight spent time in Spokane getting trained. Says she's good at it, too, that her client list is growing. Now she wants to study hypnotherapy."

Yates throws her cigarette butt on the ground and grinds it into the frost with her boot, all the while shaking her head. "I have heard it all now."

"Fat chance," I say. "Did I tell you we're identical twins and that she stole my boyfriend thirty years ago and then married him? She never even loved him. But I always did. Then he went and got himself killed in a logging truck accident a couple years ago. Me and Delight are not what you'd call close."

Mickey roars up with a load of trees, and we get back to work.

Once I get cold, I'm cold all winter. On Wednesday morning the temperature is ten degrees. While Yates drives the tractor pulling the shaker out into the sea of trees, I cuddle up to the warm exhaust pipe. When we move the shaker to a different location, I drive the tractor, teeth chattering, at top speed—five miles per—into the sub-zero wind. In the afternoon the temperature goes up twenty degrees and it starts to snow. I'm not so cold now, but when I'm surrounded by snowflakes like this I can't stop thinking about the logging truck accident. The next time I drive the tractor, through the falling snow, I remember this: after news reached town about a logging truck going off the grade, a few regulars at The Log Drive Café claimed they'd heard the truck slide, and then the impact when the truck dropped to the base of the giant white pine tree. The fools said they'd stopped talking to listen for what might come next. Others said there's no way in hell those old geezers could have heard anything, so many miles away. Two years later here I am, worried that for the rest of my life I'll relive the event every damn time it snows, and wonder again and again exactly when, during his last moments, the man I loved let go of his life. To stop thinking about it anymore, I fix my thoughts on the meal Mom will have waiting, the hot bath I'll take, and the game of cribbage we'll play before I turn in early. That's if Rooster will start and we can actually make it the twenty-five miles home.

On Thursday during the lunch break, Yates heads for her truck and yells to me, "Hop in."

The country store where we go is heated by a big honkin' wood stove. We hang out near the warmth for a few minutes, and take our time choosing cheap twelve-packs of beer.

"I'm buying mine with money from recycling the beer cans we shook out of the trees," Yates says. "I'll share."

"Yeah, well, I'm spending every penny I have," I brag. "I'll share, too."

Back at the tree farm Craig builds a pile of wooden pallets a healthy distance from the gas pump, sloshes gasoline on the heap, and tosses a match on top. I hand everyone, including Craig, a beer. Good thing we get paid before we leave for the weekend.

Thanks to the beer and the heat from the fire, we're all having a good time, laughing at nothing much. The four guys who cut, trim and tag the trees before we shake them share the rest of their beer, too, and the party is on. Here we are, a scene out of a goddamn Norman Rockwell painting. By now, of course, I know how so many empty beer cans got into the Christmas trees. Where else can we hide the evidence from the owner of the tree farm?

We end the day in one guy's mobile home near Filmore. I use his phone to call Mom and tell her I won't be home, and then slouch in a tattered overstuffed chair with dirty arm rests. I smoke, sip beer, and watch the action all around me. The others are telling stories, most of them not very funny, and everyone's laughing so hard they snort. I'm warm, I'm mellow, and I'm safe here in a corner of the living room, wrapped in the arms of this beer-stained overstuffed chair. Yates is sitting on Craig's knee at the kitchen table with three other guys in a cloud of marijuana smoke. She looks over at me and gets up, a beer in one hand, a cigarette in the other.

"I'm beginning to think you don't like men," she says, taking a seat on the arm of the chair.

"They're okay, just not all created equal."

"Amen," she says. "You ever married?"

"Yeah, once. When Delight stole the man I wanted, I married a guy from out of town and *then* got to know him. Turned out he wanted a mother, so after a couple of weeks I had to divorce him. At least now I can say, 'Yeah, I was married once.' It's like having the mumps. I was immune after that. What about you?"

"Yeah, I was married once, too. He left me a while back."

"Yates, come on back here," Craig yells. "You gotta hear this one." Yates gets up.

"Loan me a cigarette?" I say.

She tosses me a half-empty pack and returns to Craig's lap.

Sometime after midnight I'm snoozing in my chair when Craig comes over and says to me, "I think I love you, Echo."

"Hah! I don't think so," I snort. "You don't even know me."

"Well, I let you have your party, now it's payback time."

"Don't think so," I repeat, wondering what the hell he's talking about. My party? But to be on the safe side, I do stay awake most of the night guarding my pants.

Today I'm working at quarter speed, if that, after the party last night. No one else is breaking any records, either, and then, right in the middle of the frigid afternoon, Craig checks up on us and Yates stroll off into the woods with him. Here I am freezing my ass off, hung over, and shaking a load of trees all by myself while they're getting it on in next year's Christmas trees. To tell you the truth, I feel abandoned.

At quitting time we get our paychecks. It's a slow, slippery drive home, but me and Rooster finally make it. All weekend long I stay close to the stove, leaving it now and then to add wood to the stove, help around the house, eat, sleep, and play cribbage with Mom.

On Monday morning I make it down the road and onto the highway in the new snow, following my neighbor's tire tracks. Out on the highway Rooster slides around the first bend, so I slow to a crawl. The roads are slicker than snot. It'll take a couple hours to get to the tree farm, and Craig will dock my pay for being late. To make the trip even more fun, the heater is on the fritz and I could swear hypothermia is setting in. Or maybe rigor mortis. But I keep going. Someone's gotta help Yates shake the Christmas trees. I barely touch the gas pedal, moving forward no faster than if I was in a parade. Off to the right is Eagle Creek Lumber Company, all lit up in the falling snow. Good thing Weldon has four-wheel-drive. I heard him drive down the road while I was eating breakfast. He's probably already at work.

Suddenly a bridge abutment flies past within inches of my window. Snowflakes are flying sideways. Crap, I'm going in circles! When I skid to a stop, I'm facing the wrong direction. At least I'm off the road enough not to get hit. I hold my breath. My heart bounces around in my chest. My breath escapes in a gust of steam, and I can't stop shivering, from the cold and the fear. I grope in my coat pocket for a cigarette, find my lighter, and light up. Smoke drifts around me. The wipers scrape one way, then the other, across my cracked windshield, back and forth, back and forth. Fat, fluffy snowflakes drop onto the hood of my car, melt and trickle down into the crack of the hood. By the time I crawl on the icy roads the last five miles to work, I'll be over an hour late. Then, too, on my paycheck Craig had deducted the cost of the gas the first morning, which I expected, but he also cheated me out of four hours' pay. If you ask me, that's pretty steep interest on a tank of gas.

I sit in the dark, cold car staring at the snow falling in the beam of my headlights, feeling trapped in a snow globe of sadness. It's all so hopeless. I bite my lip. I will not bawl or lose control. Watching the windshield wipers flop back and forth, back and forth, I make a decision. *Hell with it. I'm not going to shake beer cans out of trees today, or ever again.* I gun the engine and crank the wheel in the direction of the skid. Rooster's tail feathers swing around, and as his bald tires search for traction we bounce off one snow bank, and another, and then we head for home.

## CHAPTER 2

Snow will be an icy fact of life for the next six months. It's falling now, outside the window of the unemployment office where I stand waiting, watching. Snow makes the world look all soft and clean and pretty. So it's a crying shame that every damn time it snows I can't stop the accident from playing out in my head. It's sort of like gravity. You drop something, it's gonna fall.

I mentally brace myself for the picture in my head of his loaded logging truck skidding sideways through big, fluffy snowflakes, skidding down and down and down that steep mountain grade. I watch Dwayne stomp the brake pedal over and over, cussing the early season snowstorm. He begs and makes deals with God. He cranks the steering wheel to pull the truck away from the edge, and he keeps doing it even after the truck flings itself into the silence and soars above a clear-cut, wheels spinning. The muscles in his arms bulge as he turns the wheel one way and then the other. His eyes are as big as door knobs, staring straight ahead, looking for an opening, and then his truck takes aim on the single giant white pine still standing on the mountainside.

Parts of the scene are filled in by details the newspaper reporter made up from what he heard around town: *An axle caught on a branch as thick as a lumberjack's waist and, for just a second, the truck hung there like an ornament. The branch snapped and the truck, the driver, and the logs dropped straight down onto the steep slope and then tumbled all the way down the mountainside to the headwaters of Hat River.* I always add: *ass over teakettle, spraying logs all over hell.* In my imagined avalanche of snow, splintered wood, and truck cab I search the shattered windshield for a sign of the man I love, and every time I don't see him I panic, knowing I will never see him again.

"Echo, you're here so soon." Leland startles me back to reality.

"Nice to see you again, too, Leland." Still stunned from my trip down memory lane, I follow him in slow motion to his desk, located in a maze of cubicles.

Leland's been my caseworker at the unemployment office for years. He's plump and soft, with clean finger-nails—the opposite of the man I lost. Leland probably doesn't even heat his house with wood. We go back a long way. He knows I remember that time in third grade when he wet his pants.

"A mistake on your paycheck is no reason to quit," Leland says. "I can try to get that fixed."

I shake my head. No need to tell him I'm still suffering freezer burn from my most recent brush with employment, if you can call shaking Christmas trees a job. And I won't bother telling him that driving twenty-five miles each way with bald tires on icy roads to earn minimum wage won't steer me out of the black hole I dug for myself trying to gamble away my grief. Sometimes the less said the better. "If I'm sitting here, Leland, you know I won't be going back to the Christmas tree farm. I need something better."

He studies me. "You have a nice smile."

"You flirting with me, Leland?"

The corners of his mouth twitch upward. The start of a smile? "There is a temporary job, Echo." A pink hand holds his place in the stack of job descriptions available to someone like me. "I think you'd be good at it."

I wait him out.

"How would you like to be the Salvation Army bell ringer at the mall?"

"Jesus, Leland. Ain't that a job you give homeless people?"

"The county's poor, Echo, you know it yourself. But the one thing we don't have is homeless people. They'd freeze to death out there. In fact, the money collected helps keep people *in* their homes. You'd be doing something good for mankind."

We stare at each other. It don't take a mental giant to weigh my options. "Sure," I say. "I'll do it."

This new job's not exactly a get-rich-quick scheme, either, but at least I can feel good about doing it. Might tide me over until the New Year. After that we'll be in 1999, the big millennium eve year. Mom's convinced the world's coming to an end, which she probably read in *The National Enquirer*. What if it's true? Poof! There goes my gambling debt.

I'm wearing a red Salvation Army windbreaker over two wool sweaters on top, flannel-lined blue jeans on the bottom, and thick wool socks in my Sorel pack boots. At an outside entrance to Hatfield's mall, I ring the little bell. I visit with anyone who risks stopping. Some people won't even make eye contact because they don't want to put money in the pot. Others I haven't seen in a long time stop to chat and reach into their pockets for change. I find myself using social skills I didn't know I had. If I can't remember an old guy's name, even though his face is familiar and he was probably a friend of Dad's, I just say, "How're you doing, you old coot?" I listen to what they say. A lot of people are lonely. If someone's had a bad year I give 'em a hug. It's not so much that my social life is picking up; it's that I now *have* one.

My nephew, Justin, stops by one afternoon and stuffs a few dollars into the red pot. "Auntie, I see you found your career niche."

"Yeah, the Santa Claus job was taken."

He stands close by a few minutes. I hand him the bell to ring, which he does with confidence and heart. Justin could have done or been anything, even gone to college, but instead he stayed in Hatfield. He's one of the lucky ones, though, with a steady job at the sawmill.

"How's your mother?" I ask. I've always been grateful Justin turned out to be such a fine young man, in spite of Delight. What *if* Dwayne had married me instead of her? Since Delight and I are twins, would *our* son have looked like Justin? As it is, I love searching his face for similarities to his father. He doesn't know I do this. He doesn't know about me and his father.

"She's baking cookies," he says, handing me back the bell. "I'm here to buy vanilla at the IGA, so I gotta get going."

"Bye, Sweetie." He walks away, so tall and strong and good-natured. So much like Dwayne.

Hatfielders call the place a mall, but really it's only a few odd stores under one roof: Ben Franklin, IGA, a pet shop, and probably the smallest K-Mart in the world. There's also a home decor shop with log furniture,

wreaths of peacock feathers, silk flowers, and candles
that stink real good. This shop's main customers are the
out-of-staters who bought up farms and ranches along
the river. All these stores open up to a common area, just
like the real malls in Spokane.

On a good day I take in a lot of money. One evening
the red pot is so full that bills stick out of the slot. I poke
'em down inside. A man comes over and says to me,
"Why don't you just take some of that money?"

"Why would I do that?"

"You don't need money?"

"Well, sure, but I like to earn it. I lost my job and I'm
lucky enough now to work for a good cause." Okay, so I
quit my job after a week and my feet are still cold, but
this is different. I get paid minimum wage for an eight-
hour day, but if people keep putting money in the pot I
like to stay an extra hour or two.

December is especially cold this year, so I stand just
inside the main entrance where the discount stores are
located. It's warmer, and it's where I collect the most
money. Then, too, when times are slow there's the parrot,
sitting in a cage on a table near the pet shop. He's lime
green, and his head is yellow.

One day I waltz into the pet shop, careful to keep an
eye on my red bucket, hanging from its tripod. I introduce myself to the owner, a woman even older than I am
named Betty. She's slender, and today she's wearing a
tweed pantsuit. Her bottle blond hair is done up in a
twist. "What's the parrot's name?"

"Moose."

"Strange name for a parrot, ain't it?" Smile, I tell myself. It's what Delight says to do when I ask a question. That way I won't sound pushy.

"He's an Amazon. His name is spelled M-o-u-s-s-e, like the dessert, not the animal. I named him that to celebrate the lemony color of his head."

"Where are you *from*?" I ask.

"New York. We moved here because my husband likes to hunt and fish."

"Oh." This worries me. Too many hunters already, and more and more accidents. Just the other day a hunter from out of state shot another hunter he thought was a bear.

"He's happy here," she says. "He got his first elk this year."

"That's good," I say. "If you need some recipes, I can get a few from my mom."

"Oh, we don't eat the meat." She says it like the meat would taste bad, as she sprinkles food into a fish tank. "We donated it to the food bank."

"Oh," I say. "Well, nice meeting you. Guess I'll get back over to my pot. See if I can get someone to feed *it*."

The walls inside the mall are decorated with murals of Santa, his sleigh, and eight reindeer. Foot traffic flows around either side of the big Christmas tree in the middle of the hallway, surrounded by piles of empty boxes wrapped in green and red paper. It's downright festive.

Later in the day, a little boy walks past with his mother, crying *wahhhh, wahhhh*. The parrot screeches *wahhhh, wahhhh*, and the little boy shuts up.

I stroll over to the parrot to get acquainted, then can't think what to say except, "Moussie want a cracker?"

"Shut the fuck up!" the parrot growls in a low mono-tone voice, his head down, his beady black eyes glaring at me.

"Same to you, you little shit. If I could get a hold of your lime jello neck I'd choke you. It's Christmas, for chrissake. Why can't you be nice?" I make a bee line for my red pot, where I'll be safe from the parrot, but I trip on one of the boxes near the Christmas tree. I pick myself up off the floor and walk the rest of the way with my head held high.

Tinkle, tinkle, tinkle. "Hi, how're you doing?" I do my job and smile, even though the parrot threw cold water all over my good mood. When someone is especially nice, I speak up to be heard over the bell, "If you know anyone who needs food, tell 'em they're giving away elk meat at the food bank." If someone has little kids, I warn 'em, "Don't get too close to the parrot. He bites."

A few days later I try again to make friends with the parrot. First I visit with Betty in the pet shop. "Parrots make excellent pets," she tells me. "They live longer than we do, which means they don't die on you and break your heart, the way cats and dogs do."

Back outside the shop entrance, I approach the parrot slowly, so as not to seem threatening. "You really are a handsome bird," I say. "I don't care what anyone says."

He lowers his head and ducks it back and forth while lifting his little parrot feet, first one then the other. Suddenly he freezes, stares into my eyes, and in his evil, low monotone repeats exactly what he said yesterday.

"You know, for a parrot you sure have a piss-poor vo-cabulary," I say, glaring at him.

He squawks like a vulture on a road kill.

I don't cover my ears. Don't want to give him any satisfaction for being nasty. Inside the pet shop, Betty is arranging boxes on a shelf. I toy with the idea of blowing the whistle on the parrot, but decide to let it go, for now.

After that little event, I ring my bell with less enthusiasm. Betty must think I'm tired, because she brings me a folding chair, says I can use it any time. All I have to do is return it to her shop before I leave for the day.

My gig as a bell ringer was going so well, but being verbally abused by an X-rated parrot reminds me of something I've known all along: I won't be allowed to be comfortable and happy. For almost fifty damn years, I've lived life on the skinny branches, always close to falling off. And I'm still working at crappy odd jobs, earning minimum wage. Goddamn parrot.

Dad always said, "It's easier to push a pencil than a broomstick." Even though he only finished the eighth grade, he meant that me and Delight would be real smart to get an education, that life would be easier if we did. But we weren't brave enough to leave. Hell, look at all those immigrants who made it to America. They had what it took to move to a better place. But then we do have that river. Most everyone around seems attached to it, which is just plain strange, when you think about it.

Up until Dwayne's accident, Delight liked to say, *Echo, there are no accidents.* Of course, she held a sizeable life insurance policy on him. Yeah, Delight and Dwayne. I'm sure no one would understand the chain of events that allowed our relationship to continue in secret. After the funeral Delight even confessed that she didn't love him, said it was a relief when he got himself killed, said she'd no longer have to wonder where he was at night. As usual, I suffered her meanness in silence. But then, I knew exactly where he'd been.

"Yates!" I yell when she comes stomping through the entrance to the mall.

"Echo!" She slaps my shoulder with her wool hat. "Missed you at the tree farm after you quit."

"I was going to call." I remember to ring my little bell and nod to people walking past. "What're you up to?"

"The tree farm hired me to sell Christmas trees here. We're set up in the parking lot outside."

"I'll come see you. We'll catch up."

"Glad you're here, girlfriend," she says, nudging me with her elbow.

"You'll want to go over and say hello to the parrot before you leave. His name's Mousse, that's M-o-u-s-s-e, and he has a pissy attitude. Maybe you can cheer him up."

Yates glances in the direction of the pet shop and sets off to meet the parrot.

Tinkle, tinkle, tinkle. "Hi, how're you doing?" I smile. I nod. I do my job. When I look over at Yates, her head is inches away from the parrot's cage, and they're glaring at each other. I don't think Yates liked what he said to her, and I can't hear what's being said now. But suddenly the parrot straightens up and looks surprised. And afraid. He lifts one foot and then the other, like he's trying to escape. Yates maintains her position.

Tinkle, tinkle, tinkle. Coins drop into my red bucket. "Thank you. Have a good day."

Yates struts past me toward the door. "See you later, Echo . . . Echo . . . Echo . . ."

My days at the mall go better, now that Yates is around to smoke with once in a while. And the parrot never insults me or anyone else again, far as I can tell. I don't know what Yates said or did to the parrot, but I'm telling you, I never, ever, want to get on her bad side. Once in a while the parrot tries to engage me in conversation. When there's no one around I hear him say to my back, "Hi, how're you doing today?" But I never turn around to look at him.

A few days before Christmas the Salvation Army is so happy with my work, they call The Hatfield Weekly News, and send out a reporter to interview me on the job. He takes my picture standing next to the red pot, me smiling, ringing the little bell, my hair doing its imitation of an osprey nest. On Christmas Eve a feature story, with my picture, appears on the front page.

*ECHO SPANGLER RINGS FOR SALVATION ARMY*
*Christmas shoppers entering Hatfield Mall this year were greeted by the timeless tinkling of a Salvation Army bell and the smiling face of Echo Spangler.*

*"She brought in more money than any other bell ringer in the history of the county," said regional Salvation Army coordinator, Syd Norton. "And there's a good reason. She's friendly, outgoing and takes the time to chat with people. Too, she's extremely dedicated to the Salvation Army and its good works."*

*"It was very rewarding," Spangler said. "It's amazing to find out how many people the Salvation Army has helped. Men from the wars, including my father, often talked about how the Army was right in the front lines helping out."*

*Spangler was born in Hatfield, one of two daughters of Gus and Mabel Spangler. She now lives with her mother, Mabel, a few miles west of Hatfield. Her sister, Delight, and nephew, Justin, live nearby.*

*Like most natives to the area, Spangler hunts and fishes. Her love for family, the area, and her belief in the Salvation Army programs made her a delightful reason to pause this year at the red bucket. She was a bright and friendly reminder of the meaning of Christmas.*

I wish Dad could see it. He loved the newspaper, even though he called it The Weekly Blabber, and when he reached for the newspaper he always said, "Guess it's time to read the front word." Well, now *I'm* the front word.

# CHAPTER 3

Mom and I've been playing too much cribbage. I pause to rearrange my cards, hoping for a miracle to gain a few points on the board, and say, "Now that it's January, guess I'll go over to the unemployment office, see Leland about another job."

"Your deal," Mom says.

I haven't been focusing on my cards. She'll win this game, too. We play a hand or two almost every evening, either before dinner or after, sometimes both, just like her and Dad did. I prefer poker, but cribbage is important to her, a ritual of some kind.

"You could write a book about the odd jobs you've had, that's for sure," Mom says. "But be a little particular this time. It's not like we'll starve. I can shoot another deer off the back porch, and we do have all those canned cherries."

There are shelves of canned cherries in her bedroom, and boxes of canned cherries stacked on the floor of the pump house that Dad insulated so she could store canned goods there. Must be that Great Depression upbringing I've heard so much about. "Why so many jars, Mom?"

"Those cherries were free. Couldn't let 'em rot."

"Let's buy a hundred-pound sack of spuds to go with the venison and cherries, then we'll be eating high on the food chain."

The dining room table where we sit butts up against the window sill. The window is large, by mobile home standards, and looks out into the side yard. There's snow on the ground, snow stacked up high on the branches of the ponderosa pine tree at the edge of the field, and more snow falling. If I concentrate on my cards and keep Mom talking, I can avoid the snowflakes and the story in my head that goes with 'em.

While some people keep their TV on low for background noise, Mom has the police scanner sitting nearby on the end of the kitchen table near the window. I usually tune it out. Now Mom reaches over and turns it up. "It's a 10-16," she says. Domestic disturbance somewhere." She turns an ear to the scanner and listens. "Over on Alder Street. Wonder who it is."

Mom will be seventy-eight in the spring. After Dad's funeral, I moved in and it's our third Christmas together. We share expenses, I try to be good company, and I let her believe she's the one taking care of *me*. When she gets grumpy, I have Tummy Dog, our overweight tiger cat who tangled with a coyote once and now has an eating disorder. He's usually hugging his food dish, even when it's empty. Tums is so fat you could bowl with him. Vet calls it emotional eating. Every night when the coyotes yip and howl out in the field, Tummy hugs his food dish tighter and stares in their direction.

"Remember that summer about ten years ago, when Justin and I picked apples near Yakima?"

Mom glares at me. "We thought you two'd been kidnapped. You didn't call, not even once. Had to send Delight down there to round you up."

"I know, I know. And when we got home, Dad had just ripped up his arm with the chain saw. You were at the grocery store and he came driving his truck down the hill from June and Weldon's. June had wrapped his arm the best she could. He seemed almost proud, telling us how the chain saw had kicked back into his forearm, right between two veins."

Mom shakes her head. "That man. There I was putting away the groceries, when he unwrapped the bandages to show me how his arm was all tore up."

"At least Dad let me take him to the clinic," I say. "Then, when the doctor on duty shot Novocain into his arm and asked him if it hurt Dad said, 'Aw, I can't complain.' When the doctor left the room for a minute, Dad said, 'That dumb bastard. Of course it hurt.'"

Mom and I smile and shake our heads. Talking about Dad keeps him with us. Someday maybe I'll get used to the big hole left in my life when he died. A year later, Dwayne got himself killed. Those two losses about buried me in grief.

Dad's accident with the chainsaw was the main reason I took nurse's aide training. I'd be able to take care of Mom and Dad as they got older. Since my sorry work history is a source of amusement for us, I relive my first job after becoming a nurse's aide. "Yeah, the outdoor jobs are too cold in the winter. But those hard-bitten old heifers at the rest home about drove me crazy. Had to leave. The residents were nice, though. Even the ones who painted brown pictures on the wall. Hah! If they ever recovered and found out what they'd done, they'd probably want to commit suicide."

"Promise me this," Mom says, looking up from her cards, giving me her I-really-mean-this look. "If I ever do that, you just take me out back and shoot me."

"Okay, Mom. I promise." She knows I'd never in a million years do such a thing.

Mom lays down a five of clubs and says, "Fifteen-two plus three makes eight." She cackles. After all, there's not much drama on a winter night, unless you count the yipping and howling of coyotes. When Dad was sick toward the end, they came in close to the house. Both Dad and Tummy would sit staring in the direction of the coyotes. One night Dad looked at me with resignation and said, "One of these nights, they're gonna come right in the goddamn house after me." I grabbed one of his rifles and a fist full of shells, ran out of the house, and shot up the sky while screaming every cuss word I knew. The coyotes left for a while and then came slinking back, even closer.

Years ago Mom and I called a cease-fire about politics, her being a fan of Rush Limbaugh and all, and believing that Clinton should be impeached, if not shot, because of the affair with Monica. And she's a good shot, too. Says it's a good thing *she's* not in D.C., she'd clean the place up. Since there's no talking sense into her, I start in on another safe topic, the weather. "Think it'll ever quit snowing?"

"I'll never forget the winter your dad went to a funeral in town," Mom says. "Some guy I didn't know, so I stayed home. It'd been snowing just like this. He was all dolled up, didn't even wear his long johns. During the funeral service it stopped snowing and the temperature dropped about thirty degrees, and I'll be damned if Gus didn't slide off the road into a snow bank on the way home.

Colder than a well digger's you-know-what. No one else out on the roads, so he walked the two miles home. With the wind chill and all, must have been twenty below."

"Mom? He walked the whole two miles in that weather? I've never heard *this* story before."

"Fifteen-two, fifteen-four, and a pair makes six," Mom says, pegging ahead on the cribbage board. "Your play."

But I'm like a dog with a bone. I fold my cards. "Well, what happened?"

"It was already getting dark and I wondered where he was. Hoped he wasn't at the tavern. Finally heard a scratching at the door and there he was, half froze to death. I wanted to shoot him for being so damn careless, but instead I dragged him in the house and thawed him out. Like to cried my head off."

"But you never cry, Mom." It's true. Even when she had the bout with cancer and the mastectomy, she handled it better than any of us. "No cancer's going to get me," she'd announced, and went on about life. She's tough, and a lot braver than I could ever hope to be. For instance, back in 1943 when she was twenty, she hitchhiked out here from Wisconsin with a girlfriend.

"That time even Gus saw me cry," she says. "I howled something awful."

"Did he almost die?"

"Might as well. Frostbit his. . . his. . . thing so bad it turned black. I was sure it was gonna shrivel up and fall off."

"Jesus, Mom, you mean his dick?" She nods, studying her cards. I forget we're playing cribbage. "Well?" I lean down so I can study her face. "Then what?"

"For a month or so there, we played a lot more crib-bage."

I'm floored. Mom and Dad growled and sniped at each other, but when it was time to play cribbage you'd think they were on their honeymoon. I never once imagined it carried over into the bedroom. "Mom, when was this? How old *were* you guys?"

"We were young then, weren't even seventy yet," Mom says, smiling to herself, studying her cards as if she's just been dealt a new hand.

The phone rings and I reach up to the phone on the wall. Before I can say "Hello," I hear sobbing.

"Oh my God," Delight says. "Oh my God!"

"Is Justin all right?"

"He just called me. It isn't him, but Echo, it's . . . oh, God, it's so awful."

"Who, Delight?"

"Weldon," she says. "Justin called and said there was an accident over at Eagle Creek. He was . . . working in-side the hog when someone turned it back on."

"Oh, no!" I groan. "Not Weldon." I'm looking at Mom. She brings her hand up to her mouth. Using the table for support she pushes herself up and limps toward the front door. "Delight, I gotta go."

Mom and I lift our coats and hats from their hooks by the door. We don't talk as we take turns sitting on the chair to slip on our boots, and we're silent as I hold Mom's arm on our way down the front steps and through the new snow. I help her into the car, unplug the engine block heater, and turn the key in the ignition while saying a prayer. Rooster starts. Then I broom most of the new snow off the windows, before crawling into the ice-cold driver's seat. I let the car warm up another minute, grateful I got the heater fixed. I turn left and drive up the road so we can be with June. Weldon had plowed the road before going to work, so the snow is only five or six inches deep now. But here come headlights down the road. I pull over as far as possible. June is in the front seat of the sheriff's car, her gloves covering her face. As the car squeaks past inches away, Mom and I each put a hand up, palm out, on our cold windshield, to reach out to her, but she doesn't see us. The sheriff nods and keeps driving. We continue up the road, tires spinning. Turning the car around in their driveway, I gun the engine to back around so I can aim the car downhill toward home. I hang on tight to the steering wheel as we skid down the snowy road through snowflakes nearly the size of white chrysanthemums, the flower at every funeral I've ever attended.

# CHAPTER 4

"I'm thinking of filing harassment charges on that parrot at the pet shop, Leland," I say as I follow him to his cubicle.

"Someone should. I can't repeat what that parrot said to my wife one day. Now she won't go near that end of the mall."

Leland sits in his chair and I sit in mine, a ratty waiting-room chair with a rip in the vinyl seat, probably from a screwdriver some dumb shit had in his hip pocket. He puts his hands on a stack of papers and studies me, and I hope he's going to tell me what the parrot said. My face is straining, stupidly, to hear more.

"Congratulations on your work with the Salvation Army," Leland says, shuffling through the stack of job descriptions. "Saw you on the front page of the paper."

"Thanks, Leland," I say. "I enjoyed it, and you were right. It was a good job."

Leland stops going through the papers, looks up and makes eye contact, full on.

"Echo, how are you at housekeeping?"

I can only groan. "Not another motel job."

"No. But have you ever thought about working at the sawmill?"

"The one here in Hatfield? I'm not thinking too highly of sawmills these days."

"Echo, I heard about your neighbor, Weldon. He was a good man and I'm real sorry."

"Leland, I'm going to tell you a little story about Weldon and my dad. Happened about five years ago. One day Dad was turning into our driveway down on the highway by our mailboxes when a speeding car hit the right front fender of his pickup so hard it knocked him out of his truck into the ditch. He ended up in the clinic with several broken ribs." I stop talking.

Leland waits.

My chest tightens first and then my throat. A tear rolls down my face, but I'm determined to finish the story. "Because of his emphysema, his lungs filled up with fluid and things were touch and go. During this same time Weldon walked down the road to get his mail, and when he walked back up past our place he saw Dad out chopping wood. He was surprised, thought Dad was still in the hospital, or if he'd just been released he sure as hell shouldn't be out chopping wood. He said, 'Hello, Gus. How're you feeling?' Dad said, 'Aw, I can't complain.' It's what he always said. Except he was still in the hospital. Right after that Dad started to get better, though, and we think Weldon saw Dad out chopping wood when he was closest to dying, when he could have gone either way. We still think Weldon tipped the scales. Dad lived three more years after that."

Leland looks at me as if seeing me for the first time. "That's an amazing story, Echo." He pauses. "Communities need men like Weldon, and your father, too. I've heard there'll be an investigation over at Eagle Creek. But here's the deal, Echo, our mill's been opening up to women, on orders from their Spokane office."

"That's big of 'em. I mean, it is almost the twenty-first century. I'm listening."

"The women we've sent over there so far haven't lasted long, but you're . . . uh . . . more seasoned. You . . ." Leland's mouth is open far enough to catch flies.

"Seasoned, Leland? Do you mean old?" Guess I'm a little sensitive, being nearly fifty years old, still sniffing out a job, any job.

"Well," he shrugs. "I mean you're an experienced worker. You can take care of yourself. You did so well with the last job, and you're not afraid of hard work. If you don't want it, I have others to send over."

"What's the job?" I ask, sighing. "Let's hear it."

Leland continues now, in his calm, determined case-worker way. "You'd start out doing cleanup, and then learn other jobs on a stand-in basis. I think you'd like the pay. Starts out at $11.50 an hour, with full benefits after a three-month probation period."

At the minimum wage I'm accustomed to, this would be like working one hour and getting paid for two. Even Delight would approve. The last time I talked to her on the phone, she had the nerve to suggest I picture exactly what it is I want in life. When I asked her to use her magical powers to picture me farting in silk, she hung up on me. "Benefits?" I ask. "I've heard of 'em. What exactly do you mean?"

"You know, health insurance, 401K, paid vacations."

"Full time?"

"Full time," he says, like I just won the lottery, and in a way that's exactly how it feels. I'm in no position to be choosy. Hell, I've been known to *dance* with a broomstick.

Lying on my back like a corpse, with Tummy plastered to the side of my face, I turn my head to stare at the beeping alarm clock and the time, 4:05 a.m. "Oh," I groan. "The mill." I close my eyes for a minute, and an odd memory flits into my head. *I'm a little girl looking at a page from the Sears & Roebuck catalog. I ache to own a pair of little girls' lacy pastel panties on that page, worn by a cute girl with curly blond hair and a big smile. I hide the catalog in the clutter under my bunk bed. My own cotton panties have holes and stretched-out elastic. Over the top of these shameful panties I wear brown cotton leggings and secondhand dresses. At school, I imagine all the town girls are wearing pretty panties, like the ones on the catalog page.*

"Move, Tummy, you big galoot." The cat drags his big butt off my pillow. I wipe the cat hair from my cheek and shove aside the mountain of quilts along with the memory of lacy panties. My eyes are still shut, but I'm motivated by the smell of coffee and bacon. I grope along the narrow trailer house hallway, touching the thin veneer walls for support on my way to the kitchen.

Mom says nothing as I sag against the edge of the counter. Her size eighteen lavender chenille robe, the elbows nearly worn through, drapes flat across one side where a large breast used to be. Mom likes to cook, and she likes to eat, and her permed hair, dyed light brown, makes her look a few years younger.

I pour a mug of coffee and flop down onto the vinyl seat of a chair at the kitchen table. "Mom, you didn't have to get up for me."

"I was awake anyway," she says, breaking an egg into the frying pan.

"I s'pose you're pretty excited about my new job."

"Well," she says, pausing as egg white drips over the side of the frying pan, "considering."

"I know, I know," I say. "But I'm thinking of calling in sick this morning. Test their sick-leave policy." I only say this to get her goat.

"I'd say it's time you put your big-girl panties on."

"Guess I should have bought me some at the mall," I say, setting my cup down and splashing coffee onto the table. Odd thing for her to say, right after I was thinking about frilly panties when I woke up. But Mom's focus is elsewhere. She stands at the electric stove with a pancake turner in one hand, a book in the other. The romance novels and mysteries she reads are all tattered, often with no covers, and by the time she's done reading one it has so much grease and dried egg, sometimes even bread dough, on the pages it's unreadable. She ends up burning the books in the wood stove, says that way she gets to enjoy the book twice. Dad always said the same thing about going to the woods to cut firewood. You sweat when you cut it and you sweat when you burn it. There's probably an old novel burning in the stove right now. This might say something about romance, but I can't think what without more coffee.

Mom and I eat breakfast without talking. The kitchen clock ticks but the police scanner is turned off, since nothing much happens between four and five in the morning in our little corner of Washington State. While I can count on Mom to be frank with me, especially since she attended that Wild Woman Workshop a few years ago, I wish I could talk to Dad. He'd remind me one more time that I should have got an education, but once that little habit of speech was out of the way, he'd tell me a useful bit of inside information about working in the mill. He never worked in a mill himself, but he'd speak with authority anyway. That was Dad. Oh, if I could hear his voice right now.

By five o'clock I'm bundled up in layers of cotton and wool, my Sorel pack boots are laced up and crunching on the snow as I carry my nerves and my lunch pail to the car. It's black as pitch outside and close to zero. I unplug the orange extension cord from the outlet on the end of the trailer, and toss the cord onto the back seat. While the car warms up I scrape the windshield clear of snow and ice, breathing blue smoke from the exhaust.

Labor Ready, that's me, farting along on bald tires between snow banks six feet high, on the way to my newest gig. I pat the dashboard to thank Rooster for starting. Delight has said so many times that we get what we think about, so I figure, what the hell? Having positive thoughts can't be *that* difficult. But I'm straining like when I'm constipated. I squeeze my eyes shut, then remember I'm driving, so now with my eyes open I picture my new boss. He's nice, nice is good, and he doesn't act like an asshole. Whoops. Delight would tell me not to bring in any bad thoughts. Okay. He'll say, "Good morning. My name is suchandsuch and you must be Echo. I'm glad you're here. First let me walk you through the paperwork, and then I'll show you where to find your safety gear and give you a tour of the mill. Now, there are no easy jobs here at the mill, and some of us are stronger than others. Don't be afraid to ask for help. Do you have any questions?" That's when I'll say, "Yeah, when's payday and where can I smoke?"

At the mill, I park under a giant overhead light next to an assortment of pickup trucks, each dangling an extension cord from an engine block heater, each plugged into an outlet on a utility pole. Like umbilical cords. They're that important. I drag my orange cord with me and find one last plug. This means my car might start at the end of my shift. Then again, it might not.

Looming in the cold snowy dark beyond the parking area is a monstrous metal building the size of Hatfield High School. Next to this building is another one, almost as big, and behind that are other hulking structures. The edges of the monstrous buildings glow an eerie yellow color, thanks to yard lights the size of small moons.

I cross the road and spot a trench in the mountain of snow and follow the shoveled path past a wall of corrugated metal until I come to a door. I open it and stand inside holding my lunch pail, like it's the first day of school. A tall, slender man in his forties walks toward me, not smiling, wearing an orange hard hat. Must be an alien, landed here from someplace else. Otherwise, I'd have seen him around. In spite of my earlier flirtation with positive thinking, no handshake is offered.

"I'm Leroy, the assistant manager here." At least that's what I think he says, since he speed-mumbled the words. The mill equipment suddenly starts up—violent shrieks of heavy metal doors slamming shut, the noise colliding into my chest with the force of a logging truck, jake brake hammering. On instinct, I cover my ears, and at exactly that moment the man yells a string of words that include "boss. . . . now." He gives off zero reaction to the sudden noise from the machinery. Who is this vaguely familiar guy, anyway? He looks a little like one of those handsome

Nazi officers in a World War II show I saw with Dad. As he motions for me to follow him, his movements are more robotic than human. He hands me a card with my name at the top and waits while I poke the card in the mouth of the clock, hear the click, and insert the card in one of about twenty slots in a vertical metal box, most of them filled. God, am I late?

Leroy takes me past a row of lockers and the closed door of a restroom. We enter the break room, with its walls of rough-sawn lumber. Cupboards line part of a wall, along with a sink and a counter with two microwave ovens. Good, there's a candy machine and pop machine. A rectangular metal table sits in the middle of the room, surrounded by metal folding chairs, maybe a dozen, none of them pushed in. Leroy closes the door, somewhat reducing the noise. Unlocking a cupboard, he sorts through file folders and hands me all kinds of paperwork, which he says to take home and complete.

I set my lunch pail on the table where I can keep an eye on it. Then we sit through a ten-minute video on safety that's closed-captioned, I guess for the hearing-impaired. In the video, the employees, all white, all male, wear hard hats, lift with their knees, and smile. I learn that if a board gets caught in a piece of equipment that the machine must be turned off, with the off switch locked in position, before the board can be safely removed. But there's more. Foul language is not allowed, so I'll have to watch myself there. No drugs or alcohol, either. Surprise. It's also important to wear a hard hat and safety glasses at all times.

Leroy shows me the lockers outside the break room, and one of them with a bent door is empty. He points toward the empty locker, then opens a cupboard and shows me the boxes of ear plugs, dust masks and safety glasses. While the pounding noise from the machinery reverberates up through my boots, climbs my legs and stomps around on my chest, he reaches into a different cupboard and presents me with an orange hard hat. This is the first job I've ever had that requires one. Dad always wore his brain bucket when he worked in the woods, and I think about this while adjusting my hard hat and safety glasses to fit.

"The sawmill has two separate operations, the mill and the planer," he says, as he starts walking. "Logs first come to the mill and . . . to length. . Then . . . debarker and on to the scragg, that cuts off four sides . . . squared-up . . . cut into rough-sawn lumber."

I nod, hoping I can remember the few words I could make out. Walking through the mill, we pass several stations, one of them with a woman standing next to three men. That's good. Once we're through the mill, Leroy leads me outside across a plowed yard lined with units of lumber the size of RVs, and on into another building.

"This building is called the planer . . . planes the boards smooth."

I'm following behind Leroy, through the deafening roar and banging noise of the machinery. He's saying something but I can't make it out. Hope it's not too important. Men stand at various stations handling boards. They're all wearing hard hats and clear safety glasses, but just like over at the mill, I can't say I know any of them. Where've I been? Hatfield only has about 1500 residents. We must hang out at different bars; there's so many to choose from. Oh, but there's Justin and another guy in a room enclosed with clear walls, flipping 2 x 4s, focusing on what they're doing. He's too busy to look up. Leroy stops walking suddenly and I plow into him. When I yell, "Excuse me, I didn't see your brake lights," he acts like nothing happened and starts walking again. So, why'd he stop in the first place?

I follow him outdoors across the yard. In the dim light of an overhead light, his movements are even more robotic, and I'm feeling leery of being out here alone with him. He leads me around the side of the mill building, where he stops abruptly. "Your first job is out here," he shouts, even though it's much quieter. "We just finished a big run of cedar. Logs get cut to length and sent up the ramp and through the debarker." He looks up about twenty feet. "See those L-shaped teeth up there?"

I strain my neck to look up. In the ten watts of light, I can almost see what he's talking about.

"Those are called dogs. They stabilize the logs on their way up the ramp. At the top, the bark peels off in long strips. Gets all tangled up. Freezes in the debarker and the dogs." He points to a steep metal stairway, more of a ladder than anything. "Need you to climb up there and remove that frozen bark." He studies me. "Okay?"

"Sure." I say, hoping this is an initiation gag like Justin told me about, like the one where an old-timer asks you to go find the knot-puller, that it's really important, that he's counting on you.

Leroy grabs a round metal bar about three feet long that was leaning against the outside of the building and yells, "Here's a chisel."

*I guess the foreplay is over.*

Gripping the heavy chisel in my left hand, I climb the narrow metal stairs up two flights, creep along a catwalk with my free hand gripping the handrail, and step onto the ramp with those metal dogs. Dead woman walking. So much for dancing while pushing a big broom. Does Leland know about this part of the job? I think I'm in shock. I don't stop to look around at the stars overhead but set to work using the chisel end of the bar to break apart a clot of tangled, frozen cedar bark. We have *dogs* holding trees on their way to losing their *bark*. That's a good one. At least now I've figured out that a debarker does exactly what it says, takes bark off logs. I lay the chisel down and with both hands hanging on tight to a dog, I kick at the loosened bark. At the next dog, I jerk on strips of bark with my stiff leather gloves, grunting and cussing clouds of steam. Frozen bits of bark break loose and fall to the ground.

Only rapists and murderers should have to do this job.

If I'm going to reach the frozen clots of cedar bark underneath the dogs, there's only one way I can see to do it. I've gotta hang from a steel I-beam that's about eight inches square. Maybe there's an easier way, and I'm not smart enough to figure it out. But this job didn't exactly come with instructions. I curl my left arm around the beam, wrap my legs around that same cold hunk of metal, and lock my ankles together. Might's well be hanging onto a capsized boat out in the ocean, sharks circling. With my right hand gripping the chisel, I stab at the ice, grunting steam in the ice cold air. My safety glasses fog up.

While I wait for my glasses to clear, I try to recall the stages of hypothermia, but can't. Guess I'll know them soon enough. Next I think of all the uses for cedar: cedar siding, cedar chests, a trunk to store your valuables in . . . like hope chests. Yeah, all I ever wanted was to settle down with Dwayne. Maybe if Delight hadn't stolen him from me I might not be up here risking my life, chiseling apart a solid mass of cedar bark with a more or less useless piece-of-crap chisel. Except he's gone, and now's not a good time to think about death.

I chisel, claw, and pull until I score another loose tongue, letting it, too, drop to the ground below. Sore, strained body parts are one thing, but after I move on to free the next strip of bark I let my imagination run wild. I picture the muscles of my left arm exploding and ripping out of the socket. My legs fail. I have to let go. Since I'm frozen stiff, I bounce several times when I hit the ground. Pieces of me shatter.

I gotta stop thinking shit like that.

Why am I up here dangling from a beam, risking my life? Even circus performers have nets. This isn't a job. It's a fucking nightmare. There's no feeling left in my arm, the one holding tight to the beam. Hell, if I fall and survive, I'll end up in a wheelchair. At least I could stay indoors by the wood stove all winter. Out loud I yell into the darkness—to Leroy, to all my old bosses, to life—"I can do this job, don't think I can't."

Slowly, one dead snake of cedar bark after another drops to the ground. I crank my head around. Down below me a man on a bobcat is scooping up the crap I've managed to pry loose. Please, God, help me hang on. Don't let me look down again.

That's it! I can't take this no more. How long have I been up here? Ten minutes? Half an hour? I drag myself up onto the ice-crusted ramp and flop onto my back. My hard hat bangs the metal. I stare into the dull gray pre-dawn sky and tears well up behind my safety glasses, spill, and freeze on the sides of my face. I roll onto my side and reach for the hand rail but my fingers are frozen in my stiff leather gloves and I can barely feel the metal. I pull myself part way up, crouch low on shaking legs, and make my way to the catwalk. Walking now as tall and nonchalant as I can, I make my way past the debarker shed on the catwalk, and down the steep metal stairs, like the lone survivor of a mountain-climbing expedition gone wrong. When I pass Leroy, standing on the ground with his legs apart, one hand on each hip, I nod to him and point in the general direction of the restroom, my face expressionless, hoping he won't notice the tears, frozen like conks on a dead tree.

Safely in the restroom, I lock the door. In the mirror I see that my face is frozen into its oldest, horror-movie scream face. I look like shit. I slam my cold, stiff gloves onto the floor, not caring that the men have missed the urinal and pissed all over, a fact I can smell. Grabbing the sink with both hands, I drop my head. Hot new tears roll down my face, stinging my frozen skin. Only one low guttural sob escapes my throat before I jerk myself up-right, a proud citizen in this work place of male wage earners.

The hot water faucet actually works, and I splash my face for a while before noticing the water is too hot. The paper towel I dry my face with is rough, only one step up from the wood chips it was made from, wood chips that could have come from this mill. I throw the used paper towel on the floor in the corner, missing the empty wastebasket. The bathroom is warm. Might's well make the most of it. I drape my Carhartt jacket over the sink, drop my jeans, unbutton two layers of wool shirts, and unbutton my dad's old pair of wool long johns. Too bad they don't have an opening in the butt like some of 'em do. Bending my stiff body, I gather the heap of clothes off the floor and scoot myself close enough so I can collapse onto the toilet. My thighs feel like popsicles. Guess I'll have to lay off the liquids.

Every cell of my body begs me to sit on the pot for as long as it takes to thaw out. Can I make myself go back up onto the debarker? Can I even get up off the pot? I check my watch. It's 7:23 a.m. Someone pounds on the door. "Okay, okay." In no hurry, I put on all my layers of clothing and grab my gloves. When I leave the restroom I don't look at the man standing there, waiting.

One foot in front of the other in zombie mode, I make my way through the roaring slamming-door noises of the mill. At my locker I cling to the bent door for support. I'm shaking inside-out from fear, and outside-in from the cold. Maybe I should quit while I'm still alive.

My head, its full weight resting against the locker door, starts to spin.

"Ready for your next job?" Leroy shouts behind me.

My eyes jerk open. I turn toward him and pull myself up to my full five-foot-seven. Even though my vision is fuzzy, I notice how blue Leroy's eyes are and why he looks familiar. He could be a younger Clint Eastwood, in that movie I saw recently called *Absolute Power*.

## CHAPTER 5

Leroy hands me a grain shovel and points to a pile of sawdust outside the back door, higher than my head. The temperature outside here is five or ten below zero. Thank God the sun is up now.

"You need to shovel all the sawdust off this platform," Leroy yells above the roar. "Got an inspection next week. Esterbrook wants this gone. Soon as you make a pile over here," he points to a spot about ten feet away, "a bobcat will come and haul it away."

"Okay," I say. "Got it." At least I know a bobcat's a piece of machinery with a bucket loader on the front, used to scoop stuff up.

A grain shovel is big, and a shovel full of frozen sawdust is as heavy as wet snow—twenty pounds or more. I bend, scoop and toss, and work fast to prove I can do the job. Before starting this new torture, I took a break alone, but I'm still not thawed out from my high-wire act with the frozen cedar bark. My body ain't accustomed to all this damn stooping and twisting, though, and my lower back now hurts like a sonofabitch. Bend, scoop, lift and toss. I stop to use a pick axe to bust through the frozen crust, and it's almost restful.

What would Dad say if he could see me now? I'd tell him I wished I'd got that education he talked about. 'Course if the teachers hadn't passed me *on condition,* the term they used when Mom talked to 'em, I'd still be going to school. At the high school reunions I'd be fifty, then sixty, maybe even seventy, still going to high school, when everyone else had already retired. I think about how I stood in for the son Dad never had. The two of us were always outdoors cutting firewood or clearing brush, hunting or fishing, while Delight stayed indoors doing girlie things. I was born first, bushy brown hair, plain looking and, it was clear soon enough, not the shiniest tool in the shed. A few minutes later, along comes Delight, cute as a button. So we're not what you'd call *identical* twins, but still, we *are* twins. She crawled and walked before I did. I had to figure out how to talk, or Delight would have done that first, too. Yeah I talked first, but no one could understand me. So I took to the outdoors. It set me apart from Delight and that way I spent more time with Dad. By seven I'd learned to chop wood, and when I sliced into my bare foot Dad said, "Don't you whine, now. Don't you be a sissy." After that I worked harder, lifting rounds of firewood that were too heavy, working faster, always trying to anticipate the next chore. All for approval that never came. Guess I'm still waiting.

With my arm and most of my weight on the shovel handle, I fumble to find my watch, buried under several sleeves on my left arm. Another hour. If I can last until then. God, I want a cigarette. Tonight the hot bath will be heaven, followed by flannel sheets. I moan, glad no one can hear me. My toes are starting to warm up and they tingle and hurt from thawing out. More bending, scooping, tossing. At last the buzzer groans, like on that game show, Jeopardy. The equipment stops screeching, slamming, and roaring, taking a few seconds to unwind. The sudden quiet is almost a shock.

"Break time," a woman says, extending her hand. "I'm Carmel."

"Echo Spangler," I say. "Feels like you just tossed me a life preserver."

"Breaks always feel like that."

She's shorter than I am, about 5' 4", but big-boned and stocky. When she lifts off her hard hat, her blonde hair is cut in a shag, like Meg Ryan's, and aside from the hat-hair you'd expect, it looks as if she didn't bother to comb her hair. Her eyes are light blue—she's probably one of those Scandinavians. Might be thirty-five. But then most women younger than me look that age. She's dressed in layers of thrift-store wool sweaters, shirts, jackets, pants, just like all the men, and she's wearing felt-lined work boots. Big feet. I'm guessing size ten, like mine.

"Cigarette?" I offer, removing my leather glove to reach into my jacket pocket for an Ultra Light, the cheapest brand I could find.

"No thanks. I don't smoke," she says. "And you can't smoke here, either. Follow me."

I throw my shovel down next to the pick axe and plod behind her, aching, stiff and slow, like I'm walking upstream. We make our way along one metal catwalk and another, drifted with sawdust, then up wooden stairs into a corner of the machine shop. We sit on a wood bench and lean against the wall of rough-sawn lumber. As soon as I can fish the lighter out of my jacket pocket, I thumb the wheel on my lighter, and watch the warm flame ignite the tobacco. I feel the love all the way down to my toes.

Carmel talks but her words are muffled, like she's talking with her mouth full in a low octave. "I'm sorry, what did you say?"

She points to my right ear and mouths the words, "Ear plugs."

"Oh, duh," I say, removing the pieces of yellow foam and sticking them in a jacket pocket.

"I said, the millwrights aren't in their shop during breaks. They're checking the equipment while it's down. We're okay here. I tried taking breaks with the men, but they totally ignored me. Leroy was there, talking about how his daughter wanted to play football at school, but couldn't because she's a girl. I wanted to tell them I think football is barbaric, even for boys, but I didn't. Being there was so uncomfortable I never went back."

I nod. "So, how long you worked here?"

"About four months."

"You made it," I say, almost too tired to speak. "Full time with benefits."

"I pick edgings," she tells me. "The edger rough-cuts large cants of wood into 2 x 4 or 2 x 6 studs. Whatever size they're cutting. I stand at the station right after the edger with three guys and we spread apart the studs to pick out scraps of wood. We send the junk wood down into a hole. And then the studs continue on to the next station."

"Saw your edgings when I got the grand tour," I say, blowing smoke away from her, feeling glad I've never been able to stop smoking. "Big honkin' mess down there in the basement. Seems a little hopeless, this cleanup job."

"You'll think you can't do it, that your body won't keep going. But then you get your first paycheck. It's like winning big at Keno. Gives you a second wind."

Oh, yeah. My old friend, Keno. "I might be too old for this shit." I snuff out my cigarette butt in the coffee can half filled with sand, sitting on the floor next to the bench.

"Looks like you're fixed on working here, and you're strong," she says. "But you gotta pace yourself. The men sure do. Some more than others. You have to."

"Guess I'm trying to prove myself. I really need this job."

"Whatever you do," she says, now on her feet offering her hand to help me up. "Don't try to stand out."

From my position on the bench I want to stand upright by myself, I really do, but I take her hand. "Thanks," I say, and mean it. Every bone and muscle hurts. I try not to groan.

"To be continued," she says.

On our way out of the machine shop, we walk past shallow tubs holding jugs of oils and fluids. Odd they let us smoke here. Carmel strikes me as capable, good-hearted, almost cheerful, not that I mind a person with a good attitude. Someday I'm gonna have one myself.

By the time I clock out at the end of the shift and plod toward Rooster, my back hurts so bad I walk as stiff as a 2 x 4. The others unplug their extension cords, wind 'em up in a coil, and start their trucks. No one pays any attention to me. They rev their engines and leave while I'm still fiddling with my cord. Carmel honks the horn of her Bronco as I grip my steering wheel and ease myself down onto the driver's seat. When my car starts, I sit and stare like I've been rear-ended.

At home, I stand inside the front door in a daze, rubbing my left eye. Tummy looks up from his nap on the couch. Mom stops cooking and folds back a page on her paperback.

"My God! What'd they do to you? And what's wrong with your eye?"

"Don't matter. Just a piece of sawdust."

"We need to get you to the clinic."

"Oh, Mom. If I'm gonna go to the doctor every time I get a piece of sawdust in my eye at this job, I'll have to go bankrupt again."

She says nothing, which is odd for Mom. Finally she announces, "You're filthy."

"No foolin'." Bits of sawdust flake around me and settle on the floor as I fight off tears. Mom grabs me by the shoulders and backs me up to the chair near the door. "You sit down, right now."

But I can't. I'm that stiff. When Mom pushes down hard on my shoulders, my knees buckle and down I go in a heap. When she pulls on a jacket sleeve, it won't come away from my armpit.

"Oh, hell," I groan. "Just cut it off me." I feel small and helpless.

"What exactly did you do today?"

"Shoveled sawdust." I'm sure as hell not going to tell her about the frozen cedar bark. She'd haul out her 30-30 rifle and head for the mill.

It takes a while, but we get me mostly undressed, my dirty clothes in a pile on the floor around me. Mom helps me into the bathroom like the old people I helped at the convalescent center. "You sit here," she orders me onto the lid of the toilet, wearing only my cotton panties and a sleeveless undershirt like wife beaters wear. I close my eyes and sag against the tank. The piece of sawdust digs into my eye. Mom hands me a bottle of eye drops and starts the bath water. A wash of eye drops does the trick, finally, and now Mom helps me out of the rest of my clothes and I slither down into the tub. In the glorious warm water, I lean back to soak and form my right hand in the shape it'd take if I was holding a can of beer. The next thing you know Mom has installed a Coors Light in my hand. It's a perfect fit.

"Thanks, Mom." What I almost say is, "I love you." But I catch myself. We don't say things like that in our family. After she leaves the bathroom, I sip my beer and doze, and pretty soon I hear the washing machine running out in the hall. Here I am, almost fifty years old, and my mom is still taking care of me. If I wasn't so goddamn stiff I'd just slip down under the water and drown myself.

## CHAPTER 6

There's a snowmobile way off in the distance and the driver is gunning the engine to get unstuck. When the alarm rings, I realize it was Tummy, snoring. The cat leaps off the bed. It's cold outside and warm under the quilts. If only I could call in sick today.

Good thing I like the smell of sawdust, because on my second day at the mill I'm back to bending, scooping and tossing. My breath steams out in great huffs, fogging up my safety glasses. Today my nose is irritated from the sawdust and cold air, and it's dripping like a faucet. I can't stop to use Dad's hanky so I wipe snot on the sleeve of my jacket. It's what the men do. Today a guy on a bobcat comes and goes, hauling away the new sawdust pile I've made. Why in hell I'm moving this pile of sawdust only ten feet away makes no sense. I'm working as fast as my sorry old body can. Using a long metal bar with a pointed end, a spud bar, I break up frozen clumps of sawdust. I get so warm I gotta stop, pull off my jacket, and throw it out of the way on the ground. Now when I wipe my nose, I start a new snail trail of shine on my shirt sleeve.

Finally, the gift of a break. When I hurry to my locker for my thermos and a bottle of aspirin, the men pretend not to see me. Up in the machine shop, Carmel is already sitting on the bench. Before dropping down next to her, I turn away to blow my nose on one of Dad's big old red cotton hankies, wad it up, and shove it in a jacket pocket.

"Hey," Justin yells as he tromps up the wood steps to the machine shop. He has someone with him. "Hi, Auntie. Meet Nose. We work together at the planer."

The man extends his hand. When I shake his warm hand, I notice his most prominent feature, his nose. His eyes are brown, behind horn-rimmed glasses. His beard is trimmed, and his hat hair is light brown with no balding. There's something else, too. The man has tufts of hair growing out the sides of his ears, like a lynx. I smile up at him, almost coyly. Where has *this* guy been?

"How're you doing, Auntie?"

I'd like to tell the truth, that I'm all fuckered out, but I say, "Great." I toss three aspirins in my mouth and wash them down with coffee from my thermos. "Think I'll go out dancing tonight."

"That's good news," he says, flashing a grin. "Nose likes to dance."

"You both know Carmel here?" I ask, not looking at Nose-who-likes-to-dance.

Justin and Nose nod and smile at her.

"Good job with the cedar bark," Nose says to me. "Way to go."

Justin pipes in, "Yeah, Auntie, I heard about that. You're really something."

"Oh, that. I wasn't up there long. But thanks." I'm happy they know about it.

"We gotta go," Justin says. "Time to get back over to the planer. Don't work too hard."

"Oh, you know me," I say, giving both Justin and Nose the best smile my tired face can manage. "I'll pace myself." After they leave, I reach into my jacket for a cigarette, smiling again at the thought of Nose's ear fur, and

Justin's attempt at match-making. And I couldn't help but notice something else. While Nose ain't exactly gifted in the buns department, at least the butt of his jeans don't include the outline of a chewing tobacco can. Snoose chewing has to be one of the most disgusting habits. Lots of the men here at the mill keep a wad of chew under their lip, including Justin.

"I didn't know Justin was your nephew," Carmel says. "Haven't seen much of him, since he works over at the planer, but he's been real decent."

"He's a good kid. Closest I'll ever get to having a son. Every minute with Justin is a good minute."

"Nose has always been nice, too," she says. "Unlike most of the men."

We sit quietly, resting. I finally blurt out what's been eatin' me. "I wonder who turned the hog on over at the Eagle Creek Mill, with a millwright in it? He was a good neighbor to my folks for thirty years. Can't think of a worse way to die. Might as well have been eaten by a goddamn grizzly bear."

"I think all the men feel bad," she says. "After they heard about it, they worked like they were on auto pilot. His poor family."

Back to the sawdust heap, where I shovel until the buzzer announces lunch break. Again, when I make a quick in and out to get my lunch bucket from my locker, it's as if I'm invisible. Maybe if the men don't look at me, I'm not really here. By the time I arrive at the bench in the machine shop, Carmel is already eating. I'm so hungry I dive head first into my peanut butter sandwich, made with Mom's homemade bread and huckleberry jelly. I'll smoke later, before eating my apple and Snickers bar.

"You have an accent," I say. "Where you from?"

"Texas Panhandle."

"I'm listening."

"It's a long story."

"If it don't require heavy lifting, I'm game."

Carmel smiles just a little and asks, "You married?"

"Yeah, once. For a while. What about you?"

Her eyes are closed and her smile's gone. "His name is Melvin."

By the way she says it I know her husband is not your average Joe.

She continues. "When I first met Melvin down in Amarillo he was so charming, so attentive. No one else had ever paid attention to me like that, or made me feel so alive and special. We got married. I remember thinking, *So, the love you see in the movies really can happen, even to me.* I wanted to be the perfect wife. I gave him whatever he wanted, even before he realized he wanted it. He worked hard in the oil fields, and I tried to take care of him like nobody ever had, not even his mother." She stops chewing and shakes her head. "And then he changed."

The break buzzer groans, like Carmel just gave the wrong answer. She stands and holds out her hand. I stub out my cigarette in the coffee can and, once again, allow Carmel to pull me up to a standing position. We both know I could do it on my own now, if I had to. Standing face to face for a second, I notice that her eyes are as blue as a robin's egg, and they're the most childlike eyes I've ever seen on a grownup. I think about this as we clomp down the stairs, along the catwalks to our lockers, off to our separate jobs.

The mountain of sawdust is now just a mound. It's darker, heavier, almost petrified, and the spud bar is the tool to use. Leroy and another man, maybe Esterbrook, the owner of the mill, come to stand in the open doorway. They shield their eyes and look up into the cold, clear morning sky, then stare out to the log yard, over toward the planer building. The other man yells above the noise of the equipment, "What do you suppose this place looks like from the air?"

Leroy scratches his neck and shakes his head. When they turn to walk back toward the line, Leroy stops not far from me and says, "Looks like you're doing some damage here."

Was that a compliment? I don't stop shoveling, but glance his way and nod, and just in case the other guy is Esterbrook, I nod to him, too. Bend, scoop, toss. I try to show how professional I am at my little housekeeping job. As soon as they leave I stop, lean on the spud bar, and wipe my nose on my sleeve.

I live from break to break, cigarette to cigarette. And now, upstairs on the bench, I light up and say to Carmel, "You were saying your husband changed after you got married?"

"Yeah, and I still don't understand it," she says, taking a small bite of trail mix and chewing slowly. It's like our earlier conversation had never been interrupted by the need to go back to work. "He became sullen and withdrawn. Then one day I forgot to buy ice cream at the store, and when I apologized, he backhanded me." Carmel stopped chewing and swallowed. "By then we had a little girl. When I came out of the shock from it, I told him if he ever did it again I'd leave."

"Well, hell. I would have said the same thing, or worse."

"Sure, but then he acted all wonderful, and that lasted until I got pregnant. After that he became sullen and angry again. I guess he just couldn't help it. The second time he hit me, I divorced him, just like I said. Boy was he surprised. The kids and I stayed in Texas and he came up here, and I never felt so lost in my whole life. I was so overwhelmed, so afraid of making bad choices." She pauses. "Do you think prisoners feel that way after they're released?"

"I don't know," I say. "Never been a prisoner, but I do know about feeling lost and making bad choices."

"Anyway, he got a job fixing forklifts, mostly in Spokane."

She must really be lonely, telling me all this. I smoke and rest and listen. If Carmel represents women who work in sawmills, they're way more interesting than the heifers I met doing regular women's work.

"Then he started calling," Carmel continues. "He even talked nice to the kids, when he'd never had much time for them before. He said he missed us and wanted to try again. I came to think that the big and loving thing I could do for us all was to forgive him and trust him again. I thought maybe my kindness, generosity and love could heal him. I'd soothe him, you know; pet him, heal his wounds."

Sounds like *The Horse Whisperer* to me. I think Carmel is a nice person, but maybe *too* nice, and way too naive. That's not a fault, I guess, but it sure can be a big honkin' disability. Take me. I'm the opposite of naive. Not that that's so great, either, but at least no one in particular kicks me around, just life in general. Hell, being naive is like getting screwed and not feeling it. *Is it in? Are you done?* And I *have* experienced that.

"So, you moved up here with the kids?"

"Last fall. It was so beautiful the day we arrived, with the aspen trees and larch all bright and yellow. Indian summer." Her eyes are closed. She's smiling again. "When we walked in the woods together as a family, the leaves showered down on us like petals. Melvin was so happy to see us that I was sure I'd done the right thing."

"And?"

"We got remarried by the justice of the peace. But Melvin was behind in his child support, and somehow he talked me into paying the amount he was in arrears. It had to be paid. That's one reason I got on here at the mill. I needed to earn as much money as I could. I knew it would be hard work, but with this job I can be home when the kids get off the school bus."

Already, I don't like Melvin. "At least you guys end up with the money."

"Eventually, after I send it to Texas first."

"But why doesn't he pay it himself?" Delight would say I'm being too in-your-face. But, Jesus, what does the man *have* that he can act like such an asshole and get away with it? And why would Carmel let him?

"Oh, Melvin got tired of going to Spokane to fix forklifts and began to work less and less. He's not a city person. For a while we all lived with a friend of Melvin's, but there wasn't enough room, so Melvin bought a big old cabin tent at the Army-Navy surplus store to put up on the friend's land."

"You're not living in it now, I hope?" I stare at Carmel, my mouth open.

The game show buzzer goes off. This time I struggle to my feet on my own.

"To be continued," Carmel says.

It's mid-morning of my fourth day of bending, scooping and tossing sawdust, of gobbling aspirins to keep my sore muscles working, of wiping my nose on my jacket sleeve. I'm shoveling burnt sawdust when *clank*, my shovel strikes metal. By the time I finish with the spud bar and shovel I've uncovered a motor about three feet high and four feet long on a concrete platform. I search out Leroy.

"I've been here eight years," he says. "I didn't know this was here."

He calls a millwright to the scene.

"Does it still have oil in the clear tube?" Leroy asks.

"Yep," said the millwright, scratching his head. "I've been working here over twenty years and didn't know this thing existed."

"Hell," I blurt. "When was this spot last cleaned?"

"Probably never," the millwright says. "I don't even think Esterbrook knows about this."

At lunch break, as Carmel and I clomp up the stairs together, she says, "The men are talking about the motor you dug up."

"They say anything about me, or just the motor?"

"Well," she said, sitting down on the bench and getting out her sandwich.

"Well, what?"

"Kurt said to Dave, 'Hey, didja hear about the motor that new bitch dug up?'" Carmel takes a small, ladylike bite of her sandwich.

"Oh."

"Doesn't think women should work in the mill. That's all. Nothing personal. At least you don't have to work with him. He's always trying to pinch my fingers in the two by fours."

"Let's not waste time on 'em," I say. "What I really want to know is if you're living in a tent now."

"Yes, I am, and it's not as bad as you think. The tent has a solid wood floor and a wood stove, and Melvin promised we'd be warm. We do have a plan. Since I work here at the mill and we can buy economy lumber cheap, he plans to build a house around the tent in the spring."

"But it's winter," I say, as if Carmel might not have noticed. "It's freezing cold."

"Oh, it's warm near the stove and in bed," she says in an almost dreamy voice. "We have lots of quilts. The two boys seem to enjoy it. They think it's an adventure, like being a fur trapper in the movie *Dances With Wolves*. But my daughter isn't happy. She's always cold."

"I have to say, living in a tent this time of year is just plain crazy."

"I know." Her eyes are closed and she's slumped back against the wall, chewing slowly. She says, "Did anyone tell you the last woman hired to do cleanup refused to climb up onto the debarker ramp to deal with the frozen cedar bark? So they let her go. Anyway, it's Ed's job. Leroy only had you do it as a test."

This information hits me hard. "Well, hell. I never even questioned doing it," I say. "At the time it didn't seem like I had a choice."

"What you just said? That's the reason I live in a tent."

Neither of us says a thing for a while. There's nothing to say and way too much to think about. What Carmel says is true. My doing something so dangerous that I could have ended up in a wheelchair or been killed, and doing it without thinking I had a choice, well that makes us alike in some basic way. The buzzer groans. Lunch break is over. Double jeopardy.

# CHAPTER 7

Compared to slinging sawdust at the mill, cleaning out the cat box at home is a picnic. In the winter, Tummy does not want to go outside and I can't blame him. After sleeping in Saturday morning 'til 7:15, I eat a lumberjack breakfast of bacon, scrambled eggs and pancakes. I haul in firewood and fill the wood box. I vacuum, do laundry, and make a run to the IGA. Mom bakes bread. I soak in the bathtub for an hour and then we play cribbage, while it snows and blows outside the tin box we live in. Just like last year, we agree that winter is worse than ever, that it'll probably never end. This is, after all, the year of Y2K. Anything can happen.

About 4:00 p.m., when it's already starting to get dark, we hear Justin's diesel pickup truck coming up our driveway. He has a plow on the front of his truck, and he's pushing snow.

"Hi Auntie. Hi Grammy." Justin stands on the welcome mat, looking like a character out of *Call of the Wild*.

"Knock the icicles off yourself, boy," Mom says, moving toward him to get a big bear hug.

"Hi, Sweetie," I say. Justin and I never touch, but he knows I'd kill for him, that he's my favorite human in the world.

"When you started at the mill," he says. "I just knew you were gonna holler out, 'Hi, Sweetie,' while I was working."

"You gotta give me some credit. I do have a few social skills."

Justin takes off his coat and boots and puts on the slippers we keep by the door for him, year round. We sit down at the dining room table. He says, "It's just that I'm finally being treated like one of the guys. They still kid me about the time I learned to drive the bucket loader. When I went to raise the bucket it swung up like a fist and lifted the dry shed roof a couple inches. I was afraid to tell Leroy, but he just laughed. Sent the carpenters up to repair the roof."

Justin loves to talk and we love to hear him, so we keep his coffee cup full and listen.

"You keeping warm, Grammy? Think the eight cords of wood I brought you'll be enough?"

"I'm warm. But your Aunt here, I don't know. Hope she gets through winter with all her digits."

"That's if I don't wreck myself completely first, end up crippled."

"You're tougher than you think you are, Auntie," Justin says, all serious. "Or at least that's what happened to me. You just keep doing what you gotta do, and the next thing you know you get used to it."

"I hope you're right. I'm getting up in years, and so is Rooster. I'd like to buy a truck someday, that is when I grow up." Justin and Delight don't know about my gambling debt. So far, Mom's been keeping my secret.

"But I like your car," Mom says. "He's comfortable. How am I gonna climb in and out of a truck?"

"I'll get a little truck, Mom. A Toyota. You and Justin can help me pick it out." I realize I'm counting my chickens too soon, with only one week at the mill and I just barely survived that.

"You'll probably have to learn to drive a forklift, Auntie. One day they let me drive a brand new one. I parked the thing out in the yard and went off to take a leak. When I came back the forklift was gone. I went around asking all the guys where they hid the forklift, thought they were playing a joke on me. Then I found Ken and Jake over the bank in the ditch trying to get the new forklift off its side and back in the yard before Leroy found out. I didn't know it, but what I should'a done was set the brakes instead of putting the forklift in neutral and dropping the forks, like with the old ones. There it was over on its side, a little scratched up. The guys told Leroy the brakes must have failed. Even the truck repair shop across the river played along, and charged the mill for a minor whatchamacallit that could have affected brake performance. They fixed it, too," Justin says, grinning. "That forklift never rolled out of the yard again."

We laugh with him. But I know that even if I survive at the mill, even if I learn to drive a forklift, I'll never be treated like "one of the guys."

Dad had a friend named Pete who used to come over to visit. We see him once in a while. When he was still in his seventies, Pete did cleanup part-time at a little mill over in Montana. He told us about that day he was working all by himself on a Saturday. No one else should'a been there. He said, "On the weekends nothing was running, so I could clean the equipment and all around it. Saw a piece of 2 x 4 stuck in a chain. Reached underneath to pry it out. About that time a millwright started up the chain to check it, and that's how I lost my hand."

On Sunday morning I take Mom to The Log Drive for breakfast—thin coffee, two-egg omelet special—$3.05, not $3.00—or you can pay with thirty minutes of dish-washing. The offer's good only until 8:00 a.m., which is early on a Sunday morning. Other than the bars lining Main Street, The Log Drive is where people meet from five in the morning to nine at night. This morning a bunch of regulars are here. Mostly of the geezers retired from working in the woods or at the mills. With all the years of accidents, this morning is like amputee day—guys with missing fingers, hands, arms, eyes, even legs.

Ed, who works on the debarker at the mill, is here. When he was working at a mill over in Idaho, his jacket got caught in a chain and he was drug through a piece of equipment and spit out the other side. He's all scarred up—face, neck, arms—and that's only what you can see. One day he told me he died three times on the way to the hospital, but they revived him every time. Each time he died, he said he heard the most beautiful music and felt so peaceful. Told me he didn't really *want* to come back. Said dying was beautiful.

This morning Dad's old friend, Pete, comes over to say hello. "We all feel real bad about Weldon," he says. "That's his empty chair, over there. We know he was a friend to your family."

"Thanks, Pete," Mom says, taking his one hand for a minute.

We nod to the men. They'd kept an empty chair for Dad one whole winter, at what they all call The Table of Wisdom. Pete goes back to the geezers and they settle into their usual banter. We order, and while we eat our two-egg omelet we hear the men talking politics, most of them agreeing that Rush Limbaugh should be president.

"See?" Mom says.

## CHAPTER 8

Dunes of sawdust, chips, and scraps of wood are heaped up all around, like a natural disaster happened here, like a tornado. This is my next job—cleaning up an area half the size of a football field—the basement of the mill.

"There's no way you're gonna clean the whole thing," Leroy says. Most of the mess from operating the mill ends up here, all over the floor."

I'm thinking, *What floor*?

Leroy continues, "Once material hits the floor or the ground it's only good for hog fuel, and all mills use it to fire their boilers. Just fill the wheelbarrow, push it up the ramp there, and dump it into the conveyor bins on that platform."

"Okay." Hard hat and safety glasses on. Dust mask in place, already fogging up my glasses. Ear plugs in. Nothing to do now but sweep and shovel sawdust, and wonder why the hell sawdust and scrap wood is called hog fuel, when it fires a boiler? I give up on the question and picture Weldon, not as someone chewed to bits by a giant chipper but as a neighbor—walking, talking, and telling stories while he and June play pinochle with Mom and Dad.

Down here in the dungeon, I shovel sawdust and scrap wood into the wheelbarrow and strain every muscle in my body to run with it up the metal gang plank. At the top I dump the crap into the bins that carry it outside onto the ground. Over and over. Repeat. When the break buzzer finally rings, I meet Carmel at the bench in the machine shop.

"God I love breaks," I say, lighting my cigarette.

Carmel takes my left hand, the one not holding a cigarette. The veins on the back of our hands look like blue angleworms. Our hands do not push pencils to make a living. She lifts her wrist up to my nose. "Smell."

To smell something, anything, besides pitch, sawdust, wood chips, dust, or hydraulic fluid just about knocks me off the bench. "Citrus? Musk? What, Carmel?"

She smiles, pulls her wrist away and rests it in her lap. "We went to Spokane on Saturday and Melvin insisted we buy a bottle of *Safari* perfume. You'd think he'd want me to pay off his back child support and then save money for the house. But now that I work here at the mill, he acts like he's tapped into the Bank of America."

"You could put the men in shock, wearing a smell like that," I say, but what I think is that Melvin's a real tosser.

"Not sure they even notice it. Melvin makes me wear it to bed. I mean, I like to smell nice, but it was so expensive." Carmel stops talking and sniffs her wrist again. "Last night, when I got up in the middle of the night, the moon was shining down on me through the clear plastic window in the side of the tent. I sat there on the cold pot wearing my perfume, looking up at the moon. And I peed, feeling sad and stupid to be living in a tent, in winter."

"Maybe you could rent a place in town." This is obvious, but I want to hear what she'll say.

"I guess, but spring will be here in a few months and then we'll build. Besides, it can be lovely in the woods. Some time after I got up in the night, the sky turned

overcast and it snowed. This morning the trees were un-
speakably beautiful. Mentally, I went away somewhere,
like maybe Iceland, where I was untroubled."

"You're one tough cookie, Carmel."

On my walk back to the wheelbarrow, I think about
Carmel's curious life. Delight would call it *dysfunctional,*
a term she used on me. And that's without even without
knowing all my secrets. On the other hand, some women
bore me silly with all those details about their closets,
and whether a minor event happened on a Tuesday, or
no, a Wednesday. As if it matters. Thank God Yates
doesn't talk like that, and neither does Carmel. And if all
I can do for Carmel right now is be her friend, well, that's
what I'm gonna do.

No wonder most women don't last at this mill. The
jobs are either dangerous or so damn repetitive it eats
your brain. Only criminals, like maybe sex offenders,
should have to work here. I'm stronger this week than
last, but I still feel threadbare like an old sock ready for
the rag heap. At least it's not so cold, here in the basement. Today I'm dressed for success, wearing a pair of
Dad's long wool underwear, this pair with a drop-down
flap in the back. It's a lot easier to go to the bathroom,
but it feels like I'm wearing a diaper.

The job continues. I shovel sawdust and pieces of
wood into the wheelbarrow, take a big breath, and run up
the ramp. Over and over. Plenty of time to think, and I
guess I'm not in the best of moods. Now I'm on a mental
kick about how my whole life has felt like The Great
Depression, always counting pennies—that is when I had
pennies to count. Poverty and grief were the two main
reasons I took up gambling, why I drove Rooster west

over the pass one day and stopped at the casino, where I won $432 right off the bat. Seemed like my big opportunity. I drove back and forth the next few months. Made a part-time job out of gambling. I was gonna take charge of my life, once and for all. What an exciting, hopeful time, knowing the next big win was only one crank of the lever ahead of me. By the time I was done with my little gambling spree, I'd opened up several credit cards—way too easy to do—and ran 'em all up past their limits. $43,000 worth. I put thousands of miles on the car, wore out two sets of retreads, and shortened Rooster's life. Built up the muscles in my right arm, too, pulling that lever. But instead of winning big, I faced paying back my debt with minimum wage jobs, when I could get 'em. Mostly I try to forget about that sorry time in my life. Gambling was the most expensive, lowest paying part-time job I ever had. And I've had some real doozies.

The wheelbarrow is full of wet sawdust now and I guess I don't run up the ramp with enough enthusiasm, because the wheelbarrow flips and all the sawdust falls eight or nine feet back down onto the basement floor. I manage to hang onto the wheelbarrow, so at least I don't wreck that. As I back down the ramp, I hear laughter. When I get to the bottom and look over to where the sound came from, no one's there. Did I really hear something or did I imagine it?

After a couple more days in the basement, Leroy sends me outdoors in the yard to sort for hog fuel. "The price is up and demand is high," he tells me. "Someone will bring you loads of material to sort, about three loads an hour. Just stand on the platform here beside this pit and use your shovel to knock everything off the conveyor except bark."

"Okay."

"The bark will go into a crusher and then into another bin. Trucks will drive under the bin, load up, and haul it away."

"Okay," I say again. "Bark equals hog fuel." Why does he explain nothing one time, and the next time he can't stop mumbling. Then I remember. I'm getting paid when I'm listening and paid when I'm honking bark.

Dark clouds in the north are moving toward me. Better work fast or I'll freeze in place staring at a cold front.

Rollers at the bottom of the pit move along the *material*, as Leroy called it, onto a steep conveyor. In addition to bark, I'm finding rocks and scraps of metal, like broken pulleys and pieces of chain, probably from the logging operation. But fast food wrappers and pop cans? A guy in a bucket loader shows up to haul away a load of reject material I've knocked off the conveyor, and then returns with another load for me to sort. I yell up to him, "Leroy wants me to go through three loads an hour."

"Well, now," he hollers back. "That depends on how busy I am and if I *feel* like bringing you three loads an hour."

"Okay, as long as I don't get in trouble and I can keep busy enough not to freeze to death."

"Cold as a witch's tit, ain't it?" He sits in the bucket loader, stares at my chest and adds, "Like yours."

Ignoring the prick, I turn to the new pile of material to sort, and never look at him again.

Friday at lunch break, Carmel holds her wrist up to my nose again.

"Oh. God, I love that smell," I say. "Maybe Melvin's idea ain't so bad."

"But, Echo, don't you think wearing perfume while living in a tent is like wearing lacy underwear while picking edgings?"

"You mean to say you don't wear lacy underwear to work?"

Carmel looks at me real serious. "Do you?"

"Nice idea, but I don't own any . . . yet."

"Me neither," she says. "But that reminds me of something Melvin said. When I get out of bed in the morning, my right cheek is completely exposed, never the left. So every time I get up I have to yank my panties out and down." She pauses, smiling. "Melvin calls it *the coriolis effect,* says it would be the opposite cheek in the Southern Hemisphere. He's so funny." Her smile turns to a frown. She sighs. "Lately my whole life is bunched up, sort of like my underwear."

I can only shake my head. "That Melvin sure does seem to have a sense of humor." What I don't say is, How can a knuckle dragger like Melvin use such big words?

Back at the sorting job, the loader man dumps material to be sorted into the pit—sometimes one load an hour, sometimes two or four loads an hour, but never three—and I do my best to sort the crap he delivers. Finally, it's Friday and payday, followed by a weekend of soaking in the tub and playing cribbage with Mom.

# CHAPTER 9

"This is a chipper," Leroy says, as if talking to the beast. "It's also called a hog. Processes scrap wood and feeds sawdust into one bin and chips into another. Trucks pull under the bins and haul the material away."

He tears his gaze away from the hog and looks at me. I nod my head. Jesus, I hope I won't be quizzed on the names of all the gizmos at the mill, and where all the parts of a tree end up.

"All you have to do is pull the 2 x 4 pieces off the conveyor, but only the ones that are at least two feet long. Don't let those go into the chipper. We can sell them for spacers. Okay?"

"Okay."

This monster is shaped like a barrel, except that it's almost as big as a city water tower. Leroy leaves me standing about ten feet from the monster's open snout, about three feet square. The spiral cutting devices in the throat of the hog are sucking in the wood scraps, being dumped into the mouth from the conveyor-shaker bin. I can feel the draft. This is like the monster that ate Weldon over at Eagle Creek.

I stare into the mouth of the chipper, the maw of death. Pieces of 2 x 4 longer than two feet pass and get sucked into the hog, but I can't move. I feel eyes on me. When I turn my head, there's Leroy leaning against the wall, arms crossed, waiting, watching. In slow motion I begin to lift pieces of wood off the conveyor and place them on a pallet. I am cheating the hog. Leroy leaves. I reach for another 2 x 4, and notice out of the corner of my eye that he's stopped again, watching me. Wish I could give him the finger.

Retired mill workers have a saying, when one of them is gone from a room for a while. "Old Hank, yeah, he probably went to take a leak and the hog ate him." They say this anywhere—at weddings, reunions, picnics, or when they get together at The Table of Wisdom for coffee. Mill work is hard and dirty and dangerous, and I guess getting eaten by a hog—that sonofabitchin' chipper—is about the worst thing that can happen. They're missing body parts, but by making jokes like that after they retire from the mill, they have the last word.

While cheating the hog, I let my thoughts take me where they will, and remember my own life or death hog story. One chilly day in April, when Delight and I were five or six years old, we walked with Mom and Dad down to the field where a pig lived in a shed. I don't remember why the Kodak moment—all of us walking hand in hand to see that pig—but I do know I was wearing red corduroy bib overalls, rubber boots and a blue-gray coat that flared out at the bottom. I've seen pictures of me in that outfit. The pig was always hungry and ate strange things. When we butchered chickens, we gave it the feet. It was funny to see yellow chicken's feet sticking out of the sides of the pig's snout as she chewed and snorted. That day there was mud everywhere. Bluebirds and robins flew from one fence post to the next. When we got to within a few feet of the pig, Mom said, "Don't get too close to the fence. That pig'll eat you alive." I remember the pig's name was Daphne, and she was given to us by a family who lived on the edge of town. Daphne was an enormous problem pig. She'd sit in the middle of the road and not move, so cars and pickups had to drive in the ditch to get into town. Then Daphne somehow knocked over a lantern and burned down her owner's barn. That's when they gave her to us. The huge pig, her hide like a filthy brush, snorted and nosed around in the squishy mud inside a pole fence. All of a sudden the pig squealed and grabbed the bottom of my coat and pulled me against the fence. I screamed. Mom grabbed my arm and tried to pull me away. Helpless inside my coat, I yelled, "Please God let my buttons pop. Let me outta here!" The pig was gonna eat me. Mom said so. I pictured my legs sticking out the sides of the pig's snout. I screamed again. My coat ripped. Mom cussed and yelled at the pig. Delight howled like a dog. I hollered 'til I was dizzy. The pig snorted and squealed louder as it pulled me one way, while Mom pulled me the other. When Dad whacked Daphne on the nose with a board, she let loose of my coat and backed off. I'm not sure what finally happened to Daphne, but I never blamed her for what happened.

With all the equipment running full tilt, the ear plugs help only a little to muffle the roar of heavy metal and the screeching tires. It sounds like a train that's jumped the tracks going 100 mph. about to smash into the mill—except the train is already inside the mill, and it can't escape. Besides the noise, dust hangs in the air like fog. Still, for me this job is the promised land, my only hope for decent money.

On my second day of cheating the hog, I wonder what the basement is like, with no one down there cleaning. Oh, no. Here comes Leroy.

"We've started running shorter lumber," he says. "I need someone to stack railroad ties."

"You do?" I ask. What he said makes no sense. I also know that railroad ties are heavier than shit.

"Yeah," he says, like he read my mind. "Think you're man enough to handle it?"

"Sure," I say. I abandon my station at the mouth of the hog to follow him through the sawdust haze. We make our way out into the yard, walking past the stations, each with workers in front of roll cases, red laser lights, coils, and grinding gears. And always, *always*, the sound of boards slamming their way through the mill.

"These ties are lodgepole," Leroy states, grabbing the end of a tie as if he's mad at it. "They're only seventy, maybe eighty pounds. Lighter than most." He grabs one, flips it sideways, and stacks it on a pallet.

It's a matter of balance and timing, I know, but still, they are 9" x 6.5" x eight feet long. I'll wait for him to leave, and then figure out how to do this myself. I nod my head to him to let him know I'm good, and wait.

"They aren't going to stack themselves," he says, finally walking off.

After a few clumsy attempts, I grab a tie, pull it over, swing one end around, and drop the fucker onto the stack. No one's gonna say *I'm* not man enough to do something at the mill.

## CHAPTER 10

The ramp in the basement is steeper, and the wheelbarrow full of sawdust is heavier than before, I swear. This morning I struggle up the ramp to the platform, dump a load into one of the conveyor bins, and back down with the empty wheelbarrow right into Leroy, standing there with a couple of kids.

"Esterbrook wants the entire place cleaned up in a hurry," Leroy yells above the dull roar of the equipment above our heads. This is Janie and Smitty. I'll bring a couple more wheelbarrows and shovels. Think you can show these two the ropes?"

Janie is much too little and cute to be shoveling sawdust in the basement of a sawmill. And Smitty is a tall, skinny pimply-faced kid, maybe sixteen.

"Sure," I say, dropping the handles of my wheelbarrow as Leroy walks off.

"Hi, I'm Echo," I say, shaking gloves with each of them. I'll have my hands full with this pair.

Janie can't be more than 5' 2". Perfect skin. Under the layers of work clothes, she appears to have the body of a young boy, like one of them mannequins in the children's department at JCPenney. She's more like a Barbie *Boy* than a Barbie *Doll*.

They look around the basement at the mountains of sawdust and scraps of wood. I doubt if either one is tough enough to push a loaded wheelbarrow up the ramp. But Smitty handles the wheelbarrow like it's a toy, and after a few tries Janie gets the hang of it, too, after I suggest she fill the wheelbarrow half full. She's quick and ends up making more trips than either Smitty or me. We get coordinated so we don't stand around with our thumbs up our butts waiting for a turn on the ramp. And Smitty is working farther out, so we don't trip over each other.

"How'd you guys get on?" I ask, at our first break.

"They're hiring on the Extra Board," Smitty says.

"Never heard of it."

"You have to be willing to do whatever job needs to be done. Might work into full time, might not, and that's okay with me. I'm taking a semester off college to earn money."

"Huh. No kidding." He sure seems young for college.

Janie tells us she graduated from high school in 1988. "I loved high school," she says, smiling her little pixie smile, flashing her perfect teeth. "I was a cheerleader. The games were always so much fun, especially when we won. Being Miss Hatfield my senior year was the most fun I've ever had.

I don't tell her that I barely made it through high school, and that, believe you me, I did not try out to be a cheerleader or Miss Anything. No way. I rode the bus home after school, and my extra-curricular activities involved chopping wood, climbing trees, and fishing up the creek.

"I dated Danny my junior and senior years," she says. "He was the quarterback on the football team. Played basketball, too, even though he was short. We got married right out of school."

I want to say, *If you have everything going for you, how come you're here doing cleanup at a sawmill?* But instead I say, "Any kids?"

"Two boys, five and seven, and a girl, eight. Tiffany is going to classes in Spokane so she can be in the Little Miss America pageant. That's mainly why I'm working. The classes are expensive. And she's learning to play the piano; that costs money. I want to give her a few opportunities in life."

When she takes off her hard hat, her hair is dark and short. Unlike Carmel, who doesn't comb her hair, Janie has put wax or whatever in her hair to make it *look* like she didn't comb it. The hard hat mashed it down. Carmel is right. Why comb your hair, except after you wash it? I comb mine before work, but you'd never know it.

At the end of the day Leroy comes down to the basement. "Tomorrow you can all work farther out. Just take the tops off the biggest mounds. In other words, slop-clean the entire basement. I'll have you go back over it if there's time. Esterbrook's selling out," he continues. "Has a prospective buyer. When you get done down here, I'll set you up in the yard."

"Yates?" I say into the phone. She'd given me her number, but I hadn't called her. 'Course, she didn't call me either. We knew we were both out there somewhere.

"Echo, girl. How the hell are ya?"

"Working at the sawmill doing cleanup. Breaking my back. Filthy work, too, but the pay's good and I think they're hiring on what they call the Extra Board. They even put a sign up in the break room, something about 'valuing diversity.' Looks like we're getting a new owner."

"Hey, thanks for the tip, girlfriend," Yates says. "I'm waiting tables at the truck stop. Hardly any tips these days. I'll stop by the mill office, see if I can scare up some diversity."

The next morning at the mill, before Janie, Smitty and I can get the entire basement slop-cleaned, Leroy sends us outdoors to sort for hog fuel and stack scrap wood. We split up. I clean around the dry sheds where stacks of planed, finished lumber are stored until trucks can haul them away. At least it's not so cold out, about twenty-five degrees.

Who knows how cull boards find their way out to the dry sheds, but that's what I'm picking up. When I finish making a stack, I walk out from between two units of lumber on my way to the next mess. Hearing a forklift coming behind me, I walk close to the units. There's plenty of room, so I don't look over my shoulder as the forklift approaches. The next thing you know, the forklift passes so close the machine touches the arm of my jacket. I freeze, staring after the speeding forklift. I yell, "Son of a bitch!" When I stop shaking I dart from unit to unit, looking over my shoulder, listening for the forklift. All day long trucks come and go and bucket loaders carry sawdust from one pile to the next. They're both big and slow, and it's easy to stay out of their way. But forklifts are small and can race around the yard like remote control cars.

When I find Janie and Smitty I say, "Let's take a break now." I lead them to a spot I'd scouted out earlier, behind several units of dried, planed lumber. "Don't worry about getting caught smoking," I tell Smitty. "Worry about getting run over by a forklift. I just had a helluva close call. Jesus, I'm still a wreck."

Smitty lights up a cigarette. "Here," he says, handing it to me.

Oh, the joys of nicotine addiction, especially when suffering a case of nerves. "The driver'd have to be blind not to see me. Still can't believe it happened."

"You sure the guy wasn't making a pass at you? Kissing you with his forklift?"

"Hah!"

"Just kidding," Smitty says.

"Not funny."

I sag against a unit of lumber, half the size of a boxcar, wishing I could sit down. Jesus, a lawn chair out here in the snow and sawdust would feel good right now. Janie stands near me and puts a hand on my arm. Smitty and I smoke silently, and after I recover a little I ask Janie a question I've been thinking about off and on. "Did you have June Starkberry for a teacher in high school?"

Janie nods and smiles. "Mrs. S, we called her. My favorite teacher. She told me I should go on to college, that I was too smart not to. But all I wanted to do was marry Danny. Poor June, losing Weldon in that horrible way."

We're quiet again for a few seconds, and then I say, "June lives up the road from us. Mom saw her a couple days ago, and she's having a hard time. Said she's leaving soon for Portland, where her daughter lives." I don't say that June told Mom she talked to a hotdog attorney in Spokane about the accident, that there'll probably be a big lawsuit. I'd say June deserves everything she can get.

"When I called her to offer my condolences," Janie says, "I didn't know what to say."

While Janie talks, it dawns on me why she's so familiar. "You look just like a girl a couple years behind me in school. Could that your mother?"

"Maybe. Susie Baker was her name then. She was a cheerleader, too. Graduated in 1969, I think." Janie pauses and looks out toward the yard. "Yes. It was '69. I've heard her talk about a thirty-year reunion."

"Well, sure. I graduated in '67. Whatever happened to her?"

"She went away to Butte, Montana, for business college," Janie says. "That's where she met my father. They settled in Hatfield. He worked in the mill, but then he ran off with a bar maid from Spokane. My mom eventually married again." Janie looks down at her boots. "Unfortunately, he moved in with us."

"One more mystery solved," I say. "Small world."

"I agree," Janie says. "But then I've never seen Leroy before. Guess we don't travel in the same circles."

"Glad to hear I'm not the only one," I say. "I don't know most of the men at the mill."

Janie, Smitty and I sort and shovel and stack cull lumber all day. No need to wear ear plugs out in the yard, which makes it easier for me to listen for a forklift roaring toward me. I also think about how Spokane is the closest big city where you can go to be anonymous, to study for a new career like Delight is doing, or where you can go to cheat on your spouse like Janie's father did. Spokane's also where you go to live if you can work up enough courage to leave home. Hatfield's a bit like Outer Mongolia, the edge of the world. Take the 1960s. No one threw bricks or burned their bras in Hatfield. That decade came and went without us. Then, too, our fashions run a decade or two, hell, maybe three, behind Spokane, and I doubt *they're* so up-to-the-minute. My own personal fashion statement hasn't changed since the 1960s. Jeans and flannel shirts or tee shirts, during the two weeks of poor sledding we call summer. 'Course the 1970s brought a flood of city people moving back to the land. The woods are still full of abandoned shacks banged together out of old wood doors and windows. Rusty vans and school busses converted to homes, their windows broken out, sit around in the national forest with their tires rotting into the whortleberry bushes.

Our cleanup work in the yard continues. Whenever I hear a forklift, I hide between units of lumber. At break times, we don't get caught smoking until the electrician, Sparks, sneaks up on us and yells "BOO!" We jump but hang onto our cigs, and he asks to see what brands we're smoking. He selects a cigarette from Smitty's pack and I strike a match on my jacket to light it for him. I usually use a lighter, but wanted to be cool. Inhaling deeply with his eyes closed, Sparks says, "Don't let the forklift drivers catch you smoking here, and if you do get caught, you're on your own. I was never here."

The next day while we're working outside, a man drives his truck under the sawdust bin to load up. He jumps out of his truck, climbs up the ladder on the outside of the bin, pulls the rope that releases the sawdust, and watches, dumbfounded, as the load buries his truck. We stand leaning on our shovels as the driver mouths four-letter words. He'd forgotten to take the tarp off the box of his truck, and now with all the sawdust heaped around it, we can hardly see his rig.

When the truck driver comes over to apologize for making such a big mess, I start laughing. When I stop to catch my breath, I say, "I'm sorry to laugh, but it's funnier than hell. I've never seen anyone do that before."

"Echo," Smitty says, "You're not being very polite."

"Yeah, I know," I snort, laughing like a hyena. Maybe I need a good laugh, but I laugh so hard I nearly wet my pants. I just can't quit.

Leroy stomps over to us, frowning, shaking his head. By now the truck driver is laughing, too. He says, "I've been driving truck for ten years, and I've never pulled a boner like this."

A *boner*? I think. A *boner*? And I start a new round of hysterical laughing.

"Once sawdust hits the ground," Leroy says, struggling not to smile, "we gotta 'hog fuel' it. You know what to do, Echo."

Leroy leaves. It takes a few minutes for me to settle down. Laughing felt so good for a change, and now I hate to give it up. Not that it's so funny, mind you. Even before the truck driver pulled that boner there was too much cleanup to do. We'll have to work overtime. He needs to get on his way, which means digging out the truck so he can remove the tarp and get another load of sawdust. The truck driver grabs a shovel and helps. Work is more fun, now that I work on an actual crew, throw a snowball or two, and find things to laugh about. And my body is complaining less about the hard work. *Adversity is good for you—it helps prepare you for more adversity.* Whoever said that, maybe it was Benjamin Franklin, hell, maybe it was Delight, sure knew what they were talking about.

It takes a few hours to get the truck driver on his way and then a few days to get the yard cleaned up enough to suit Leroy. Then he assigns us to help out in the planer building, where the rough-cut lumber gets planed smooth on all sides. After the forklift drivers deliver the unplaned lumber to the planer, the boards are moved along rollers and chains through different stations, where it's graded, planed and cut to dimension. It's always amazed me that 2 x 4s end up 1-1/2" x 3-1/2" and 2 x 6s at 1-1/2" x 5-1/2". After the lumber is stamped for species, length and grade, it's banded into units again and stored in the dry sheds—one of the areas in the yard we just cleaned.

The doors of the planer building are always wide open to the cold north wind so forklifts can come and go with units of lumber, and bobcats can pick up sawdust, shavings and chips. Justin said the floor heaters died a couple years ago, and Esterbrook never got 'em fixed. The only heat in the building comes from two giant turbo heaters hanging down from the metal overhead trusses. They're heated with water piped in from the boiler. The area under them is warm, and you can get warm, but you also have to eat sawdust stirred up by the blowers.

The main job of our clean team is to pick up cull boards and sweep sawdust during the hours the men are working. The regular cleanup person at the planer, Tripp, carries a broom around and drinks coffee most of the time. We don't think it's coffee in his thermos bottle, either, because he doesn't take sips—he gulps. He does so little that it takes all three of us two days to deal with the sawdust and cull lumber he let pile up. While you wouldn't want to eat off the floor when we're done, at least, according to Leroy, we did some damage.

When Leroy first asks me if I can drive a bobcat, I say, "Sure." And I don't see any reason why I can't. If men can do it, so can I. In the driver's seat, there's a vertical lever on each side of my legs. No gas pedal, no brake, and no steering wheel. I sit a while, feeling stupid. Maybe what to do next will come to me. Leroy smirks and shakes his head in that robot way he has, then walks over to the bobcat. He shouts, "Lever on the left turns you to the left, lever on the right turns you to the right. Push both levers forward to go ahead, neutral to stop, back for reverse."

Okay. Okay. So I ease forward on both levers and take off. Out in the yard I have a little room to learn, but I hit a hole and panic. I jerk both the steering levers toward me, to neutral, but I over-correct and throw the rig into reverse. Me and the bobcat rock and roll. It rears up on the back wheels, then down onto the front wheels, then the back wheels kick up again. I hang on for dear life to the levers, which are thrown forward and back with the bucking. Jesus, this is worse than the mechanical bull at that bar in Spokane. I give up, let go of the levers, and throw up my hands. The bobcat stops. As soon as I stop shaking I climb out of the bobcat and let Smitty try it. Leroy explains things a little more to him, and he does all right. Smitty teaches Janie how to drive it and she maneuvers the thing like a champ. She says she doesn't have a driver's license, doesn't even drive without one, like some people do.

About an hour before the shift ends, Smitty and I are shoveling sawdust in the mill while Janie drives the bobcat. Even above the pounding roar of the mill, we hear the thundering rotors echoing up the valley toward us. Smitty and I run to the big open doors and watch the helicopter drop down in the yard, like we're an unofficial welcoming party, and watch the rotors blow snow and sawdust all over our clean yard. The prospective buyer for the mill has arrived.

"Jesus, you two!" Leroy yells, pushing us indoors none too gently. "At least *act* busy."

# CHAPTER 11

The pit under the planer machine is just that—a concrete hole eight feet deep by twelve feet long and about six feet wide—and it's filled close to the top with sawdust, chips, and scraps of wood. All four of us descend into the pit, but it's so full we can't stand up.

"We have a problem," Leroy says, squatting down to talk with us. "While the machinery is shut down for lunch break, I want you three musketeers to clean here. We're running white fir. It's real dry, and when the pit is this full a spark from the planer could start a fire."

Leroy's hunched over, showing Smitty, Janie and me how to use what looks like the exhaust hose on a clothes dryer. The hose is attached to an intake pipe, like a vacuum. Then Leroy grabs a shovel and uncovers a much larger pipe that's buried in a corner of the pit. The pipe's sole purpose is to snort up sawdust, except scraps of wood get caught in it. "After you pull the scrap wood out of that pipe, just push the reset button on the wall there. You'll have to work fast. You only have half an hour." He climbs up the only two metal steps that aren't buried by sawdust, opens the door of the Lexan-walled room that houses the planer machine and the pit, and leaves.

The vacuum hose carries static electricity, and right off the bat I touch metal and get a shock.

"Know why you got a shock?" Smitty shouts.

Even though the planer equipment is shut down for lunch break, there's still loud noise. The vacuum hose sounds like a monster shop-vac, so I have to yell back, "No, tell me, Einstein."

I gotta hear this. I kill the switch on the hose.

"Friction from the dry sawdust passing through the inside of the hose builds up in you as energy. When you touch metal, the energy is released."

Janie and I stare at Smitty. "Well, here you go," I say, offering him the hose. "Your turn."

"Thanks." To the hose he says, "Gertrude, may I have this dance?"

With Smitty hunched over, dancing around the pit with the hose, sucking up sawdust, Gertrude doesn't always suck so good. Sticks keep getting caught. When this happens, he switches off the hose to unclog it. Another time he gets his foot too close and falls down in the sawdust yelling, "Help! Help!" Janie and I play along and pull the hose off his foot. We laugh so hard that I almost pee my pants. For a moment I stand still as a post and think, What price will I have to pay for having this much fun working?

Janie and I get in the groove and dance, too, all bent over. We feed shovels full of sawdust over to the mouth of the pipe in the corner, while Smitty makes a game out of seeing how long he can go in between shocks. But over the roar of the vacuum hose and pipe, we hear the buzzer announcing that lunch break is over, which means all the machinery will be turned back on. And Leroy was right. We don't get the pit all cleaned up. In fact, we hardly did any damage at all. And now it's our turn to eat lunch.

After our break, Leroy puts Smitty and Janie to work sorting hog fuel. He says to me, "You'll usually clean the pit when the planer is off, but today I'm going to let you work in here with it running." He says this like he's doing me a favor. "We gotta get the pit cleaned up."

"Okay," I say, reaching for Gertrude. Odd that it's all right for me to be in the pit now with the planer running, when it wasn't okay earlier. But I set to work alone. Over the deafening roar of the hose, I hear studs slamming through the machinery overhead, but being in the pit is easy compared to other jobs I've done at the mill. I check my watch. It's been almost an hour. Time for a quick smoke break.

When I return to the planer room, I walk past the station where Nose and a man named Dave are feeding lumber into the machinery. I stare at Nose's back a while, and wonder where Justin is working. When I go around to the side of the planer to enter the pit, I see dark orange flames and black smoke curling up. "Fire!" I yell. Dave and Nose flip the switch to turn off the planer. Dave calls the fire department and another guy rounds up a fire extinguisher, while Nose sprays water on the fire in the pit. With so much smoke, it's hard for them to see if they're actually putting out the fire, so I take it upon myself to lay on the floor in the slop and sawdust, looking into the pit to see if they're putting out the fire. I keep yelling, "Still sparkling down there, still burning." My eyes are burning, too, from the smoke, but I'm operating on adrenaline. What I'm doing is important.

A rough hand on the back of my jacket grabs me up off the floor like a rag doll. Before I can see who is jerking me around, I hear Leroy beller, "Echo. You get the hell out of here. It's not safe."

The butt-wipe puts me in the pit to clean while the planer's running, and now he's worried about my safety?

I yell, "Hey, Nose. Leroy's taking my place. Leroy, you lay down here and let 'em know when it quits sparkling." As I stomp out of the planer room I hear Leroy yell, "Keep spraying. Fire's not out yet."

All of us are sent out into the parking lot. The fire department shows up, bringing their big water hoses right into the mill. You'd think water might hurt the machinery, but Justin tells me that over the years there have been lots of fires with water sprayed on everything. Some of the equipment looks a little scorched in places, but it still works fine most of the time. Within an hour the fire is out. It's almost quitting time anyway, so Leroy sends us all home for the rest of the shift, with pay. The millwrights stay to fix the damaged wiring.

The next day Leroy calls a safety meeting. He's fuming. "Why wasn't the pit cleaned out? Somebody's head's gonna roll. Echo! That's your responsibility."

I didn't see *this* coming. What an asshole. I guess he wants to put me in my place for telling him to lay in the muck and watch for sparks. It was a peon's job, but Leroy told me to leave. Somebody had to do it.

In my defense, Nose pipes up, "Good God, Leroy. She just got there when the fire started. Her crew had only worked in the pit for a half hour before that. How in the hell could she get the pit clean. And she can't go in the pit while the planer's running." Nose is aware that it's against OSHA regulations and he knows that Leroy put me in the pit when he wasn't s'pose to.

Leroy turns and walks off. The meeting is over.

It would be just my luck if Leroy tries to make me a scapegoat. That'll be the end of my sawmill career and the big paychecks. My gambling debt will follow me around like a pack of coyotes. I'll never get a truck, never go to the dentist, and never experience that distant thing called *benefits*.

## CHAPTER 12

There's Dave at the trim chain and Dave at the edger, and one or two others besides. This new Dave, the safety inspector who arrives the day Tri-State International, alias TSI, takes over the mill, is Safety Dave. He's big and he's all puffed up, with thin red hair and a fat red face, plus he has what you'd call jowls. To me he looks like Howdy Doody, that puppet on a TV show I watched as a kid. Rumor has it Safety Dave did various jobs at the TSI mill near Spokane, and he was always hurting himself. Lost his index finger down to the first knuckle, and another time he fell down a set of stairs. He kept screwing up their accident rating, so the goons-that-be made him a safety officer covering several of TSI's mills. Picture a fox guarding a chicken coop.

When I got to work this morning, a big note at the time clock said SAFETY MTG IN BRAKE ROOM. MUST ATEND. Meetings are at least a chance to get warm and rest while getting paid for it. And maybe this'll be a safer place to work from now on. Hell, maybe I'll raise my hand and say it ain't safe to work when you're froze half to death.

Here we all are, sitting at the break table or standing around holding our hard hats. Carmel stands on one side of me, Yates on the other. She applied for a job, got hired on, and this is her first safety meeting. She'll sure liven up this joint. Nose and Justin stand across the room from me.

Safety Dave says, "Good morning." He waits like he expects us to say something nice and friendly in return, but no one does, so he continues. "By now you know who I am, and that I'm here to help. I want you all to be extra careful. Mills in the region are still getting an occasional log with nails in it, thanks to the environmentalists who don't believe trees should be cut for any reason. We all know these crazies use toilet paper and live in houses built from trees. Anyway, when a log first comes into the yard at the mill and goes through the debarker, a nail could get past the metal detectors, even past the scragg. These nails can be spikes, six to ten inches long. If a board with even a piece of one of those nails comes through the mill, that nail can catch on a chain and send the board flying. Or it can bust the teeth off the band saw, maybe even cause it to come loose. If you hear the hum of bees, or what sounds like a monster cat in heat, yell as loud as you can, 'board loose!' or 'band saw loose!'" Safety Dave ducks like he's dodging something. "Now listen up, people. It might seem safer underneath a machine, but if you value your life, for cryin' out loud don't crawl under any of the equipment while it's running, and especially not the scragg."

"You should all know this rule, too." He nods his head up and down, like a doofus. Someone snickers. "Do not touch anything of a biological nature. In other words, if you encounter anything that is *ooey, gooey* or *chewey*, let your supervisor know. He'll take care of it."

Then he holds up a new orange hard hat. "Never get caught without your brain bucket on. Your brains are your most important asset," he says, his red face straining like he's going to the toilet. "And here's another thing. There'll be no cussing or arguments. On a different note, no one will ever go in the pit when the machinery is running."

Nose looks right at me through his horn-rimmed glasses. Just a kindly look and a slight smile. That's all. But it's enough of a signal that my shoulders relax from up around my ears. Don't guess I'll be in any more trouble about the fire in the pit.

Next, Safety Dave announces he'll outline the rules to follow if there *is* another fire.

I whisper to Carmel, "It's Howdy Doody time." She smiles. It's the first time I've seen her smile since she talked about Melvin saying her underwear experienced *the Coriolis Effect*. I feel like putting an arm around her.

"If there's ever a big fire in any part of the plant," Safety Dave continues, "you will hear a warning bell." He pushes the red button. The bell actually rings like a monster telephone, not like the game show buzzer here in the mill that announces the beginning and end of our breaks. And it's not like the regular buzzer over at the planer building, with its *Ahooga, Ahooga* sound. "Stay calm," he says, "but go as quickly as possible to the parking lot. There'll be a head count. One of the forklift drivers will meet the fire trucks when they arrive and lead them to the fire. That's it, kids. Party's over."

"Hah!" Yates whispers, nudging me with her elbow. "That man's never *been* to a party."

"God, it's great to have you here," I tell Yates as we leave the break room. I saunter off toward my broom and shovel and Yates heads to her new job—tail sawing. Her first gig as the newest employee on the totem pole is a hard, dirty job, even worse than picking edgings. Tail sawing is so awful and the wood is so heavy that the men usually transfer to a different job as soon as possible. They like easier jobs with more down-time, so they can stand around picking their noses. Maybe it's their way of meditating.

Leroy turns me loose to do general cleanup in the mill, and I clean where I can watch Yates handle the edgings after the scragg cuts 'em off a log. Then there's the square of log that remains after the edgings are cut off. Those monsters are called *cants*. Yates and three other workers at tail saw shove the log edgings down a hole and also turn the cants to position them for the next set of saws, the head rig. Some cants are over two feet across, and eight or nine feet long, although most are smaller. Yates steps back and throws her weight against the cant to turn it. Being new at the job, she's slower than the guys next to her doing the same work, but with only a few minutes of instruction from Leroy, it looks like she knows what she's doing. That's Yates for you.

At lunch break she limps as we climb the stairs to the machine shop.

Carmel shows up, too, and there's just enough room for our three butts on the bench. I sit in the middle. Since Yates and Carmel work on adjacent lines, they've already met. Without speaking, Yates and I light our cigarettes. Inhaling, I stare at the drill press set up in the middle of the shop.

Yates groans. "I'm already black and blue on my right side, from my waist down to the top of my boots. God, I'll be glad when Friday gets here. The thought of cashing my paycheck and buying food keeps me going."

"Life is good," I say, leaning back against the wall, closing my eyes. "Cold, but good." I know Yates understands that I mean life is in no way perfect, but it could be a lot worse.

"You're not really hungry, are you?" Carmel asks.

"Not really. Found some sardines and crackers on sale the other day. I'm good."

"I'm glad you're at the tail saw now," Carmel says. "With a new person on that line, it slows things down and I won't get buried in edgings."

"You better watch out, though. I'll get faster," Yates says. "I'm already learning the tricks of the trade. When I send a slab into the hole I have to lift up my right foot and step sideways, and do it fast so the slab doesn't hit my leg."

"Sounds a little like line dancing," I say.

Yates nudges my arm and smiles. "Nothing like black and blue to make you scoot your boots."

"I'm buying you a drink at The Tool Shed on Saturday night," I tell her. "We need to celebrate your new dance skills."

# CHAPTER 13

Yates and I pull up to The Tool Shed about the same time. She parks her old silver four-door Subaru, featuring dents and rust, in the sea of pickup trucks. It's 8:00 p.m., and even after a day of rest, I'm still pooped. I yawn as I get out of my car, hanging on to Rooster for support.

"Congratulations on your new job, Yates. Sure glad you signed on."

"Hardest work I've ever done. If the pay wasn't so good, I'd go back to waitressing."

"So, it's harder than calling in spotted owls?"

She snorts. No reply required.

When we walk into the bar I catch the first whiff of that old familiar smell—what is it? Stale beer, yeah, but something else I can't put my finger on. Whatever it is, I immediately feel more alive, and very much at home in my skin. Guess I'm an alcoholic at heart. While other women battle weight gain, I have to fight off the urge to drink and gamble.

"Let's party!" Yates hollers, nudging my arm, half knocking me into a booth on a torn red plastic seat cushion. Guys at the bar turn and look at us, then resume their drinking and talking. We're next to a dirty window with a flashing neon Pabst Blue Ribbon beer sign.

"Careful," I say. "I'm not a slab of lumber."

Crick, the bartender and owner of the joint, appears. "What'll it be, ladies?" Crick has a ponderous beer gut, along with rosy, round cheeks, a nose like a red light bulb, and a handlebar mustache. He has a copy of *How to Win Friends and Influence People* up at the bar, and practices on his patrons.

"Well, now, Crick," I say, "I think tonight I'll live on the edge a little and order a Flaming Blue Jesus. And bring Yates here whatever she wants. I'm buying."

"Whatever beer you have on tap," Yates says, unzipping her buckskin jacket, revealing a tight low-cut black top.

"You're a cheap date," I say, pretending to ogle her cleavage.

"Yeah, but I can really pack 'em in, once I get started."

The place isn't crowded yet and our drinks arrive right away. Crick sets fire to mine and we chant, "Burn! Burn! Burn!"

"You'll want to huff and puff and blow out the flames before you drink it," Crick says. "Cheers, you two."

"What? You think I'm not tough enough to drink fire?" I say, blowing out the flames on top of my drink.

Crick winks at Yates, not at me, and leaves. We clink our glasses together before diving in.

"Oh my God," I say, already a little drunk. "This is so good. Lots of calories. Which is fine. All my jeans are too big in the ass now, thanks to the weight I lost on the job."

Yates shakes her head. "You need a pair of tight pants. You got a good figure. I'm taking you shopping one of these days."

"Lookie who's here," I say, hinting in the direction of the bar, fastening my eyes on him. I've been in here a few times, but I've never noticed him before. "Maybe I should have gussied up a little."

Nose heads for the bar. When he glances in our direction I lift my glass to him, wishing my drink was still on fire. As soon as he claims his beer, he walks over.

"You met Yates?" I ask, by way of introduction.

"Not formally," he says, reaching out to shake her hand.

The man sure does clean up nice. Does Yates notice his ear fur? Yates glances at me. Is she reading my mind?

"Join us, why don't you," Yates offers, scooting over in the booth to make room for him next to her.

If she and her cleavage makes a pass at Nose, I swear I'll deck her.

"Just for a while. Thanks," he says, sitting across from me. He takes a drink of beer from his glass, puts his elbows on the table, and leans a little forward, "Echo, I have to say again how much I admire your spunk. Before you signed on, three other women tried your job. Heard Bullfrog ran one of 'em off, and one refused to climb up on the debarker ramp to chisel off the frozen cedar strips. The work was just too hard for the third one." Then he lifts his can of Hamm's beer toward Yates and adds, "And you have one of the hardest jobs in the mill, but I see you're doing all right."

I'm embarrassed, and Yates seems to be, too. It's an awkward moment. I mean, a man just complimented us, for chrissake. We both smile and shrug, and I look around the smoky, noisy bar to the corner where two guys are playing pool under a bright shop light. One man is bent over, ready to break apart the balls. His pants are tight and he has nice buns. Later, at closing time, he'll probably troll for a date. When I look back at Nose he's smiling at Yates and I notice he has nice teeth. Next thing

you know, Yates and her fishing lure earrings are studying the tight jeans on the guy playing pool. She knows
how to troll, too. I sip and smile at Nose. The Flaming
Blue Jesus is working like a prayer.

"Hey, Justin," I yell as he walks toward us, Corona in
hand. I was staring at Nose and didn't see him come into
the bar.

"Hi, Auntie, I mean Echo," Justin says, scooting into
the booth next to me.

The booth is getting a little crowded, which is more
than fine with me. I flash my warmest, happiest smile.
"Hi, Justin." I'm proud of myself for not calling him
Sweetie, and I can tell he's relieved.

"Excuse me you guys," Yates says. "I'll be right back.
Jukebox is calling my name." Nose gets up to let her out
of the booth and, to his credit, he doesn't watch her walk
to the jukebox. She's got quite a wiggle.

"Up in the *real* break room, in the machine shop over
at the mill," I say, "we talk about how things might get
better now that Esterbrook sold out."

"They sure are big on the drug and alcohol thing,"
Justin says. "You heard what happened to Tripp, didn't
you?"

Yates returns to the booth. The juke box is playing
*Boot Scootin' Boogie.*

"Well, I heard Esterbrook made Tri-State agree not to
fire anyone for three years," I say, smoking, swaying a
little to the music on the juke box, *Cadillac black jack,
baby meet me out back* . . . "So, what happened to
Tripp?"

Justin shakes his head. "A few guys saw it happen. On
Safety Dave's first-ever visit to look the place over, Tripp

waltzes right over to him with his broom and strikes up a conversation. Almost knocks Dave over with his booze breath. So Dave escorts him out the door to the police station for a breathalyzer test, then on to the clinic for a urine sample. No drugs detected, but Tripp was pronounced legally drunk and he got legally fired."

"They'll have to hire another cleanup person," I say. Janie and Smitty won't be helping me too much longer.

"Tripp didn't do much," Nose says. "That Esterbrook. Had some things figured out, but not others. He hardly ever laid anyone off or fired people, but he didn't pay attention. Several guys started talking union. 'Course management never wants that, so we'll see what happens. The new owner hasn't mentioned a pay raise, but we were promised one. And we'll see how serious they are about safety."

I'm sipping and listening, mesmerized by Nose's voice—that and the music on the juke box, *Get down turn around go to town boot scootin' boogie.* I catch myself smiling stupidly in a way that just ain't appropriate for the time and place, so I put on my serious and thoughtful face, and say, "Huh, really?"

"Hell," Yates says. "I didn't think the pay was low. When I cashed my paycheck at the IGA yesterday after work, I felt like I'd won the lottery."

"You earned every penny of it," Nose says. "Hard work should be rewarded."

"So, Auntie," Justin says. "Which is worse, being a mill worker or picking apples in Yakima?"

I take this as my cue, my turn to talk, so I say, "I hereby claim the trophy for the most shit jobs ever held by a Hatfield resident."

Nose orders another round of drinks.

"Make that another Flaming Blue Jesus," I yell. Pool balls clack, someone yells "rack 'em up," everyone talks louder and louder. Can't get away from noise, here or at work, so I just join in. I'm thawing out pretty good, feeling all relaxed. "A few summers ago," I begin, enjoying the fact that everyone's watching me, waiting. "Justin and I drove down to Yakima to earn money picking apples. Camped in the orchards with the other pickers, mostly Mexicans. Right off the bat a group of guys took us aside and warned us not to ask any questions. That first night, to break the ice and let 'em all know we wanted to get along, I bought a half-rack of cheap beer to share.

Justin chimes in, "Remember when I asked those guys if they were bank robbers, and they glued their eyeballs on us?" He laughs. "No one said a word? They all sat there drinking beer, staring into the campfire?"

"Well, I didn't think it was so damn funny," I say. "We were warned not to ask questions. Honestly, Justin. That night I couldn't sleep, I was so worried we'd be slashed to pieces. But in the morning they were all gone."

"And then," Justin says, "when we were thinning apples a cop car drove through the orchard. By the time it made a U-turn and came back through, some of the pickers had hunkered down in the branches, hiding and watching. When a second police car came through, you could only see three pickers in the trees besides us. Maybe they *were* bank robbers, but probably just illegal aliens.

Justin and I reminisce every now and then about our little apple-picking adventure. I have the feeling that for him it was one of the highlights of his young life, and that makes me sad.

"Justin didn't call his mother and I didn't call mine," I say, "so my mom sent Justin's mom, that's my sister, Delight, down to find us and bring us home. When Delight found my car parked under an apple tree near our tent, we called it quits and followed her home."

"She sure knows how to wreck a party," Yates says.

Crick shows up with our round of drinks and lights mine. Now all four of us chant, "Burn, burn, burn!"

"Make a wish," Yates yells.

A little dizzy already, I close my eyes. It's hard to think above all the racket in the bar, the shrieking laughter, louder and louder voices, the juke box playing *Can't get no . . . satisfaction,* and I know my wish for sure: I hope I get on at the mill permanent, full time. Oh, and I'd like to get to know Nose better. Then I open my eyes and blow out the flames.

"Auntie, tell the rest of the story," Justin shouts.

"Oh, yeah," I say, taking a gulp of my drink. "After two months of picking fruit, we only earned enough to meet our basic expenses and buy beer and cigarettes."

"It was a living," Justin says, laughing at himself.

"Yeah, like the living I've been making all of my life, until now." I glance at Yates. She's probably thinking the same thing, hoping she'll get on full time at the mill.

"Were you driving the same car, those days?" Nose asks.

"Oh, yeah. Rooster, my '68 Ford Galaxie. One of my longest-lasting relationships. In the past twenty years, he and I've gone 163,000 miles together, mostly to and from odd jobs."

"At least you can consider yourself well traveled," Nose says.

"Yeah," I snort, a little out of control. "I wonder where the hell I went?" Steady girl. Do not blurt anything about the trips back and forth to the casino.

"That's over six times around the world," Nose says, standing up. "Old Rooster. He's a classic. Looks good next to my yellow truck in the parking lot at the mill, the old International. Great truck. 1968 was a good year.

I smile up at him, grateful that he called my car *him*, happy that he asked about Rooster when he already knows exactly who owns that faded old red car. And he called him a classic. I wish he'd stay and talk some more about his special truck. I wish I had the nerve to tell him so. Who knows, maybe if he'd stay I'd ask him a few half-way intelligent questions.

But he says, "Gotta check in with the boys at the bar, then go home and get my beauty rest."

Yates chokes on her beer and has a coughing fit. His comment about beauty *is* funny. Nose ain't what you'd call handsome, by any stretch, but I think he's good-looking. In fact, the more I drink, the sexier he looks. Yates and Justin and I raise our drinks to Nose in farewell.

"What a great guy," Justin says.

"I s'pose he has a date?"

"Not that I know of," Justin says, leaning toward me. "Oh, Auntie. You're interested, aren't you?"

"Maybe." The room starts to spin as I ponder what it'd be like if I didn't have to be so damn strong and capable all the time? When I'm around Nose I go all soft on the inside like Jell-O, like I always did with Dwayne. And I don't even know his real name or anything else about him. I'm exhausted. I rub my eyes to keep them from crossing.

Crick delivers a third round of drinks, and says I get to light this one, but when I try to set the drink on fire with my cigarette lighter I fumble and drop it on the table. On the third try I succeed, and it's all I can do to blow out the flame and hold my glass up to clink Justin's bottle and Yates' glass of beer. "Whaddaya think, you guys? Ya think maybe Nose is stronger 'n me? And for crying out loud, what kinda name is Nose, anyway? Guess I talk too much. Next time I see him, I'm gonna talk more, ask less questions."

## CHAPTER 14

"Need you to stack off-species today."

Leroy's taken to speed-mumbling again, and I swear he said *off-feces*, which, of course, could be classified as *ooey, gooey* or *chewy*. I try to check my smile. Guess I'll have to trust him. "Okay," I say, following him outdoors. It's another cold-as-a-moose February morning, and it took me most of the weekend to thaw out from last week. Saturday night at The Tool Shed helped.

"We're running mostly red fir, but also lodgepole. So, you need to hand-stack the lodgepole pine that comes through. Just stack the 2 x 4s on one cart and the 2 x 6s on the other cart."

"Okay."

"You do know that red fir is darker than lodgepole, right?" he asks.

"Yes, I do," I say, tryin' to be agreeable "Red fir is really Douglas fir, and today lodgepole is the off-species. Right?"

"Right. And if you find time on your hands, go ahead and do a little cleanup under the shaker bins."

I nod, knowing I will *not* find time to do any extra cleanup. Does he take me for a fool?

So I stack *off-feces*. Like to freeze my ass off doing it, too. The mill runs lodgepole, red fir, larch, hemlock, and cedar. I gotta learn which is which, as well as the difference between heartwood on lodgepole and the color of sapwood on the red fir. It's confusing.

The next day the mill runs lodgepole and I stack white fir. The mill cuts the lumber green instead of dried, and it seems like this white fir grew in a swamp. The boards are so wet they almost drip. They stink, too. Dad always called it piss fir.

After almost fifty winters, I'm starting to hate the season. The wind never stops blowing. It snows constantly. My feet and hands are cold all the time. The boiler room where the units of lumber are dried in kilns is my new favorite place, because it's warm. During breaks I visit with Yates, Carmel, sometimes Janie. Smitty has been assigned to clean the pit but only when the planer isn't running, which means we don't see much of him.

At one break with Carmel, she tells me she overheard the men talking about what happened after the fire was put out in the planer room. The sawdust had been sucked up into the bin as usual. A truck pulled under the bin, loaded up, and hauled the material to Lewiston, Idaho, to a holding barn at a paper mill. But the holding barn caught fire and burned down. Apparently, the sawdust re-ignited when it got some air. We should have used that sawdust, but they wanted to earn an extra buck by selling it to another mill. Plus I guess Leroy thought the fire was all the way out. Now the big boss, Park, is mad at Leroy because TSI has to pay for that holding barn and all the sawdust that was lost.

Way to go, Leroy. You really stepped on your dick that time.

Then Carmel tells me, "We had to shut off the edger this morning because the conveyor that takes the edgings down to the basement stopped. I volunteered to go see what the problem was and found a wadded up foil-lined gum wrapper by the metal detector. I picked out the gum wrapper and threw all the edgings and sawdust off the conveyor onto the floor, so I could get back to the line in a hurry. One of the guys must have tossed that gum wrapper on the conveyor."

"And I'll bet one of 'em did it again, too," I say, thinking about the extra mess she made in the basement.

"Yeah," she says, staring at me, like *how did you know*? "It happened again as soon as I got back to the line. They did it three times. But even though I enjoyed my time away from them by going down to the basement to fix the problem, I hurried so they wouldn't enjoy their rest too much. It was a stupid kid's game."

"Maybe you're outworking the men, making 'em look bad, pissing 'em off." She looks tired. Has dark circles under her eyes, and seems a little shaky.

"I hadn't thought of that," she says, closing her eyes and leaning back against the wall of rough-sawn lumber. "It rots my socks the way the men get away with murder."

On Friday the weather breaks. Warm spring weather. It's a miracle. A delayed January thaw. And now, here comes Leroy.

"I'm going to ask you first, Echo. The debarker slopes have got to be cleaned, now that things are melting. Can you work tomorrow? It's overtime."

There's no time to ponder this question that ain't a question. Forty hours a week of being cold and straining every muscle in my body is already too much. But time and a half. Jesus, how can I turn that down? And I do want to pass the probationary period.

"I'd love to," I lie.

"I'll be here myself," he says, walking away. "See you in the morning."

On Saturday morning, with all the machinery turned off the mill is like a cemetery. I don't even need ear plugs. And while it's not exactly hot, it is sunny and mild compared to last week. Would have been a nice day to take Mom into Spokane to the discount stores.

The debarker slopes are actually the concrete sides of a giant trough. At the bottom, the bark collects in a wet slop of dirt, sawdust and melted snow, and bobcats come along now and then to scoop up the glop and dump it somewhere out in the log yard. Bark and crap gets stuck on the slopes. It has to be cleaned off, pushed to the bottom, and today that's my job. I'm wearing rubber boots over my work boots. And just in case my rubbers spring a leak, I put a plastic bag over each of my socks. In the afternoon, I'm shoveling the last of the bark off a slope when my feet fly out from under me. I fall flat on my back and slide fast down the slope about ten feet, sail into the air, and land on my feet in the wet bark, mud and ooze. The miracle is, I keep my balance. I look around. No laughter. Good, no one saw me, so no accident report to fill out. Even full time employees can lose their bonus if they fill out those damn forms. If a lowly worker on probation like me has to fill one out, I could lose my bonus *and* my job. The bonus is based on the average of how many board feet a day the entire mill puts out for the month. These extra checks are nothing to sneeze at. My first one was $280. No-sir-ree, my bruised ass will heal up and my two boots full of gunk will get dry. Leroy will never know.

At the last break of the day, I'm alone in the break room when Leroy peeks his head in and says, "How bad did you hurt your back?"

"How'd you find out?"

"One of the millwrights saw you," he says. "Since you went back to work he reported it just in case. I was wondering how you got so filthy."

"I'm only dirty," I lie. "Not hurt."

Early Monday morning in the yard, I'm coming out from between two units of lumber near the dry sheds, carrying my shovel, when a forklift goes past. It's still early, still dark, but thanks to the overhead yard light I can see the driver is a man everyone calls Bullfrog. He's built like a frog, and in a former life he was a Navy Seal. The last time a forklift strafed me, I didn't see the driver, and now I wonder if it was this guy. Nose did say a forklift driver ran off one woman. Bullfrog looks at me. Eye contact. He spins the forklift around. I think maybe he forgot something and is going back to get it, but the forklift comes straight at me. I duck between the units. That dumb-ass looked right at me. I hide and watch, and after he's gone I step out from between the units, keeping my eye on him. I'll be damned if he doesn't spin the forklift around, and take aim on me again. I leap between the two units, lean against the stacks of lumber, and gulp cold air. There's no mistake about what just happened. Like a deer on the edge of the woods, I skirt the units and make my way to Leroy's office.

"Bullfrog just tried to run me down with the forklift," I tell Leroy, my voice shaking.

"That's ridiculous," he says, both hands on his hips, legs apart, feet planted. "Frog does a good job and he's worked here almost twenty years. He wouldn't do that. He has cataracts. Must not have seen you. Maybe the light was in his eyes. You'll want to be real careful about making accusations."

"Well, it happened. When he missed me the first time, he . . ."

Leroy turns and walks off. My heart races. No one's ever tried so hard and with so much determination to hurt me. This was no accident. It's not even break time yet, but I don't care. In slow motion I climb the stairs to the machine shop, walk to the bench, and sit down for a smoke. A millwright is pounding on a piece of metal at a work table, but he ignores me. Exhaling, resting, my hard hat and safety glasses still on and ear plugs still in, I sit surrounded by the clanging, screeching and roaring of the mill. My eyes rest on the shiny steel workbench, next to the millwrights. Why doesn't Leroy believe me? There must be a way to get even.

Over the noise of the mill, I hear the vague sound of sirens coming closer. Did Bullfrog manage to run over someone else? At the top of the stairs I look down on the line, and see two ambulance drivers rush in with a gurney to where the edging crew works. They kneel down next to someone on the floor. Not Carmel! Not dear, sweet Carmel.

# CHAPTER 15

The teddy bear drapes because it's filled with tiny beads, and his expression is one of pure love. In the short drive between the shopping mall where I bought the bear for Carmel and the hospital, I become attached to him. Now I hate to give him up.

"Oh, thank you," she says, her voice no more than a whisper. She reaches for the teddy bear and holds him to her cheek. "How thoughtful."

I look away at the TV, the white walls, the curtain separating her from another patient. "How are you?" I ask. "At the mill they said you passed out."

"Exhaustion," she says. "At least that's what the doctor thinks. They ran all sorts of tests. And I guess he's right. You know I can handle the work if I get my rest, but I can't sleep."

"Are you cold at night? Is that it?"

"I didn't want to tell anyone. The reason is too weird. It's Melvin. I don't know why he does it, but at night he catnaps, and when I fall asleep he shakes me or jabs me in the ribs with his elbow to wake me up. When I ask him why he does it, he says 'do what?' I kept getting more and more tired." She grips my hand. Her voice is weak and she talks slowly, as if she's far away and there's a thick fog.

"Carmel. You have to get away from him. Find a place in town. You can afford it now."

"He'll stop doing it. I know he wants me to keep my job and all. He's probably mad at me. He wrote me a four-page letter saying how I'd been hurtful to him about money, about how selfish I am. I couldn't believe it. I tried to stay calm, you know, because he gets so angry. But I told him to stop blaming me for all our problems, and while I was at it I said to stop asking me if I miss him when I'm at work. I told him that I don't like to lie, that I don't miss him when I'm at work, that I'm too busy."

Her grip tightens on my hand.

"Do you know what he said? He said, 'Thank you for sharing.'"

It's hard not to blurt out that I think Melvin's a freak. Instead I say, "That's when he started to wake you up at night?"

"Yes," she says, letting go of my hand. "But, Echo, he can be so good with me and the kids, and fun, too." She smiles. "The neighbor's dogs bark a lot. Melvin read about a dog repellant spray in a bio-technology catalog. He's real smart, you know, and he reads a lot. Anyway, he says we should hire a retardant plane to drop a load of this dog repellant over the neighbor's property. It isn't easy to leave a man who comes up with stuff like that."

"But Jesus, Carmel. You deserve your rest. And a house with a toilet that flushes."

"One of these days." Carmel squeezes my hand again. We both look at our calloused, rough, red hands, our bulging veins. "I'll be back to work soon," she says. "Thanks for coming to see me." She hugs the teddy bear to her neck.

At the mill, Leroy has me stand in for Carmel until she gets back. So, here I am, picking edgings. And she's right. This job is as bad as cleanup. If I want to survive my probationary period, I have to do what I'm told. I know that. At least I'm not far from Yates, and I can look over at her once in a while for moral support or whatever it is I get from her. And I do get something. Strength maybe. It has to do with the parrot. I've gotta ask her again what she told Mousse to make him act so nice.

A surly man named Dave works as the first person on the line, spreading apart the edgings. As the second person on the line I pick out the crap that doesn't look like a 2 x 4 or a 2 x 6 and send it down a hole into the basement. The other two are Kurt and Mumbles. The four of us stand side by side in front of a flat bed about waist high, the size of a king-sized bed, with rollers that move the boards along from the edger to the stackers. The men don't want me here. They don't want Carmel here, either, but at least she knows what she's doing and works faster. I try to do exactly as Leroy told me to do. I sort and push and drop edgings into the hole almost, but not quite, fast enough.

At break time, Yates and I climb the stairs to the machine shop bench. Sometimes Janie joins us, but Yates doesn't like being around her. Anyway, Janie often takes her break when Smitty does. We do not talk until after our cigarettes are lit.

"Janie does real well, for being so little," I say, fishing.

"Wish she'd stop talking about her kids so much. If I hear one more time about that Little Miss America contest, I'm going to throw up."

"Don't you find it interesting?" I ask, feeling like a go-between. Maybe I should hang a sign around my neck. The doctor is in. Delight would be proud. "Sure," I add. "Parading little girls around like that is a little strange, but then so are lots of things."

"Now, if Janie was working here to save money for her daughter's education, well that would be different. I never hear her talk about *that*." Yates stabs out her cigarette on top of a Pepsi can. She shakes her head in disgust. "Don't get me started."

Yates isn't usually so serious and dramatic. 'Course, I don't know her all that well, really. I say, "I do think Janie's a good mother."

The buzzer sounds. Break is over. Brain bucket in place. Safety glasses on. Ear plugs stuffed in my ears. It's back to the line.

I'm sorting and moving edgings right along, when Kurt lifts the ass-end of a board he's turning, pulls it back and knocks off my hard hat, which skitters across the floor behind me. I abandon the line and chase it down, adjust it on my head and hurry back to the line. My heart is pounding as I work furiously to sort through the pile of edgings and lumber that built up in front of my station on the roll case. What an asshole. If he does that again, I'll be ready for him. I'll grab a board and pretend to slip. The board will hit him behind the knees and knock him down, maybe even onto the chains. It will look like an accident.

After this I try to flip boards in a way that pinches Kurt's fingers a little to let him know he'd better not mess with me again. Then Mumbles, who always has his mouth so full of chew you can't understand a thing he says, spits a gob on the pile of edgings and boards right in front of me. That does it. I stand with my arms folded. Suddenly I hear the roaring-train hum of millions of bees, interrupted by the sound of a gunshot. A board comes flying out of the edger, hits the bang boards, spins around and causes a bunch of other boards to pile up on top of the line that is already a mess. Boards and edgings crisscross all over the roll case. Everyone except me yells "Fuck!" By that time, I don't fucking *care* enough to cuss. Seems like a wreck on the line is the next bad thing that could happen, and I'm not at all surprised. It's a simple case of the old domino theory.

The rollers and chains go down. The whole mill stops production. It's a one-person job to crawl up onto the line, then onto the rollers next to the edger to undo the mess. And it's my turn. I ponder the situation. I should refuse to go onto the roll case to straighten things out, but I don't want to give the bastards the satisfaction of knowing they got to me. I crawl up onto the roll case and separate the edgings from the lumber. The goons stand around, not helping in any way. About five minutes later I have the mess sorted enough that the machinery can be turned back on. I step from in front of the edger and walk along the boards on top of the rollers. That's how you get off the roll case. When I'm almost off, Kurt starts up the chain. I'm still too far from the edge to step off so I make the immediate decision to run and jump so I won't get knocked into the opening for the edgings and land on the conveyor. When I jump, I trip on a board moving along the edge of the roll table and tumble onto the concrete floor. My right elbow and hip hit hard, the pain shoots all around in my body. I pull myself together on my side and tell myself, *I will not groan. I will not groan.*

Kurt tries to help me up. He says, "God, I'm awful sorry."

I slap him off. "Get away from me, you sonofabitch." I slowly get to my feet, grab my hard hat and glance over at Yates, who nods to me. This is how I know for certain that somehow, some time, Kurt will get his. Revenge will be sweet.

## CHAPTER 16

During Carmel's absence, I discover that it's a helluva lot easier—and safer—to push a broom around and honk sawdust than it is to pick edgings. My three layers of clothing had helped soften the spill off the roll case, but I ended up with sore muscles and bruises the size of saucers. I'm back to doing my usual cleanup job in the mill and planer, with Janie and Smitty. It's almost fun, compared to picking edgings with that bunch of idiots.

This morning I'm alone sorting for hog fuel outdoors, and the second the hog-fuel conveyor stops because of a jam-up, I dash for the spot under the turbo heater to get warm. When the conveyor starts up again, I hurry back out the open side doors to my job. I know they call this material hog fuel because the chipper, or hog, spits out the sawdust and chips. And paper mills buy the stuff from us to burn and heat water in their boilers. I'm like a pig rooting around for truffles as I pick out rocks and pieces of metal, like nails and barbed wire. Suddenly, there's an explosion at the transformer box not far away on the outside of the mill and a glowing ball of electricity about five feet across skips along the utility wires to a big pole above the mill. Then I hear a second explosion, just inside the mill. Jesus. Flames curl up the side of the building, and even though I don't hear a warning bell, workers pour out of the open mill doors. There's Yates, and pretty soon I see Carmel and Janie, all of them safely outdoors. I join them in the parking lot.

Janie runs over to stand by me. "You all right?" she asks. "Someone said you were pretty close to the action."

"The fire wasn't after me," I say. "Quite a show, though. Better than the Fourth of July. How about you?"

"Actually, it's embarrassing," she says. "I'm afraid of fire and I trampled a couple guys on my way out. They hit the floor hard. I'm probably in trouble."

"Their egos won't allow them to say anything," Yates says. "You're safe."

"Nothing like giant buildings and lots of smoke to make a person feel small and helpless," Carmel says.

We four women and Smitty stand together as fire trucks arrive and drag their hoses into the building. The millwrights chop a hole through the outside wall to the control panel that's on fire. They stop. One of them sprays the control panel and wiring with a fire extinguisher, then they quit spraying to see if it helped. But the flames leap higher. One fireman uses foam, which does a better job. All the wiring is scorched.

Yates says, "Well, looks like it's back to watching *Days of our Lives* on TV."

After a while, Leroy announces, "If you work in the mill, go on home and file your unemployment claims. You'll get paid for the rest of today. I'll let you know when to come back. Everyone working in the planer building come in to work in the morning, as usual."

"What about me?" I ask, since I do cleanup at both the mill and the planer.

"Nah," he says. "Don't bother coming in."

"Hello?" I groan into the phone when it rings at 7:15 in the morning.

"Hey, it's me," Yates says. "Want to go to a Willie Nelson concert in Spokane tonight? I scored two tickets. A guy I know at another mill got the free tickets, but he has to work tonight. We wouldn't leave until around three o'clock. Plenty of time to drag our butts down to the unemployment office first."

"Sure. I've always liked Willie Nelson. Might take my mind off being unemployed again. I wonder how long we'll be out of work."

"Look at it this way," Yates says. "Even on unemployment we'll earn more money than we ever did before working at the mill."

When Yates arrives later I hardly recognize her, all dolled up with makeup, new fishing lure earrings, a buckskin jacket with fringe, boots with spike heels, and black pants so skin-tight she has camel toes.

"Mom, this is Yates, my friend from the tree farm and now the mill."

"First name's Lu Ann, Mrs. Spangler," she says, reaching out to shake Mom's hand, "but I prefer Yates. Nice to meet you."

"My, don't you look pretty?" Mom says. "You can call me Mabel."

I'm all ready to go, wearing my teal down-filled three-quarter-length car coat. While Yates looks all sleek and sophisticated, I look like a mid-sized sedan, like one of those new PT Cruisers. But my coat is warm and it has deep pockets. As for makeup, I slathered on moisturizer and pulled out the chin hair that threatened to get caught in my jacket zipper.

"You both be careful," Mom says. "And remember, if you're not in bed by ten, it's time to come home."

Yates laughs and says, "Oh, Mabel, you are a dangerous woman!"

Mom never says things like that. Sometimes I wonder how well I knew the old girl.

"Don't wait up for me, Mom. It's gonna be late before we get home."

On our way out to her old Subaru, Yates says, "Your mom is one cool lady."

"She keeps me in line," I say.

The concert starts at seven. I smuggle a six-pack of 16-oz Milwaukee Ice Beer into the concert, thanks to my deep pockets. The way I figure it, why the hell not? Yates is the designated driver, although she brought a few beers along herself. When we get to the stadium and find our seats, we see a few guys from TSI in the audience, including Leroy and Bullfrog and their wives. That's just duckie. They're sitting a couple rows above us, practically breathing down our necks. The two men must be friends. Of course they'd kiss each other's butts. Of course my complaints about Bullfrog trying to run me down in the forklift would fall on deaf ears. And now I'm laid off. I don't care if they see me drink a few beers. I'm on my own time.

A group with fiddles, banjos and mandolins plays first. I can't sit still. Yates has crossed her legs, and her boot bounces up and down to the music. When Willie Nelson appears on stage, everyone jumps up and claps. Yates whistles a fierce blast. I want to cover my ears, but in order to do anything at all with my hands I'd first have to set my open can of beer on the floor and concentrate on not kicking it over. Just can't take the risk. After we sit down, Willie sings a song he made up about mill workers.

The words of the song tell me he knows a little about the work we do, and I'm impressed. Maybe in a former life he picked a few edgings. I take a swig out of my third Ice Beer while he sings one of my all-time favorites, *Blue Skies*. I hum along with him and sway from side to side until Yates nudges me with her elbow and whispers, "Knock it off, you." So I stop humming but keep swaying to the song, drinking my beer, grinning, feeling no pain whatsoever. I love Willie Nelson. When the clapping starts I open my next can of beer, and by the time he sings his final song, *On the Road Again*, I'm on my fifth Ice Beer. I'll save the last one for the road.

Hundreds of people, including us, wait after the show to get Willie's autograph. But a slick looking man, like a hairdresser or a used car salesman, comes out onto the stage and says, "Mr. Nelson is not signing autographs tonight." Just in case he changes his mind, we hang around for a while. We drove a long way to get here, and right now time no longer matters. Maybe there *is* no such thing as time. Why not wait and see? Yates agrees, and we wait half an hour without talking. I give up and open my last can of beer. By now there are maybe a dozen people waiting, mostly women. I finally have to go to the bathroom, and on my way back I see Willie Nelson come out from behind the curtains to give autographs. Yates and I get in line. I smile and sway a little. One by one, each woman who gets his autograph gives him a big hug and kiss. He kisses on the mouth, too, not on the cheek. When it's my turn, I tell Willie, "The show was jus' wunnerful. We came a long way and it was more than worth the drive. We work in a goddamn sawmill, too."

"Well, young lady," he says, looking directly into my eyes. "When things get tough at work, just remember this: they need you." He scribbles his name or something like it on my program.

"Thanks," I say, on the verge of tears. I whisper in his ear, "I love you," but when he tries to kiss me on the mouth, I point to my cheek and he kisses me there. Yates is next, and she plants a big one right on his mouth. I'm no prude, but theirs is a kiss you might see in an X-rated movie.

All the way home, I doze, perfectly comfortable believing that Yates can handle the drive between Spokane and Hatfield. The last thing I remember, Yates is humming, *On the Road Again.* The next thing I know, I'm out of the warm car and into the icy blast of air. I stumble up the porch steps, hanging on to the icy hand rail, and open the door to a warm house. The kitchen range clock says it's two in the morning, and I'm glad Mom's not waiting up for me. I throw my overstuffed coat on a chair, grope my way down the hall and fall into bed, clothes and all. I'm dead to the world when the phone by my bed rings. I pick it up, but can't think of one thing to say.

"Echo?" Leroy says.

"Uh huh."

"We need you to come into work at the mill this morning. The construction crew needs a cleanup person. Can you be here at 5:30?"

"Sure," I say, straining to focus on the clock near the bed. Through the blur, I see that it's 4:35 a.m. "I'll be there."

I crawl out of bed, staying on my hands and knees all the way to the bathroom, and then drag myself up onto

the pot. By the time I pee (and pee and pee some more)
I'm awake enough to walk upright to the kitchen and
make a pot of thick, dark coffee, the kind that puts hair
on your chest and probably on your chin, too. Sitting at
the table, I doze off smiling, waiting for the coffee to finish dripping, thinking about last night. Leroy saw me at
the concert, drinking one Ice Beer after another, but I'll
show him how well I can hold my liquor.

Leroy and a tall man, big as a planet, are standing at the
time clock when I arrive a few minutes early. They aren't
wearing hard hats yet, and the big man is mostly bald. A
reverse Mohawk. Then, too, the building stinks like
charred wood and burned plastic from that coating on
the wiring. My stomach takes a turn sideways.

"How're you feeling?" Leroy asks.

"Fine, why?" And I do, too, aside from the smoky
stench in the air. I'm wide awake on a caffeine buzz. I
touch my cheek where Willie Nelson kissed me.

Leroy and the fat man stare at me, so I say, "Where do
I start?"

They continue to stand and stare. I wonder where they
found the big guy. He's carrying too much weight for the
old axles. Now it looks like they're waiting for me to
speak. Maybe I'll tell them about the kiss. Instead I say,
"I mean where should I start working?"

"Just do general cleanup, plus watch for fires when
the crew is working," Leroy says. "They'll be welding,
making sparks. You're good with fires. Just try to keep
them from burning down the rest of the mill. They
should be done in a couple weeks. George here will be
your boss."

"Okay," I say, nodding to Mr. Gross Vehicle Weight, hoping not to slip and call him GVW. I do the work Leroy told me to do, and even though I pace myself I start to wind down after a couple hours. I take my breaks alone, away from the construction crew. That way I can sneak an extra cigarette when they're all too busy to notice. The break room is warm and smells better than the rest of the mill. As the day wears on, I feel like snail ooze. I'm dippy with fatigue so I take a quick snooze.

Back to work. With no heat out in the mill, not even the turbo heater, my legs are like popsicles at first and then I no longer feel them at all. When I blow my nose, my hanky is black with soot.

At home after work when I take a bath, I have to start with water that is barely warm and gradually add hot water. Even so, my legs and feet feel like they're on fire. I soak my face with a warm, wet washcloth and blow my nose again. More soot. After my bath I sit by the wood stove, close my eyes, and think about Willie Nelson. I touch my cheek where he kissed me, and think about blue skies and May, when we'll actually see spring weather or at least a few sun breaks. I beg off the cribbage game and go to bed early.

The next morning my eyes are blurry. I feel like hell and this time, it's not a hangover. It snowed again during the night, and on my way to work I get stuck in our long driveway about five feet from the highway. It's not the first time I've been in this situation, sitting in my car facing the wrong direction, heart pounding. This morning, though, a man comes along the highway in a four-wheel drive diesel pickup truck, puts a chain on my bumper and pulls me out of the driveway onto the highway. It's a miracle the bumper doesn't pull off. Now I'm unstuck, but still facing the opposite direction from the mill. I don't have the energy to turn the car around and drive to the mill, and I can't deal with our long uphill driveway again until it's plowed. Instead, I make my way to The Log Drive to call the mill's answering machine and tell them I'm on my way to the clinic. Don't want 'em to think I'm a flake, that I'm AWOL. Now that I found a real career, miserable as it is, I want to keep it. Sure, one of the men might kill me off, and I might freeze to death, but I need the money. And the mill needs me. Willie Nelson said so.

## CHAPTER 17

"You have a severe sinus infection and bronchial pneumonia," the doctor on duty at the clinic says. "Here's a prescription for antibiotics and a note for your teacher." He looks like a recent high school graduate, with his twelve mustache hairs and the pimple on his chin.

In slow motion I lean toward him and reach for the goods. "Thanks," I whisper.

"You're going to have to lay low, get lots of rest and drink your liquids. Lots of water, no beer," he says. "Let's see, it's Tuesday. Give yourself until next Monday before going back to work. And it would be real helpful if you'd quit smoking."

"Yeah, yeah, I know."

After stopping by the drugstore to pick up the prescription, I drive to the mill's main office to drop off my note from the doctor. I leave it with Sharlene, the office manager, so I don't have to walk all the way from the parking lot to Leroy's office. At home I crawl into bed and sleep the rest of the day, waking up only to take a pill and pee. Then it's back to bed with the cat. The next day I watch TV and doze in the recliner next to the stove. I don't even play cribbage. Mom reads books and feeds the stove and makes me her famous graveyard stew, which is buttered toast with sugar and a poached egg on top, swimming in warm milk. This is way better than chicken noodle soup when you're sick. I'm sure Mom has saved our lives by feeding us graveyard stew, but we only eat it when we're sick.

On the third morning I awake to the aroma of baking bread. I must be getting better—my smeller works. Even though I'm sick, I'd have to say I'm feeling grateful I get to stay in bed. And when I think about Mom's homemade bread, I feel even better. In junior high, in one of my hungry growth spurts, I'd eat half a loaf, still warm from the oven. We always counted pennies, and got only one pair of shoes a year no matter how much our feet grew, but we could whack off a piece of bread and eat it any time we wanted to. I was never hungry. Mom or Dad would sometimes shoot a deer right off the back porch. And in the spring, after a winter of no work because the woods were shut down with snow, we ate perch Dad and I caught through the ice at the slough. Today fish and game wardens would put Dad in jail, but the perch eggs sealed in their clear sacks were a springtime treat for us. Mom rolled the pink egg sacks, about the size of Dad's thumb, in seasoned flour and fried them in the skillet with the perch filets. Makes me drool to think about it. I can still hear Dad grumble, "Damn *Corpse* of Engineers ruined the fishing when they built that dam. Stupid sonsabitches!"

I dream I'm waiting for Hat Ferry, across the highway from our mailbox. I'm naked. Mousse, the parrot at the mall, is nearby on a tree branch. He tells me it's okay that I'm naked. But with no clothes on I'm ashamed, so I leave to find my clothes. As I walk along, a shirt simply appears on me, a long shirt that, fortunately, covers my ass. It's not something I would have picked out at the thrift store, mind you, but I'm happy to be wearing it. The alarm rings, butting in on my dream. I wipe cat hair off the side of my face, sink deeper in the covers on my back, and stare into the dark. It's Monday. First day back to work. I drag my tired body out of bed, still coughing but mostly recovered.

Driving to work, I think about my dumb dream. Guess it means I feel vulnerable. Then there's the issue of the man's shirt. Odd, but it is hard to feel feminine while working in a sawmill. God, I'm still tired. Hope I can look busy today while pacing myself.

The minute I clock in, the construction crew needs me to haul their building scraps to the area out back called the bone yard. This means driving a bobcat. They assume I know how, and I don't tell 'em otherwise. Because I'm afraid the bobcat will start bucking and snorting like it did before, I drive it at a crawl. They yell, "Get that thing out of *turtle* and put it in *rabbit* speed." I finally manage a speed in between.

Later in the day Leroy puts me to work upstairs in a room next to the machine shop that has old files and parts, like nuts and bolts. He gives me a pile of rags, a broom and a dust pan. The dirt is an inch and a half thick in places, and I wear a dust mask, which isn't real convenient for my coughing fits. When I ask the new boss, George, for a Shop Vac, he says to try the home appliance store. So I do what I can, wondering again where they found this guy.

When I grab a small garbage can to dump the dirt into it, it's got old clothes in it that smell like death and decay. Even in the cold temperature, the can smells like a road kill in summer. Uh oh. This is *ooey, gooey, or chewy.* According to Safety Dave, this one's for management.

"Leroy," I say, showing him the garbage can. "The next time you get rid of a worker, the garbage can is not the best place to hide the body." I think I'm real funny.

"What the hell?" Leroy says, all serious.

"Bio-hazard. I'm not s'posed to touch it," I say, setting the garbage can on the floor of his office and walking out.

The next thing you know, I'm outside sorting units of studs that were scorched by the fire. "Just stack the burnt lumber on this cart and the good lumber on the other cart," George says. "We'll band them into units and sell the scorched boards out the back door. It's good for rabbit hutches and chicken coops."

So I sort and stack. At least the air is fresh out here. Pretty soon, here comes Leroy. "That was a dead packrat under those clothes in that garbage can," he says. "Emptying it is your job, which I assume you'd like to keep."

When he leaves I want to kick myself. What the hell's gotten into me? Leroy is responsible for the final decision on my probation. Talk about shooting myself in the foot. From now on, I'm gonna practice my best greeting card behavior.

After two weeks of repair and reconstruction, the mill is ready to start up again. On a Monday morning, The Big Boss, Park, and Leroy kick off a safety meeting.

"Oh, look," Yates say, nudging me with her elbow. "It's the Park and Bark show."

Leroy announces, "We'll be working some overtime to make up for the down time. I want you all to be extra careful, but the more boards you get out the bigger your bonus checks."

"Remember, kids," Safety Dave pipes in, "no drugs, no alcohol, no cussing or arguments. He pauses to make sure he has everyone's attention. And you gotta wear your hard hats." To make his point, he's the only person in the break room wearing one right now. "You'll stand taller and be a more imposing figure. Also, if your head is involved in an accident, your hard hat will keep your gray matter from splattering all over the mill. Mind your Ps and Qs, and at the end of each month with no accidents, we'll give you a dinner party, right here on the premises."

We *always* wear our hard hats on the floor. Right now, though, without our brain buckets on, it's as if we're missing a part of our heads. I look around the room, and what do you know? My eyes land on Nose. I study the tufts of hair growing out from the sides of his ear lobes. Then there's his trimmed beard and his long nose holding up his glasses. The man *is* interesting looking. He glances my way. My face grows hot, and I act like I'm looking at the clock over his head.

"We're moving folks around so we can work at top efficiency," Leroy says. "Justin and Nose will continue to feed the planer. Jane will work the eight-foot stacker at the mill. We've hired a new guy on cleanup. We're amping up production to keep competitive."

While he talks I notice that today his eyes are the color of polished steel. Robot eyes. The guy's just another redneck with a college diploma. He'd have me and Carmel and Yates wearing aprons here at the mill, if he thought he could get away with it.

On our way out of the break room, Yates whispers, "I'm glad to see that Safety Dave has his brain condom securely in place."

"Hah," I say, shaking my head. "That's a good one, Yates."

She heads to her station and when I stroll toward my rake and broom, George stops me. The man next to him is so good-looking he doesn't seem real. He could be George Clooney's brother. Even his clothes sparkle: new Carhartt jacket, open to show off his new plaid flannel shirt. His blue jeans aren't faded and he's wearing shiny, high-end work boots the color of caramel.

"This is Riley," George tells me. "Smitty took a job in Spokane."

"Hi, my name's Echo," I say, shaking the handsome man's hand, wishing I could have told Smitty goodbye. This new guy looks like trouble, and I don't need any more of that.

"For now, Riley will clean in the basement," George says. "You can clean around the hog."

"Okay." I leave to get the grain shovel. At least by now I know how to do all the different cleanup jobs, and there's plenty of work for Riley. Hell, there's enough work for a whole crew of prisoners. They wouldn't be any worse than some of the men already working here.

I shovel sawdust into the conveyor-shaker bin that feeds the hog, until the buzzer announces my favorite thing about working in the mill—recess. By the time the equipment shuts down, I'm pocketing my ear plugs. Seconds count now. I dangle my safety glasses around my neck from their elastic band and head for the machine shop, already reaching for my cigarettes. Yates arrives at the bottom of the stairs at the same time, and without a word we tromp up the stairs together to the bench in the corner. Before speaking, we light up. Then our butts drop to the bench, suddenly, like two puppets on one string.

We sit and stare and smoke.

"Sometimes I wish I didn't smoke," Yates says. "You ever think about quitting?"

"Well, hell. Of course. And I will, too, someday, because of all the health risks. I'm not *that* stupid."

"I think I might be in trouble," Yates says, as she takes a drag on her cigarette.

"What'd you do now?" I ask, leaning back against the wall, exhaling.

"Kurt. You know what an asshole he is. Anyway, there was a wreck down the line and we stood around waiting for things to get going again. Kurt starts in on me, the old women-don't-belong-in-a-mill routine, guff like that. I came back at him. Told him, 'Keep it up and I'll beat the shit out of you and then I'll slap you for shitting.' Right away he told Mumbles, said, 'Hey, Mumbles, you're not going to believe what this bitch said.' Carmel was standing close enough to hear me. Everyone thought it was funnier than hell, even Kurt, but I don't trust him. Be like him to file harassment charges."

"That's hilarious. Did Carmel laugh?"

"No, but she smiled real big."

"I don't think Kurt will file charges," I say. "He's too big a chicken. Besides, he knows you saw him turn on the roll case while I was still on it."

We sit quietly, leaning back against the rough-sawn boards on the wall, smoking and resting.

"Did you see the new cleanup person?" Yates says. "The man's a real looker."

"Yeah, I met him. Riley-The-Handsome is working in the basement. Just hope he can hold up his end of a broomstick."

Over the next few days of job-sharing with Riley, I never once see him do any work. He mostly visits. And I never see any dirt on him, either. His jacket stays clean. His blue jeans stay clean. If you do cleanup at the mill, you end up with dirt on all your clothes, plus sawdust in your teeth, inside all your clothes, even in your underwear.

One day I ask him, "Riley, how do you stay so clean?"

"Oh," he says, "I only do enough work to keep from getting bored. When I'm done here I go to the gym to work out. Hate to show up there all dirty."

"You're shittin' me!" I say. "At the end of a shift, most of us don't have enough energy to lift weights."

"You gotta work smarter, not harder," Riley says, big smile, white teeth, lots of charm.

Sounds like something Delight might say. Seems to me, Riley's one of those get-by-kind-of-guys who don't do much. They look good and suck up to the bosses. Whatever gets 'em what they want. Leroy shows up. "Echo, the pit over at the planer is getting out of hand. You go over there and do general cleanup until the planer is shut off for breaks, then clean in the pit."

One good thing about cleaning the pit is that I have to enter the room where Nose is working. He's feeding boards as fast as he can and has to pay attention, but he always seems to know when I'm in the area. If he glances my way, I always smile. I owe him that much for sticking up for me when I got in trouble. Once when I'm not looking his direction, a knot hits my hard hat. I look around but don't see where it came from. I'm no rocket scientist, but the second time it happens I figure out it was Nose who threw the knot. I smile all over. He's flirting with me.

After I work in the planer building a few days, Leroy comes up to me and says, "That Riley is the best cleanup person we've ever had."

I stop working. My lips lock together. I stare at Leroy and then past him to the boards moving along the line. Why would he go out of his way to find me and say something so stupid, unless he's crazy or just plain mean? I can't think how to ask Leroy why he thinks Riley is so hot without getting in trouble. I'll bet he's pushing my buttons because my probation is up soon. Well, I'm not biting. Besides, I already went too far with the dead packrat.

"Don't you have work to do?" Leroy says.

One morning about six o'clock, I'm out in the yard picking up stray boards. It's the middle of March, still freezing, still dark except under the light where I'm working. I hear the sound but keep on picking up boards. I'm on high alert. A forklift engine revs, and Bullfrog drives into the light and past me. We make eye contact and I nod real friendly. When he reaches the darkness, the forklift spins around and I watch, jaw dropped, as Bullfrog roars straight toward me. I dart into the narrow space between the units of lumber to hide. I shiver and try to calm down. My heart is pounding. The S.O.B. *had* to see me. As he leaves the area, the roar of the forklift engine fades away. I wait several minutes and hear nothing. So I step out from between the units. My eyes sweep the darkness beyond to make sure it's safe. There are boards to pick up farther out in the area lit by the yard light. Relieved that Bullfrog has found other ways to waste his time, I go back to work. Without warning, the forklift roars around a stack of units into the light and Bullfrog guns his engine as he speeds toward me. Now I'm farther from safety. I run as fast as I can to dive on the ground between the units, spitting snow and sawdust, shaking all over from cold and fear and anger. Only a fool would doubt that the crazy asshole is trying to kill me—again.

From my hiding place on the ground, I stare past the yard light into the shadows. I don't see or hear the death machine, so I run behind the units, around the side of the mill and over to the planer building to find Leroy.

"That story is even more ridiculous than the last time you told it," Leroy yells, glaring at me, his hands on his hips. "Bullfrog wouldn't do a thing like that."

"Why don't you ask him yourself," I say, thinking how this sounds like *déjà vu* all over again.

Just before the end of the shift, Leroy and George, his brown-nosing assistant, call me into the office.

"Echo, Bullfrog's story is a little different from yours," Leroy says. "He claims you walked right into the path of his forklift this morning, and more than once. He wants you to wear a safety vest with reflective stripes on it when you work out in the yard."

"Hell, no. He'll nail me for sure if I wear one of those." My ex-husband told me once that when he was in the Navy, the guards had to wear big circles on their jackets with a bull's-eye. He wasn't sure why, probably so they'd be the first ones to get hit by the enemy, and when they got shot and yelled it would warn the officers. Sounded like a tall tale to me at the time. Now I'm not so sure.

"If you can't be more careful in the yard around the forklifts, then you'll have to wear a vest for safety reasons." Leroy is furious. His face is red. Leroy and George have me backed my up against the wall of the office. They're only inches away from me, and somebody's breath smells like dog shit. George yells in my face, "Are you going to wear one or not?"

"Well," I yell back, trying to sound strong and fearless, knowing my voice is shaking and I sound weak. "Are you guys going to wear a reflective vest when you work outside? Will everyone else have to wear one?"

"No, just you."

"Well, then, I'm not going to wear one, either. I refuse to be a target."

The buzzer announces the end of the shift. Leroy has the last word. "I'll order you a vest, and you *will* wear it."

I slip away from the wall and the bad breath. After I collect my things from my locker, I clock out on my time card. To calm my nerves, I light up a cigarette as soon as I get out the door, and Carmel joins me in the after-shift parade to the parking lot. We're both dragging-butt tired. "Survived another day," she says.

"I'm beginning to wonder if it's worth it," I say, opening my car door.

"You hang in there," she says.

"Thanks, Carmel." Her words don't change what happened, but at least I don't slam the car door and take it out on Rooster.

All evening I think of ways to get even with Bullfrog. I don't want to worry Mom so I don't tell her about the latest event at the mill. Besides she might get trigger happy. We play only one game of cribbage and, of course, Mom wins. Then I stay up late writing a full report to Park about how Bullfrog tried to run over me those times and what happened in the office with Leroy and George regarding the reflective vest.

In the morning I deliver my three-page report to Sharlene in the office. After I clock in, Leroy sends me over to the mill for a few days and has Riley take his turn at the planer. At the mill I visit with Carmel, Yates and Janie at break time. I do general cleanup, plus George introduces me to one of my "other duties as assigned," which is to stand in for someone so they can go to the toilet. Leroy and George usually do this little task. George acts like nothing happened yesterday, as he instructs me on the timing of my new gig. At 6:17 a.m. I'm to relieve Mumbles on the edging crew. At exactly 7:23 a.m., Dave, who works the trim chain, leaves to go to the toilet. I only stand in on the jobs I know how to do. One guy, I notice, takes almost half an hour. As I turn lumber and deal with cull boards, it occurs to me that the women manage to go to the toilet at break time.

While working at the mill I learn a few important things: I'll have to be more careful while working in the yard to avoid accidentally strolling into the path of the forklift; I will not have to wear a reflective vest; and I can set my watch by the men's bowel movements. Another thing I learn is that Janie is having trouble with her new job on the eight-foot stacker. The men are trying to bulldoze her out, to make things so uncomfortable for her that she'll just quit. You'd think they'd want to protect someone so nice and little and cute, but no.

One morning when I relieve Mumbles I notice that Janie has a black eye. Did she get smacked in the face with a 2 x 4? As soon as the buzzer goes off for first break, I hurry over to her.

"Janie. Sweetie. What happened to your eye?"

"Walk with me to the rest room," Janie says. "If anyone asks, I tell them I bumped into the cupboard door in my kitchen, but Danny got mad and hit me when I came home with a bigger paycheck. My new job on the stacker pays more than I earned at first, and I've worked overtime, but he's sure I was screwing the bosses or I wouldn't earn so much money."

"Oh, Janie," I say. "Are you hurt anywhere else?"

"I have bruises on my arm where he grabbed me before hitting me," she says, staring down at the floor as she walks. "I don't know what got into him. He's pushed me before when he got mad, but I still can't believe he hit me."

"I'm real sorry," I say, putting my arm around her like she's a child. "Is there anything I can do?"

"I don't think so. He was as surprised as I was when he hit me."

Surprised? Like Bullfrog was when he tried to run over me? Hah! *He* sure as hell isn't sorry. But how can I protect Janie? This is what I'm thinking about as I make my way toward my broom and shovel.

"Hey, Echo!" Dave says, pointing under the eight-foot stacker. And there, in a space about three feet high, are Yates and Riley layin' in the sawdust, arms and legs locked together, kissing with a great deal of passion. And my first thought is this: That dumb ass Riley is s'pose to be over at the planer cleaning out the pit.

# CHAPTER 18

Yesterday it snowed in the morning and melted in the afternoon, and last night Mom and I heard frog music. Which means spring is officially here. And while it don't exactly mean daffodils anytime soon, we do have plenty of mud. There's mud on the road up to our house, mud in the log yard and parking lot at the mill, and mud keeping the logging trucks out of the woods. There's still several feet of snow on the ground, but it's melting fast. It's the end of March. Spring breakup has arrived.

The mill is running lodgepole and white fir today, which means I'll probably work under the debarker in the shade. This is good. I'm taking meds for a sinus infection and I'm s'pose to stay out of the sun. Uh-oh. Here comes George.

"Echo, how'd you like to stack white fir out in the yard?"

Like I have a choice. "I'd love to."

So I'm stacking white fir in the sun on the south side of the mill, my boots firmly planted in the mud. I'm proud that I can handle two 2 x 4s at a time. 'Course I've seen Justin and Nose handle six at a time. The temperature soars into the seventies, breaking all records for this time of year, and I'm sweating like a hog. We even have flood warnings. For the next three days, I stack white fir. When I take a break, I don't feel well enough to smoke so I find some shade and pour cold water over my head. A couple hours later, after the white fir is all stacked,

George instructs me to stop the melt water from running onto the floor of the planer. "Don't want the place turning into an ice-skating rink tonight when it freezes," he says, handing over my friend, the spud bar.

Near the open doors, I find a dam of partially melted ice and jab it repeatedly until it breaks apart, then I chisel a trench so water can run away from the building. Even with a headache and fever, my thoughts are on my future. In about ten days I'll either get on full time at the sawmill or . . . I won't. Sure, this is a glorified shit job, but with bonuses and overtime it pays almost triple what I pulled in at other jobs. And now I'm paying off that gambling debt and saving for a truck. But it's not a done deal. I did refuse to wear that reflective vest. And Leroy's impressed with Riley. All he got for making out with Yates under the eight-foot stacker was a verbal warning and an order to stay away from her on mill property.

Carmel is already sitting on the bench in the machine shop when I arrive for the afternoon break. My odd jobs don't always allow regular breaks, and some days I only see her in passing.

"Hi, Chickie," I say.

Carmel smiles, but it appears to require effort. "Hi back."

"You okay?" I ask.

"I keep thinking about the dream that woke me up this morning," Carmel says. "A handsome older man with a kind face and a trimmed beard had charmed several women. And then it was my turn. When he came toward me I was wary, but he kissed me and I thought, *Well, this isn't too bad.* I even felt a little thrill. He said, 'You love me, I can tell.' When he walked away I waited to see what would happen. Strangely, he stuffed a little blond puppy in a clear plastic bag. I could see that the puppy would suffocate, but I just stood there and didn't do anything about it. Then he threw the puppy at my feet. I couldn't stand the cruelty of it. I tried to run away but couldn't. I felt so helpless that I groaned. Melvin shook me awake, and I just laid there feeling stunned, wondering what the dream meant and why I didn't try to save that puppy. What kind of person wouldn't save a puppy?"

"Maybe you were the puppy?" I say, without much thought. When Carmel says nothing, I ask, "Is Melvin letting you sleep now?"

"Yeah. He's being nice, actually. Even considerate. Anything I want to do, he wants to do, and he's always making us laugh. He also talks a lot about spring and the house he's going to build for us this summer.

"Is he still fixing forklifts?"

Not really," Carmel says. "Mostly he's reading books about climbing expeditions to Mt. Everest, like *Into Thin Air*. I know he could find work, but I don't think he wants to. He *is* older, you know. The other evening I risked joking about the job thing, and said, 'Well, lots of men your age are retiring. No wonder you don't want to work.' He said, 'I always did fold under peer pressure.' So, you see, he's an all right guy. Not that a sense of humor replaces working, but at least he's not beating me up any more or keeping me awake at night."

"That's one way to look at it," I say. "It's all so damn complicated. The other day when my sister Delight and I talked on the phone, I told her how hard it is to work here. Justin works here, of course, but I wanted her to understand how different it is for women. She said, 'You know, Echo, problems and obstacles are merely opportunities in disguise.' Carmel, I've been thinking about that, wondering how it applies to my life. But I can't get my mind around it. I've even tried to think how it applies to your life, and Janie's, and I'm not getting anywhere."

Carmel says, "It's like when I laid in bed after my bad dream, Melvin said, 'Well, the key to this whole deal is . . .' And I waited and waited for the rest of it, holding onto that string of words, trying to be polite. He never did tell me what the key to this whole deal was. I've been so annoyed with him, and at the same time I'm thankful I'm not all alone. How stupid is that?"

"There's sure a lot of mystery about life. I don't think anyone's got it figured out, not even Delight."

"Mumbles fell asleep and drove off the road on his way home from work yesterday," Leroy tells me this morning at the time clock. "Need you to stand in for him, picking edgings."

"Okay," I say, wondering why Riley can't do it. At least I'll be working with Carmel. To find out how long I'll be doing his job, I ask, "Is he going to be all right?"

"Hurt his back pretty bad. He was relaxed when the car hit the tree, or he might have been hurt a lot worse."

So I go to work as the fourth person on the line picking edgings. We're lined up like soldiers in a parade. One of the Daves is first, Carmel is second, and Kurt's playing third. While you can't call the job exactly fun, at least it's one I know how to do. So I work on speed instead of technique. No time to gawk around at what others are doing, but I do notice when George relieves Dave on the trim saw so he can go to the bathroom. Must be 7:23.

Mostly I'm paying attention so Kurt doesn't pinch my fingers in the edgings. Suddenly a squeal. It's the mother of all wrecks on top of the roll case—scraps of wood caught on each other, all of 'em tooth-picked in a great big pile.

"Shit!" Dave yells.

Carmel switches off the equipment. The chains and rolls stop turning. Kurt leaps onto the roll case like a cat, pulls edgings apart, and throws them on the floor.

"Yes!" I cheer. Riley will have to pick them up. While visiting with Carmel, I watch every move Kurt makes. She tells me, "We can't drive to our tent because of the mud. We have to park the Bronco and walk in a quarter of a mile." Now Kurt is walking along the boards on top of the roll case. I study the length of his steps and the distance from the edge. The on/off switch is in front of Carmel. I glance over at Yates, who reads my mind and nods encouragement. I step closer to Carmel, as if to whisper to her, and I can tell she knows I'm up to something. Just as Kurt gets to the edge of the roll case and is ready to jump off, I flip the switch on.

The rollers start turning and Kurt leaps sideways into the air. For a second it looks like he'll tumble head first onto the concrete floor. But I'll be damned. Instead of planting his face on the floor, he lands on his feet like a cat.

"Oh, no, I yell. I didn't know you were still up there." Which is ridiculous. He was right in front of us. But that's what he said to me a couple months ago. "Oh, Kurt," I shout again, louder so I'll be heard. "Goddamn, I'm awful sorry."

"Calm down," he says, dusting himself off. "Anybody can make that mistake."

Too bad I didn't switch the machine on a second or two sooner. He isn't hurt at all, but at least now he knows it's his turn to be nervous. I almost got even, and I'm feeling real damn smug.

In an instant, George arrives from his stand-in position on the trim saw. "What the hell happened here?"

If Kurt squeals on me, I'm toast. There goes my sawmill career.

"We're good," Kurt says, reaching for a 2 x 4.

The four of us soldier on, separating pieces of junk wood from good boards. When I glance back over at Yates, she's busy turning cants, but she's smiling. If she was standing next to me, she'd nudge me with her elbow.

Even after the lunch break, the edgings from the wreck still litter the floor.

"You seen Riley today?" I ask Janie at the last break of the day.

"He was just joy riding on the side of a forklift," she says. "He visits a lot with the guys. Otherwise I haven't seen him. But that's not unusual. You know how it is, doing cleanup."

For one thing, joy riding on forklifts is against all safety rules. Then, too, Yates has been playing the I-have-to-go-to-the-bathroom game a lot, so while George stands in for her she's probably off meeting Riley for a little R & R. And doing it in spite of the scolding they got and the fact that Riley's married. Once when Riley took off his gloves to pick his nose, I noticed his wedding ring. Yates does have an odd taste in men, take, for instance, Craig, that old hippie at the Christmas tree farm.

"So, how are you doing, Janie?" I ask.

"Fine, I guess," she says. "I mean, Danny's been nice enough, and he's sorry he hit me, but now I'm afraid of him. I don't want to be close to him, but I do it because I'm afraid of what will happen if I don't."

"Can't blame you for being scared," I say. "I'm no expert at being married, and Mom and Dad never hit each other. Even my husband of two weeks, imperfect as he was, didn't abuse me."

"I think I'll get over it," she says. "He's just having a hard time right now. Problems with his job." She sighs. "I'm having problems with my own job, too. The men don't want me on the line. They keep yelling at me to work faster, but I work as fast as they do. And there's more. Last time I talked with my mom she said my stepdad's been beating her up again. The neighbors heard her screaming the other night and called 911."

"Oh, Janie. God, I'm sorry."

"Well, I know one thing for sure," she sighs again. "Things can't get much worse."

A punch in the face from her husband sure changed her personality. How about I start a rescue service to help Carmel and Janie, and now Janie's mother. Mom can help.

## CHAPTER 19

No phone call first, no nothing. Ever since Dwayne got himself killed in that logging truck accident, my old friend, Mitch, stops by out of the blue–but only on a Saturday night around the time of a full moon. He says hello to Mom and then takes me out for a few drinks, although we never go to The Tool Shed. Now I'm glad. Wouldn't want to run into Nose.

Tonight, as usual, after too many drinks on my part, Mitch drives us to the old high school parking spot near a stand of Doug fir trees, overlooking Hat River. We talk a few minutes but soon run out of words. He's not interested in my work, and when I ask him a question about his life he kisses me for a few seconds and the next thing you know he's reclined his seat and muscled himself on top of me. This all happens real fast, given my size. I figure he must have been a wrestler at one time. A quick fondle or two, the sound of zippers, lots of tugging and grunting, and the next thing you know I'm looking over his shoulder at the moon, which is a bit of a blur since the windows are all steamed up. While Mitch is goin' at it, I roll down the window an inch or so. An owl hoots, *Who? Who?* and I think, *Why? Why?* Suddenly Mitch stops humping me. Just like that. He'd never win bronc riding at a rodeo. That takes eight seconds, which is why sex with Mitch doesn't count. After sharing a quick cigarette, he starts his unmarked sheriff's car, and we drive through the moonlit landscape without so much as a word.

At home when I get out of his car, he says, "Echo, it's been fun."

He doesn't expect a reply and he doesn't get one. He waves and drives off down the road, and when he reaches the highway he honks, signals right, and heads toward home and his wife. I think about the owl's question, and remember another thing Delight likes to say, *You get what you think you deserve.* While I stand here pondering what I deserve, the moonlight shines all around me and bounces off the patches of frozen snow. I know only one thing for sure; I will never again ask myself "Why? Why?" at least not with Mitch.

On Monday morning I park Rooster next to Nose's classic yellow International pickup truck. The truck on the other side of us wears a bumper sticker, HUG A LOGGER. YOU'LL NEVER GO BACK TO TREES. "Oh yeah," I say, slamming my car door. I know all about loggers. Dwayne might have been weak about his convictions, but he always hugged me like a big friendly bear, and wouldn't let go. And he's still hanging on. When I walk toward the mill, I look back at my red car parked next to Nose's yellow truck. That's us, ketchup and mustard.

My day starts with general cleanup in the planer room. When I walk past Nose and he tosses a knot at my hard hat, I smile at him and experience a twinge of guilt because of Mitch. But I won't see him again. When I first got acquainted with Mitch he was a sheriff, practically a celebrity in the next county over. Said he was separated.

You should be able to trust the law. Besides that, he's good-looking and can be charming. I mean, he treated me like I was special, even attractive, and never once mentioned my crazy hair. That alone was a miracle. So in a weak moment after Dwayne got killed, I *went out with him*. Then it happened a few more times before I realized that going out always meant a drink or two but no dinner, and a quickie in his unmarked sheriff's car.

George interrupts my thoughts. "Carmel has an appointment. Need you to pick edgings over at the mill."

So I work at the edger with Kurt and Dave and a new guy, also named Dave. I'm the second person on the line, and I concentrate on working as fast as I can while keeping my fingers out of the way so Kurt won't smash 'em.

All of a sudden the mill is filled with the screams of a cat in heat. Kurt yells, "No! No! Shit! The band saw's coming off. Hit the . . .!"

Everyone disappears, out of sight, gone. I dive under the scragg, where you're never s'posed to go—ever—into a space about three feet square. And who crawls in crawls in after me but Kurt. It's a tight fit, let me tell you, and the scragg is still running, still sawing slabs off logs to make 'em square. All the machinery is operating. Even with my ear plugs in, sounds like I'm under a locomotive, roaring downhill toward a crash. I can feel the vibration, the whirring and whining of the saw blade just inches away. But it's better to take your chances under the equipment, better to get hit on your hard hat or even on your back with a board, or, God forbid, get crushed by a log, than it is to get ripped to shreds or cut in half by the band saw. The thing's shaped like a giant rubber band, only it's made of steel with teeth several inches long, sharper than razors, and if that thing goes flying around the mill, it can bounce *all* over hell.

Stan, the guy babysitting the band saw, finally catches on. By the time he shuts off the machine, the saw is hanging off the wheel, ready to take flight. All the equipment goes down. The mill becomes silent. And here I am, holding onto Kurt's arm like he's life support. I jerk my hands off him and peek out from underneath the scragg.

Leroy yells, "All clear. You can come out now." Like we been playing hide and seek.

I'm spooked. When I stand up, my legs wobble. Those trouble-makin' *inventamilists* putting nails in trees just ain't right. That's probably what caused the band saw to go haywire.

We all take an early break while the millwrights replace a busted part and reset the saw.

After Yates and I drop our butts onto the bench in the machine shop, I can hardly light my cigarette, my hands are shaking so bad. At last, we both lean back against the wall and puff smoke like a pair of chimneys, staring at nothing in particular.

I take another long drag on my cigarette and say, "Stan must have been asleep at the switch."

Yates looks my way and exhales slowly, her foot bouncing up and down like it's gonna take flight. She doesn't, apparently, see the need to reply.

"Want to hear Delight's latest?" I ask, to get my mind off what just happened and maybe stop shivering. She's still kickin' her foot up and down like a crazy person, so I keep talking. "She said, 'Echo, you just have to ask the universe for what you want, and ask at a level above the roof line.' And you know something? That just didn't *resonate* with me."

Yates blows smoke and shakes her head. "Sure obvious she never did work that threatened to pop her muscles and shred her all to pieces."

"No," I say, "and I hate her for that."

"So do you know what you want so you can ask the universe for it?"

"Yeah, it's a toss-up between world peace and a permanent full-time job in this hell hole. You?"

"I'm thinking about going back to California. Come with me, why don't you? We could find jobs that pay well and aren't so fucking hard and dangerous."

"I don't know," I say, getting the shivers all over again. "The thought of leaving Hatfield is worse than that band saw coming loose."

Yates' foot stops bouncing up and down. She uncrosses her legs, sits up straight, fills her lungs with air, and hollers, *"Hoo, hoo-hoo, hoo-ah . . yeeyowuhhh. . hoo, hoo-hoo, hoo-ah yee-owuhhh!*

"Jesus, Yates."

"I had to scream or do something dramatic. I just couldn't *help* it."

"Good God! I sit here thinking about California, wondering if my nerves could take moving to a place with more sunshine and a summer longer than a few weeks, where I'd get an easier job that I wouldn't know how to do, and you push me over the edge with that ungodly noise."

"Well, don't take it personal," Yates says. "And unless you have a hot date Friday night, I'm taking you out to

The Tool Shed to celebrate, whether you get on full time or not."

When Yates nudges my arm with her elbow I almost fall off the bench, weak as I am from the near-death experience with the band saw and from hearing the call for the spotted owl. But at the same time, I'm comforted by this friendly reminder that I am not alone.

Yates and I pull up to The Tool Shed about the same time. She's riding a late-model Harley, and revs the engine before turning off the beast. Odd she never mentioned a motorcycle. Dad always said that anyone who rides a *murdercycle*, as he called 'em, had a death wish.

Yates removes her white motorcycle helmet and hangs it over a handlebar. The fringe on her buckskin jacket sways this way and that as she dismounts. She's wearing tight black jeans and motorcycle boots.

I open the door for her, since she's busy running her fingers through her hair. She told me once that men find it sexy. In the dimly lit room, I head toward the bar. "I gotta ask Crick a question."

Almost every bar stool is taken, and we wait while Crick serves up a couple beers from the tap. He says to us, "What'll you have?"

"How about a bandaid? Took a sliver out of my thumb at home."

"Don't have one," he says. "Hey," he yells to the guys at the bar. "Anyone here got a bandaid?"

Crap. I'm a spectacle now. But Yates is already on it, and a guy named Hank who's pushing eighty, has his wallet out to check.

He wheezes, holds up a flat brittle package, and says, "How about a condom? 'Course, it's been in my wallet about fifteen years. You never know when you might get lucky."

"Thanks anyway," I say, putting my arm around him. "Don't know how much good it'd do me, or you, either, you old coot."

All the men have a good back-slapping laugh on Hank, and someone buys him another beer.

We leave the bar and find an empty booth.

"Congratulations again, pardner," Yates says.

"Thanks. The letter in my pay envelope said to come to the office on Monday to fill out the paperwork. Full-time employee. A 401-K plan. The works."

"What can I bring you, ladies," Crick says. "Sorry we couldn't find you a bandaid."

"Coors Light," I say. "Guess I'll manage without a bandaid. Don't need no flaming drinks tonight, either. My new job status is excitement enough."

"You got on," Crick says. "Good for you."

"I'll have whatever beer's on tap." Yates says before strutting her stuff toward the juke box.

Our beers show up quickly, and when Yates sits down we clink glasses and both say "Cheers."

"Will you look who's here," Yates says.

Nose must be a regular. My heart jumps. Before leaving home, I applied a little mascara and lipstick, just in case he showed up. He looks around the room and smiles when he sees us. As soon as he claims his beer at the bar, he walks over.

"Echo just got on full time at the mill," Yates yells. "We're celebrating."

"Good job," Nose says. "You earned it."

I look at his ear fur and smile. "Thanks." Without asking him to sit down, I pat the seat next to me and he folds into place like he belongs there.

"Hey, Justin," I say as he walks toward us, a Corona in hand.

"Good job, Auntie, I mean Echo," Justin says, scooting into the booth next to Yates. In the background, Willie Nelson is singing *Blue Skies, nothin' but blue skies, from now on.*

"Sing it Willie," I say. "That's exactly what my life feels like right now."

"So," Justin says. "You and Yates getting along with George?"

"You mean GVW?"

"Auntie!"

"Well, you gotta admit, the man's the size of a load of logs."

Justin nods his head. "He earned it. At lunch break he brings in two grocery sacks. One holds a loaf of white bread, a jar of mayo, sliced meat, a gallon of milk. The other bag holds his snacks. By the end of the shift, those two bags are empty."

"The man eats enough food for a whole safety luncheon," Nose adds.

Crick delivers another round of drinks.

Nose raises his can of beer. "Hamm's!"

"The beer refreshing," I sing, in my goofiest alto voice.

"Hamm's!" Nose finishes in a low growl like a large bear.

All the stress of the week melts away as we hoot and all try to say "Hamm's!" in a lower voice than Nose's growl. I feel instantly bonded with this man I know so little about. After all, he can sing this jingle from my favorite old TV commercial. And his low growl's a real turn-on. Here I am with most of my favorite people. I have a full time job with benefits. And I'll never again go out with Mitch. It's been a long time since I was this happy.

"Now that you're a full-timer," Nose says to me, "you should know that Park only *acts* like he's in charge of the mill. Sharlene, the office manager, has a lot of pull and sometimes tells the bosses what to do, even The Big Boys in Spokane. And when old Esterbrook got in our hair by trying to help in the mill, she'd ask him to leave so we could get our work done. 'Course, he had a crush on her so she could get away with it."

With that, Nose finishes his beer. "Well, guess I'll be on my way." He gets up and extends his hand to me.

I hope my eyes and smile speak the words I'm not able to say, that I wish he'd stay. His warm hand holds mine longer than a normal handshake requires. I study him without blinking or looking away, and think warm thoughts about his brown eyes, his strong back, his capable hands. What would those hands feel like on my bare skin? Maybe I'll find out one of these days. For now, it would be nice if he'd just kiss my hand like the men did in the good old days. Good grief. I've never thought such a thing in my life, not even with Dwayne.

Nose leaves our booth and I watch as he stops to say goodbye to the guys at the bar. They talk a while, look our way, and laugh. Probably about Hank's condom. Glad I could make their night. When Crick delivers another round of beer, Justin doesn't drink his, so Yates and I drink up.

"Why the hell not?" I say, laughing hysterically. "Gotta have at least one lush in the family. Delight doesn't drink. Delight doesn't smoke. Don't know what *she* does for fun."

"I know one thing for sure," Justin says. "Every couple months a man named Mitch stops by to take her out to dinner, like last Saturday night. She always comes home early with a big smile on her face."

# CHAPTER 20

Mr. Gross Vehicle Weight himself catches me at the time clock Monday morning. "Big inspection coming up," he says. "There's a bunch of paper towels on the ground out in back of the planer. It's all gotta be picked up before the inspectors get here."

"Okay," I say, taking the plastic garbage bag he hands me.

I head out the back door and walk over to one of the dry sheds, and when I see pieces of toilet paper and *not* paper towels, I know right off the bat what's been going on. The toilet near the break room in the planer building is out of order. Instead of using the blue porta-potties, the guys have been going to the toilet outside behind the units. Those porta-potties stink something awful. They put those little round wafers in 'em and they're s'pose to act as deodorizers, but they just make the toilets stink bad. Makes you want to throw up. So the men do their business here. I walk back to George with the empty garbage sack.

"You didn't pick up that mess?"

"Nope. Hazardous material. Could contain diseases and therefore I don't have to touch anything that's ooey, gooey, or chewy, just like Safety Dave said. That's human waste out there. It's ooey, maybe even gooey."

"Well, somebody's gotta clean it up."

"Have the planer crew do it. They're the ones who shit down there."

George storms off, probably to find Riley. I follow along behind a safe distance so I can listen, but when he hands Riley the plastic bag, I can only see his mouth moving.

I busy myself picking up cull lumber. Pretty soon here comes Riley. He hands George the plastic sack, and I imagine he says, "That's hazardous waste. I don't have to touch it."

George points in the direction of the room the pit is in, and Riley walks off, leaving him holding the bag. It's not that he has to clean up the poop, just the paper, but that's bad enough. And he does it, too. Someone has to. Then he goes around at break time and tells all twelve guys at the planer, including Nose and Justin, "After this, anyone caught shitting down behind the units is gonna get his ass fired."

This morning, on my first day as a genuine, full time employee at TSI, I'm happy I do cleanup. I skulk around and catch anything out of the ordinary going on. For instance, while I'm sweeping near the planer office, a truck driver stomps in to see Leroy. "Where the hell did you get your millwrights, out of a crackerjack box?"

"What happened?" Leroy asks calmly.

"When I drove under the chip bin and pulled the release chain, the goddamn chip bin doors fell into my truck under a fucking ton of chips. How I can a guy stop the chips from comin', if they're layin' in the bottom of my truck? Now my truck's buried. I'm on a tight schedule and I can't leave."

To see what happens next, I get busy cleaning around the office door. Leroy phones the machine shop. Pretty soon the two millwrights who'd repaired and installed the chip bin doors walk past me into Leroy's office. Leroy yells, "This happens one more time and you're both fired. What the hell did you use on those doors, super glue?"

The millwrights don't say a thing.

"Well, don't just stand there with your thumbs up your butts, go get some shovels, Leroy hollers. "You, too, Echo."

At break time I hurry over to the mill to see Carmel and Yates. On our way up the machine shop steps, I say to Carmel, "I was worried about you when you didn't show up to work on Friday."

"My life is so stupid," Carmel says, sighing. "Melvin was cooking dinner on the little propane camp stove we use, and he caught the tent on fire. We tried to put it out by beating the flames with our coats, but just couldn't. So we all grabbed things and ran out of the tent. The poor kids were so scared. Melvin managed to rescue the *Safari* perfume, of all things. Then we just stood outside, watching the tent burn down."

"Oh, Carmel. What're you gonna do now?"

"There's more. We waded through the mud to the Bronco and drove to the motel on the edge of town," she says. I took Friday off so we could find a house to rent, and we did, but it's a dump. He wants to save money to build a house."

And finally Yates says, "Good luck with that."

Oh, yeah. I remember the last time I cleaned the debarker slopes. My feet flew out from under me, and I slid on my back into the goo and slime in the trough. But today I'm wearing boots with better tread. Right now it's

lunch break for everyone else and the mill is quiet. My
mind wanders to Carmel's situation for a few minutes.
And then I think about Delight, who has told me more
than once: *Echo, you have to follow your bliss.* And I
gotta wonder, is Mitch her idea of bliss? Mitch—the two-
timingest, no make that three-timingest creature that
ever lived. Should I tell Delight about me and him? I
picture Mitch sitting in his car smiling at me. Who *knows*
how many women he has on the string? Who can *tell*,
with a sub-species like that? The next thing you know,
both my feet slip out from under me and I fall on my butt
and slide. I get going so fast I take flight. I stop suddenly
when my legs slam into one of the metal cross beams that
hold up the building.

Sick to my stomach from the pain, I sink down into a
squat in the bark and dirt and slop. After a few minutes
of groaning and cussing, I crawl back up the slope on my
stomach using my arms. My numb legs drag along behind me. "Oh, sonofabitch'n hell. Groan, goddamn, my
legs are broken." I gain a few inches but slide back down
the slope. "Piss on it!" I let myself slide back down into
the mud and bark, and nestle in. After resting a few
minutes I lean over to feel my legs. No bones are sticking
out anywhere, but I'm filthy and when I struggle up onto
my hands and knees and finally all the way upright, I'm
barely able to hobble, stiff-legged, over to the metal
ladder. Hurts like hell, but I can walk.

When lunch break comes around and everyone else is
back on the line, I wash up in the restroom and sit alone
in the break room. I take three aspirins for the pain, and
eat my tuna sandwich, apple and chips. After lunch I
clean in slow motion until the equipment is shut down

for a break. Then I trudge back to finish my work on the debarker slopes, glad no one saw me get hurt. Won't have to file an accident report.

When George puts in an appearance, I ask, "What's that slime on the debarker slopes?"

"Oh, that. I forgot to mention it. That's hydraulic fluid from a ruptured hose."

"You might tell me next time?" I say. "That stuff's slicker than snot."

"You're not giving me shit, are you? Cuz I'll tell you a thing or two. Shit moves downhill a lot better than it moves uphill." He stomps off, obviously still mad because I refused to pick up the toilet paper. He's right. I feel like shit, and I do move downhill real fast.

My first week as a full-time employee is shaping up to be about as interesting as I can stand. Will I ever walk again without pain? Now that I've finished cleaning the debarker slopes, I pace myself doing general cleanup in the planer building. Thinking about what George said, I mimic him, mouthing the words, *I'll tell you a thing or two. Shit moves downhill a lot better than it moves uphill.* Muffled screaming interrupts me and I clean closer to the sounds. There in Leroy's office, a tall, blond woman is screaming at Riley and Leroy. "What kind of place you running here, that a man has time to make out with some slut in the parking lot in the middle of the day?"

Yates and Riley got caught.

At the end of the shift Yates invites me to sit in her car and talk. "We were just necking, for chrissake," she says. "His wife's lucky she didn't show up with his lunch pail a few other times."

"So now what happens?"

"Leroy put us both on probation. Told us again that we have to stay away from each other on mill property. Too bad, too. He's *such* a hunk. You would not believe how sexy he is."

"So are you going to?" I ask.

"Going to what?" Yates studies me, like she's surprised at the question.

"Stay away from him."

"I'll see him anytime I can. There are other places to meet, besides here at work. His wife has no clue who she's dealing with. Hell, he doesn't even love her."

"Maybe he'll leave her, then," I say.

"Good God, I hope not. It's not like I want to *marry* him. I just want to screw him."

My instructions on Monday morning are, "Need you to stand in for Yates on the tail saw."

"Where is she?"

"Taking a few days off," George says. "She had a little accident over the weekend."

So I stand in for Yates. Not a job I'm real experienced at, but the men aren't too bad to work with. Maybe she has 'em trained to work with women. But where is she? Did Riley's wife catch her? Riley loiters around, pretending to clean. He visits with the men and leans on his shovel a lot. *He* doesn't seem unhappy.

The sections of log in front of me are monsters. The first piece I turn feels like a refrigerator, but I do the best I can to muscle each cant into position for the next step—to be cut into 2 x 4 or 2 x 6 studs. Scrap pieces of wood, like the slabs, get sent down the hole under the line onto a conveyor to end up at the chipper. And just like Yates did at first, I don't always remember to dance sideways when sending a log edging down into the hole. My shins still ache. Now, as bruises pile up on my right thigh, I keep thinking about Yates. What could have happened to her? Suddenly a log edging slams into my thigh, and I remember what she said about this job: there's nothing like black and blue to make a person dance.

# CHAPTER 21

"Yates?" I say into the phone after dinner. "What's up?"

"I hope you're sitting down," she says. "I sure can't. You're not going to believe what happened."

"Try me."

"I did a dumb thing."

"You?"

"Echo!"

"Okay, okay. Let's hear it."

"Well, I didn't hear from Riley after his wife caught us in the parking lot. I just couldn't stand it. I mean, he knows he can call me, that no one else would answer my phone. On the other hand, it's not like I can just call him up, you know. *The wife* might answer."

"You didn't call him at home, did you?" I already know what she's gonna say.

"Yeah, and, of course, *she* answers. I calmly ask to speak with Riley. 'Honey, it's for you,' she says, all sarcastic. 'Hello?' he says. "I say, 'Hi, it's me, wondering when we can get together. I know you can't talk right now, but maybe you can call me later from a pay phone.' And do you know what he said? 'Stop trying to wreck my marriage. Do not call me ever again. Leave me alone.'"

"Oh, Yates. I'm sorry." I want to ask her what in the hell she was thinking, calling him at home, putting him on the spot like that. But instead I ask, "Did he call you from a pay phone?" I already know the answer to that one, too.

"No. The asshole did not call. I waited all weekend. By Sunday night I couldn't stand it anymore. It wasn't late. I knew I had to work Monday, but I went out to The Tool Shed and got drunk anyway. Crick had to take me home. 'Course then I had to slap him and his big old beer gut off me at the door. At least I think I slapped him off. Hell, I was drunker than a skunk."

"I heard you had an accident."

"What else did you hear?" she asks. "I can take it."

"That's all," I say. "But I can hardly stand not knowing. So?"

"After I got home drunk and got rid of Crick, I turned on the oil stove in my living room as high as it would go and then I took a shower. Put on a pair of panties and went in the living room to grab the pair of socks I'd left on the floor. When I bent over, I managed to lean my ass against the hot stove. Melted my nylon panties right into my skin. Jesus, did that hurt."

"Good thing you were drunk," I say, "or it might have hurt a lot worse."

"Hah! Drunk as I was, I knew it was bad. Called 911 and told 'em, 'Hey, I burned my ass on my stove, can someone come and get me?' I guess they thought I was kidding. The dispatcher said, 'Could you repeat that?'"

"Jesus, Yates. That's unbelievable. When you coming back to work?"

"I can't even sit down. At the clinic, it took 'em a while to cut the piece of nylon from my butt cheek. Hurt like hell. Now all I can do is lay on my left side or stand. Hurts to move at all. But I heal fast. Doc thinks I can go back to work next Monday."

"Riley will be there."

"Yeah. I'm talking with Leroy about working swing at the planer instead of days at the mill. That way I can avoid the man completely."

"I won't tell anyone what happened," I say.

"Hah!" she snorts. "It would have taken the mother of all gag orders to keep that one quiet. I'm sure everyone in the county already knows about my accident. You know how those ambulance drivers talk. I'm sure I'll be the butt of a lot of jokes for a while. I guess at work I'll act butch about it. Pretend nothin' happened."

We laugh at the idea. "Yeah," I say. "The truth is our friend, but acting like nothin' happened—that's a close second. And since you can't drive to the store, tell me your grocery list. I'll make a delivery before I go to bed."

I already know her list will include beer, cigarettes and a lottery ticket. And I'm right, except for one odd request: a magazine about birds, like *Audubon,* which the IGA actually has on the shelf.

A week later Yates is back at her job, and I'm doing general cleanup in the planer building and in the pit. Working in a different building from Carmel and Yates, and cleaning the pit when the equipment is down, puts a dent in my social life.

After The Big Boys do an inspection, management always posts their report in both the mill and the planer. Now on a quick trip to the rest room, I notice the inspection report posted on the bulletin board. They comment on every aspect of operation, and on the last page I read three words that make me want to dance with my broom: *Housekeeping is excellent.*

At the end of the day I see Yates walking slowly toward her old Subaru. By the time I get to her, she's already reached her car.

"Hey! Look at my new sex toy," she hollers, waving an inflated rubber donut in the air. "I found this at the drugstore for people with hemorrhoids," she says, showing me the rubber device the color of faded roses, the same color as my car. "Also works if you have a bad burn on your ass." She turns and indicates where the burn is—in the middle of her left cheek.

"How'd you do at work today?"

"I just took my pain pills and did my job the best I could. Otherwise, I pretended nothing happened. But I can tell you this—the affected area, as the doctor calls it, hurt like a sonofabitch."

"I can only imagine," I say. I don't mention my own bruises—my wrecked shins from the fall on the debarker slope, and the bruises on my thigh from doing her job last week. "You still thinking of changing shifts?"

"Leroy's working something out. Says he'll know tomorrow. Looks like I can do an easier job on swing," she says, easing herself down onto the rubber donut.

I tell her, "I'm putting in a bid to do cleanup on the graveyard shift. That way I can get away from George. I'll get a pay differential, and do a better job of cleanup with the machinery shut down all night. Hell of a lot quieter, too."

"Think you can sleep during the day?"

"Tired as I get, I can probably take a nap standing up, like some of the men do, like Riley does. Speak of the devil, did you see him today?" I ask. "He must have been working around the mill. Didn't see him at the planer."

"It's easy to avoid him. He keeps his distance, and so do I. Anyway, I was concentrating on each chunk of wood I was turning. That way I didn't notice my burn so much."

"Need help at home?" I ask. "I'll come over."

"Thanks, but I'm okay. Can't get my burn wet, so I'll just change my bandage and take a spit bath. Then I'll eat a TV dinner and lay on the couch with a beer and the remote control. Oh, and by the way, I have a new roommate. Remember Mousse, the parrot from the pet shop? He wasn't cheap, which means I'm making payments on him."

"Your shittin' me!"

She smiles. "He's good company, Echo. And I'm teaching him to say 'You are very beautiful.'"

The police scanner is awful damn quiet, for a Saturday night, and I'm grateful. Enough happens at the mill that I look forward to my evenings and weekends at home with Mom. Playing cribbage again, Mom is rearranging her cards and I'm thinking about why Yates bought Mousse. She said she'd been lonely, feeling sorry for herself about Riley. But I still don't like that damn parrot. Holding grudges serves no purpose whatsoever. I know that. But I'm good at it.

Mom lays down a five of spades, I snap a five of diamonds on the table, and say, "Two points," and move my peg forward a whopping two holes. Mom says, "Delight sure likes that hypnotherapy business. Wants me to do a past-life regression with her so she can practice. I might even change my first name. I've never liked *Mabel*. Maybe when I find out who I was before, I'll know what to call myself now. Maybe you'll want to do hypnotherapy, too."

My lips disappear in on themselves. Maybe Delight should have bought the parrot. Practice on *him*. Who knows how many past lives that parrot has had. While I sit gripping the rest of my cards, trying to think if I want to know about my past lives, I hear the familiar screech-clunk-bang down on the highway, followed by the slamming of car doors.

"Jack-in-the-box," I say, laying down my cards. Mom always acts like a kid when it happens. We've all hit deer, but so far I've been lucky, knock on wood. Nobody wins when a car hits a deer, but Mom and I have figured out a way to come close.

Mom can move surprisingly fast for being so old. She jumps up, grabs her 30-30 Winchester and a box of shells out of the cabinet and heads for the door. With our rubber boots and jackets on, we make our way down the edge of the road, Mom with her cane, me carrying her rifle in one hand, a big flashlight in the other, glad that the rifle weighs only six pounds and that the mud is partially frozen.

A woman's voice carries uphill. "You should have seen the deer! You always drive too fast at night. Now what are we going to do?"

"Hello!" I yell, flashing my light toward the woman's voice. "We're coming to help you."

When we reach the scene of the accident, the young deer is still kicking. The newer model mini-van has suffered a dented right front fender.

"You folks all right?" Mom asks, a little out of breath.

"Yes," the man says. "We aren't hurt."

His wife is crying. "Oh, that poor little deer."

"Happens all the time," I say. "This is a deer crossing. There's a sign back down the road, showing a deer leaping out."

"I saw it," the man says, "but that same sign is everywhere."

"So are the deer," Mom says. "Cover your ears."

She drops a shell in the chamber of her rifle and takes aim on the deer's head. One loud, sudden shot and the animal stops kicking. "We'll take care of the deer for you," I tell them. "You should probably get going so someone doesn't come along and plow into your car."

"Thank you both," the man says, opening his car door. The woman gets in her side of the van and they drive away slowly, their emergency lights flashing.

I grab the doe's front legs and start dragging it up the road. The deer is mostly hair and bones, not much meat, but it's awkward to handle, especially while carrying the flashlight. I'm grunting less than I have with past road kills. Working at the mill is starting to pay off. When we get the deer up the road and into an empty corner of the woodshed, we flip on the light. Mom helps me tie a piece of clothesline rope around the deer's hind legs before I toss the rope over the rafter to hang up the deer. The doe can't weigh more than seventy-five pounds, the same weight as a wet railroad tie at the mill. I put an old metal wash tub under the animal's head and plunge Dad's hunting knife into the throat to cut the jugular veins so the blood can drain out. Then I make one clean slice from top to bottom to remove the innards, like Dad taught me when I was about ten. The guts steam in the night air as they spill into the metal tub. I'm much better at gutting a deer than I am at hunting. The last time I went hunting with Justin, I shot a deer and only wounded it. He chased down the deer, wrestled it to the ground, and finished the poor thing off with a knife.

Mom stands watching. Finally she says, "I think I'll give it a try."

I reach into the tub for the heart and liver. Mom's favorite parts. "Give what a try?"

"Hypnotherapy. A character in one of the books I just read tried it and found out she was a queen in a former life. Besides, maybe it'll be good for Delight. I think she needs help now.

"What do you mean?"

"Justin says she's depressed or something, that she sleeps all the time. She told him she blanked out while driving her car the other day and ended up in the neighbor's field. Wrecked his fence. And she didn't remember getting there."

I stand over the tub of steaming animal guts, my hands wrapped around the still warm heart. "That's not like Delight," I whisper. "She needs to go to the doctor."

"Justin's taking her on Monday," Mom states matter-of-factly, staring at the round, dripping dark mass in my hands. "Get the liver, too, don't forget."

"Mom! Why didn't you tell me this before?"

She doesn't say anything, just folds her arms and goes blank in the face.

"Mom?" I'll look at her until she tells me.

"Well, I know you and Delight aren't . . . close. I'm so worried and scared for her and I just couldn't stand telling you about it and seeing that you don't care.

Suddenly I'm not interested in the deer, its liver or its heart, nothing except my sister. I drop the heart back into the tub. Tears well up in my eyes. My own heart feels swollen and bruised. "But Delight has all the answers," I blurt. "Maybe it's nothing at all. Maybe she's fine." I reach toward my mother, wanting to touch her.

"Don't you dare! Not with those bloody hands," she says, an edge to her voice. She probably wishes I was sick, and not Delight.

I reach back into the tub for the heart. Like everything at the mill, this job must be done *now,* not some other time. There's not much in my life that can wait. Nothing can be put on hold–not illness, not even death. When Dwayne and Dad died, I just kept going, kept doing. We all did. Then there was Weldon. If only the world would hold still for a while. And now Delight might have something serious wrong with her, and I have to finish gutting and skinning a goddamn deer. Then it has to be cut up into pieces to cool overnight in the refrigerator. Tomorrow Mom will cut the meat into steaks and roasts and wrap them for the freezer. She'll probably make her special mustard. The show will go on.

Around midnight I drag the tub of guts out into the field for the coyotes. The snow is gone, and the tall grass is damp. When I dump the contents, I remember what Delight likes to say: *In an abundant universe, there is always enough.* As if the coyotes smell what's in the tub, they start their yipping down by the river.

Above me is a quarter-moon. A dry moon, Dad called it, sitting in the sky like a bowl, keeping the rain from falling. A cup holds things, but I can't do it anymore. My chest hurts like I've been kicked by a hoofed animal.

Delight, the chosen one in the family, the Christ Child. She got it all—the looks, the niceness, the smarts, and she got Dwayne—but none of it was her fault. Well, except for Dwayne. Maybe nothing is wrong with her at all. On Monday we'll find out. And that night I'll start working graveyard at the mill.

It's so quiet and peaceful out here under the stars and the dry moon. Even the coyotes stopped howling. I reach for the handle of the old tub and head back to the house. An owl hoots in the pine tree near the edge of the field. It doesn't sound like a spotted owl.

## CHAPTER 22

"That asshole's been parking on the road across from my trailer, watching me," Yates says, spitting a piece of tobacco onto the machine shop floor.

"Which one?" I ask. "There's so many to choose from."

"Riley, of course, the poster boy for assholes everywhere." She's kicking her boot up and down. "Why's he doing that?"

"Maybe he knows he's with the wrong woman."

"He even called me a couple times. Oh, he doesn't say anything, just listens while I say, 'Hello? Hello?' all pathetic-like. 'Who is this?' I yell into the phone. I mean, the man chooses his wife and then I get drunk and burn another hole in my butt. What the hell's he want from me?"

"Sounds like he's having trouble letting go of you."

"He never even *had* me. Jesus, we were just fooling around. It's not like I wanted to grow *old* with him."

I grunt to let her know I'm listening. Guess I'll tell her about Delight tomorrow night. I switch to thinking about Mitch and how I never once thought of calling his house. Now I can't remember what I even saw in him.

"The man's a goddamn psychic vampire."

"Sounds like a freak in a horror show," I say. "Next time tell him if he keeps stalking you you'll call his wife and then the sheriff."

"Maybe I'll do just that," Yates huffs.

*Ahooga! Ahooga!* The buzzer announces the end of our break.

It's my first night of graveyard shift and Yates' first night on swing. Since her last break starts at 8:30 and my shift actually starts at 9:00, I came to work early to grab a smoke and shoot the breeze with her. Thought we'd spend some quality time together. She'll leave at the end of her shift at 11:30 and I'll work all night. Hope I don't tip over from exhaustion around midnight, end up eating sawdust.

The equipment runs full-tilt until the end of swing shift, so in the meantime all I can do is dance around with my broom and shovel, doing general cleaning. When everyone else is gone and the machinery goes down, I get serious. With a dust mask on, I use the air compressor to blow sawdust out of the crevices. Then I rake, shovel, sweep, use my boots—whatever it takes—to shove the sawdust down the holes under the machinery onto the conveyors.

Before you know it, I'm winding down, working slower and slower, fighting to stay awake. Shortly after midnight my feet freeze in the sawdust when an odd movement catches my attention. My mind's eye sees what it sees—a hose the size of a boa constrictor swinging back and forth above the eight-foot stacker. The giant snake whips around and grabs me like a rag doll. Then the band saw starts up, spins faster and faster, breaks loose and takes off after me, too, like a heat-seeking missile. With all my strength I pull away from the snake, drop to the floor onto a pile of sawdust, and run like hell. All the equipment wakes up at once, and instead of gears grinding, an eerie, pitiful moaning echoes throughout the mill. I leap onto a roll case, and stare over my shoulder at the boa constrictor hose whipping toward me. When I turn to run, the snake knocks me down and drags me into the hog. No one's around to hear me screaming. In the morning, when the day shift starts, Leroy notices the mill isn't clean, and finds pieces of me—a hank of fluffy brown hair, yarn from a dirty sock, a button. Safety Dave collects a chunk of my flesh in a baggie, takes it to the clinic, and has it tested for drugs.

My heart gallops in my chest as I lean on my broom and close my eyes. Scared shitless but glad to be alive, I let loose the pent-up air from my lungs. My crazy imagination takes a rest, but my body is still convinced it actually saw what my mind only imagined. The machinery sits silent and innocent, ready to . . .

"How's it going?" a man's deep voice booms behind me.

Afraid to turn around, I clench the broom handle, ready to swing.

"You all right?"

I turn slowly to face this new threat. The man is wearing a uniform, like a Maytag repairmen on the TV ad. Both his hands are trembling, like he's freezing cold or crazy. Is this the *The Twilight Zone*?

"Name's Slim," he says, reaching toward me to shake hands.

But I'm too spooked to shake his hand, especially since it's already shaking.

"Echo," I say, still gripping my broom. "I do, uh, cleanup."

"Well," he says, dropping his hand. "I'm the head of security. Get around the whole place about once an hour."

"No one told me about you," I say, trying hard not stare at his hands.

"Folks call me Shaky Slim," he says, holding up both hands. "I don't mind. This here's a mystery disorder, like palsy. Skips generations, you know, but I got lucky. I'm carrying on the family tradition."

This guy has to be all right, with an attitude like that. I reach out to shake his hand. "Sorry to be so unfriendly. First night on graveyard." When he shakes my hand, my entire arm shakes and we both smile. "I'm glad to know you're here, Slim. Real glad."

"See you around," he says.

I nod, wishing he'd stay and hang out where I can see him while I sweep and shovel sawdust.

As I finish up around the trim saws, I hear, "How're you doing now?"

Slim's real friendly. I s'pose he gets lonely, here in the middle of the night. He tells me that besides watching out for lumber theft, vandalism, and people starting fires, he follows a system. Special keys are located throughout the mill and on the outside of the building. He makes regular rounds and at each location he turns the key in a recording box he carries with him on a shoulder strap. The box has a clock in it and each key is different. By turning a key in the box the time gets recorded. He says this used to be the boiler man's job, but he put all the keys in one handy place where he could turn them in comfort. The guy got caught, of course, and that's when the mill hired Slim.

"Security is important," he says. "They need me so they can keep their insurance."

By three o'clock in the morning I'm spooked again. I hide from the machinery in the boiler room and smoke a couple cigarettes to calm my nerves. On graveyard shift, I can smoke almost anywhere, any time. 'Course, I'm careful. Wouldn't want to burn the place down and end up jobless, sitting at the unemployment office with Leland again. The old metal folding chair I sit on is only six or seven feet away from the massive boiler. One leg of the chair is bent, so it would be easy to tip over sideways. No danger of getting too relaxed. No risk of falling asleep.

Janie is now the boiler room attendant, which means she babysits the dry kilns where the lumber is dried before going through the planer. From where I'm sitting, I watch what she does. She monitors the control panels for the boiler that heats the water that fires the kiln that dries the lumber. All the coils and pipes, switches and indicators remind me of the dashboard of a spaceship, like on *Star Trek*. Janie watches the gauges and writes down numbers. No way could I ever keep all this crap straight.

Janie is little and the two doors of the dry kilns are about the size of barn doors that swing open from the center. To open a door, she grabs a handle as long as a crowbar, swings it out, and pushes with both feet while running backward. She does the same with the other door. She says, "I'm small, so I learned early on to use physics in my favor." Next she uses a meter to check the moisture content of the lumber inside the kiln, to see if the wood has reached the specified dryness. Inside the kilns, flat beds on wheels, called dollies, hold units of lumber. Janie hooks a forklift to the dollies and pulls them out into the yard. She unhooks them, and pulls dollies of wet lumber from the yard into the kilns to be dried. This is big job, and I have new respect for her.

The temperature of the dry kiln is automatically set, so Janie doesn't have to mess with that, but she keeps a careful record of the units she moves. She does a few other odd jobs, too, like sweeping out the boiler room and cleaning around the bin near the boiler where the hog fuel is stored. And she shovels up the bark that spills outside and hauls it in the bucket of a bobcat to the hog fuel pile.

We visit off and on throughout the night. I'm worried about Delight, but I'm not in the mood to talk about it with anyone.

"I get home from work in time to see the kids off to school," Janie tells me, "and I sleep during the day while they're gone. I'm awake to cook dinner and be a mom in the evenings, until I leave for work about 8:30. But pretty soon school will be out for the summer, and that complicates everything."

Graveyard shift in the boiler room must be wearing on Janie. She looks older, more tired. I ask her, "Is your husband feeling better about your job?"

For a while, she doesn't say anything. "Danny likes it better when I'm home all the time, but I'm working because there isn't enough money. Now we can pay off some bills and I can afford to take Tiffany into Spokane for her Little Miss America training. If I didn't work here, we couldn't afford it. And even though Danny doesn't want me to drive, I'm saving my bonus money for a car."

"So other than not wanting you to work, he's all right?" I'm fishing. I know I'm being nosy.

"The good news is that he hasn't been violent, but he baits me and tries to pick fights. I want to be nice and reason with him, but he doesn't hear me. His voice gets louder and he just won't quit, and I'm so afraid he'll hit me again. The next thing you know, I'm sobbing, moaning like an injured animal. I hate myself for that. And then he comforts me and tells me I don't say my feelings right to him, says my communication skills need work. But there doesn't seem to *be* a right way to talk to him. I don't know what to do. At least I'm not around him as much, now that I work graveyard. Except for weekends."

A growing, boiling fist of anger toward Danny centers in my chest. "How about if I go to your house and clean his clock?"

Janie touches my arm. "Thanks, Echo. But I have to believe things will get better." She looks at her watch and sighs. "Break time's over. Don't let something get you out there."

"Don't let something get you in here," I say.

"It's safe in the boiler room," she says. "As pathetic as it sounds, this place has become my sanctuary."

At the end of my first night on graveyard shift, I sit in the parking lot a minute to let my car warm up before leaving. I fall asleep with the motor running. Luckily, my windows are cracked a little, and my cigarette burns down and scorches my fingers before setting my clothes on fire. "Ow, sonofabitch!" What a way to wake up. I hold my scorched fingers on the cold window before heading home. Driving along on the drowsy line between awake and sleep, night and day, I finally crawl up our driveway. When I drop onto the chair near the front door to take off my boots, I fall asleep bent over with my fingers on my boot laces. No telling how long I stay like this, but sometime later I wake up to finish untying my boots, pull off my filthy clothes, and drop them into the laundry basket Mom now keeps near the door. Then I make my way to the bathroom, where I fall asleep sitting on the toilet. Finally, I wake up enough to shower and crawl into bed.

After only about four hours' sleep I wake up to Mom puttering in the kitchen. I smell venison roasting, probably with onions, potatoes and carrots, and her special blend of spices. My stomach growls. At the thought of eating road kill for lunch, I push Tummy off my pillow and drag my tired, grumpy body out of bed. The spring weather calls at me to go outdoors, to work a little in the yard. Even though summer isn't here yet, I know how short the season is, that it'll be like waiting at the train station, and then the train won't stop for me. And just because it's May doesn't mean we won't get snowed on. Today the grass is neon green especially in the yard. Time to mow the quack grass we call our lawn. I'm tired but if I keep busy, maybe I won't worry so much about Delight. Mom doesn't talk about her, either. Maybe today we'll hear the results of her tests.

When I come back into the house after mowing the grass, Mom is sitting in her chair sniffling. This can mean only one thing. She got a call about Delight.

I close the door and sit on the chair to take off my boots. If Delight was all right, Mom wouldn't be crying. This can't be happening. I sit and wait, hoping she'll tell me, but she just blows her nose.

"Mom, what is it?"

"Brain tumor. They don't know if it's cancer or not. Justin is taking her back to Spokane for more tests tomorrow. Then they'll know more."

I sit on the floor by her feet and rest my head against her knees.

Later, after a dinner of venison steaks, I do the dishes and we play a game of cribbage. As usual, Mom gets to deal and I peg three points on the board, my reward for losing the first deal. It's something. But then my eyes close for a quick rest, and Mom yells "go!" She wins the game, again. Time to head to work and my second night of graveyard.

While I work, I imagine the equipment coming to life. George, Leroy, and Esterbrook himself get chewed to bits. Next the guy who said I had underwear hair, all those years ago, wanders in looking for me. A dog on the debarker grabs him by the throat and debarks him right down to the bone. The thought makes me smile. What is happening to me? Was I always this wicked, deep down, or is it because the mill is such a tomb in the middle of the night and that reminds me of all my losses? Now Delight faces surgery on her brain.

At times I swear I hear moaning, always interrupted by a strange, spooky silence. It's as if all the equipment is gathering into a deadly force. Maybe I imagine these things to entertain myself while I work, or maybe I'm finally losing my mind.

If Janie wasn't here, too, I couldn't work graveyard. Once in a while I see Shaky Slim, but I mostly work alone—shoveling, sweeping, picking up cull lumber, hearing noises, imagining evil things happening. It doesn't help that Sparks, the electrician, has managed to wire the motion sensor light outside the boiler room bass-ackward, so it goes *off* when it senses movement. The thing was installed to light the path, but as soon as I walk out there, the light shuts off. I have to stand still so it'll come back on. That Sparks is a real magician.

On another break with Janie in the boiler room, I plop down on the metal chair, and light up a cigarette. She looks even more tired tonight. "You're walking a fence at home, Janie. You need your sleep to do that."

"I'm not doing so well in that department, either. I get home from work just before six, before Danny or the kids get up. As soon as I get out of the shower, Danny grabs me and insists on sex. It doesn't matter how tired I am. He didn't used to be like that. It's like I'm a small home appliance. One morning I fell asleep during sex. He flew into a rage, said I was aloof, unavailable, unloving and only interested in work." She pauses. "I'm sorry, Echo. "You probably didn't want to hear all that."

"That's okay. You deserve better. Let me know if I can help you." I yawn loudly and close my eyes, just for a minute before going back to work. The last thing I remember is thinking how Mom is getting awfully psychic these days. Don't want *her* helping Janie by taking matters into her own hands with that gun of hers.

Arms grab me. I jerk awake. An alarm is buzzing on and off, on and off, like the mill's break buzzer has gone berserk.

"Echo! Wake up," Janie says. "You fell asleep. You were groaning like an old dog. You're all right now."

"Oh, my God! Oh, shit! Janie, is the boiler on fire?"

She squats down to put her arms around me. "Too much water pressure built up. It happens once in a while. I need to go outside to turn on the relief valve."

The alarm continues. I grip Janie's jacket.

"Echo, sweetie. Let go so I can take care of it."

But I can't. Tears well up and spill down my face. Janie puts her arms around me again. "Echo, I'll be right back." I study Janie's face as she pulls away, leaving me sitting on the chair with the bent leg, alone with my fear and overwhelming need for sleep.

Later, on the drive home at dawn, I stop for a nap. I drift off to sleep. After a few minutes I wake up to the honking of Canada geese down by the river. The rest of the way home, I manage to stay on the road. I crawl up the porch steps to the door, drag off my boots and dirty clothes, and collapse on the living room floor. Around noon I awake from my coma to the familiar sound of pots and pans and the murmur of the police scanner. Still on the floor, I'm covered with the blanket from the recliner. There's a pillow under my head.

"Mom," I groan. "Turn that thing up."

She stands with both hands on her hips, looking at me. She's been baking bread. There's flour on her red apron and on her dark blue pantsuit. "You must be gonna live, if you want to hear what the police scanner's yammering about."

Finally, it's Friday night. I drive slowly to work, more tired than I have ever been in my life. If only I can make it through the night, it will be the weekend.

After clocking in, I do the general cleaning until swing shift ends and the machines shut down. At the end of swing shift, I see Yates for a quick visit. She tells me, "I ran into the guy who gave me those tickets to the Willie Nelson concert. I'm seeing him now." She nudges my arm. "He's helping me teach Mousse how to sing *Blue Skies*. He's a good student." She winks and adds, "The parrot's a fast learner, too."

"So Riley's leaving you alone now?"

"Who?" she asks. "Oh, yeah. He's history."

"Good," I say, surprising her by taking her hand. I hold it while I tell her about Delight and the good news, that her tumor is about the size of a golf ball, and the doctors believe they can remove it, even though it surrounds a main artery. Then I tell her the bad news, that they still aren't sure it's benign, but they'll know on Monday when they operate.

Yates hugs me and doesn't let go. I lean into her, and we both brush tears away before saying goodbye.

After midnight, I do a slow-mo once-over with the air compressor, working like I've been drugged. Janie is cleaning up hog fuel spills around the blue bin, so I wait for her in the boiler room. Even before my butt drops onto the metal chair, my eyes are closed. And before you know it, I wake up on the floor, spitting sawdust. The metal folding chair and I must have toppled over sideways, and now the chair is snuggled up behind me in the spoon position, like a lover gone cold.

A small, ungloved hand gently touches my shoulder. "Echo," Janie whispers. "It's time to go home."

I groan. As if she had nothing on her mind, she's babysitting me like I'm one of her pressure valves. Finally, my first sleep-shy week of graveyard shift is over, and I didn't get the place all that clean. Oh, well. There's always next week.

On my way home I drive slow and careful. About half a mile from home my eyes lose all focus. I pull off the road, roll my window all the way down for air and slap myself in the face, but I finally give in. Geese are honking down by the river as I roll the window up most of the way, lock all the doors, and let sleep have its way. About an hour later when I wake up, surrounded by fog, the geese are still honking. Suddenly they stop. When I turn the key in the ignition and Rooster crows to life, the geese start honking again. Driving east toward home, along the edge of the fog, the sky glows a lovely shell pink, the color of fine lingerie. I wonder, as I sometimes do, how silky underwear would feel against my skin. Maybe someday. I turn onto the driveway that leads to the house, the same road that continues on up to June's. I stop the car. The velvet blue mountains all around are glowing. It's as if I'm noticing them for the first time, and I'm reminded of the one thing I know for sure:  this place is my home in the universe.

## CHAPTER 23

Thanks to working the graveyard shift, my skin might stay lily white through the entire spring and summer. No new age spots. No risk of skin cancer. Not even a farmer tan. When I wake up in the afternoon on Saturday, I stay indoors, eating everything in sight, watching television until it's time to play cribbage.

After our game, Mom reads and I stay at the kitchen table, noticing, as if for the first time, the pictures on the living room walls. Maybe working graveyard is messing with my mind, because those pictures have hung there for years and I never looked at 'em. There's the wedding photo of Mom's parents, two glum people with thin lips. The grandfather I never met wears his hair parted down the middle. Not a good choice. His hair was fluffy, too. There's a high school graduation picture of me, hair tamed down, almost smiling, thin lips almost not there. And the photo of Delight, with her big smile and upside-down tulip hair style, as if she always knew she was special. And now we might lose her.

The police scanner is turned down. Not much happening. Still in a semi-coma, I stare out the window. Just a few weeks ago the field was tan and knee-deep with dead grass and weeds. New plants somehow broke through it all, and now the field is green. Not far from the house, a robin hops. He listens, head tilted, like Mom does when she listens to the dispatcher on the police scanner. The robin studies the ground and suddenly stabs his beak straight down into the soft earth. Bingo, the bird scores an angleworm. Of all the birds, I'm most like a robin: I'm nothing special but I always show up. I work hard, and sing a little. So what if I've been a thumb sucker in the night, afraid of the mill equipment. Next week, by God, I'm gonna be more of an adult on grave-yard shift.

Mom rocks in the recliner, reading her latest bodice ripper. A paper grocery bag, filled with other ratty paper-backs, sits near her chair. When she finishes reading this batch of books, she'll put the bag out in the woodshed to burn in the stove. One time she read most of a bag of books twice. She realized it when she found a piece of bacon in one of 'em, used as a book mark.

"Want to drive over to see Delight?" I ask her.

She tosses her book on the floor and pushes herself up, already reaching for her cane. In minutes we're out the door, sitting in Rooster while he coughs and sputters to life. Before he's even warmed up, we're lurching down the road to the highway.

We find Delight dozing on the couch under a quilt. She'd started the quilt—a red maple leaf design—when we were eleven years old, and finished it a few years ago. By then the red leaves had started to fade. Justin, standing nearby, is off work a few days to help his mother. Delight half opens her eyes and looks at us. Does she wonder who we are?

"You in any pain, honey?" Mom croons.

Delight says nothing but folds her legs up so Mom can sit on the couch by her. I want to kiss her face, now that I know in my heart how important she is to me. When I get down on my knees in front of her and she realizes what

I'm about to do, she closes her eyes. After I kiss each cheek, she opens her eyes and stares at me, surprised. But I believe she knows I love her, in spite of our being at odds with each other the last fifty years.

While Mom stays next to Delight on the couch, I talk with Justin at the kitchen table. He tells me, "The mill is giving me time off with pay, under the circumstances."

"That's good. How're you holding up?"

"I'm just doing what I can, hoping for the best," he says. I notice he hasn't shaved in days, and I know Delight used to nag him to shave every day. "Mom's using self-hypnosis, trying to outsmart the tumor. And she might do it, too. She's done some amazing things. Helping people to quit smoking is the least of it." He looks at me. "Not that I'm suggesting you quit," he says, smiling.

"Can't hurt to expect the best," I say. "Your grandma is worried half to death, besides being mad as hell about it."

"Being worried and mad doesn't help," Justin says. "Mom told me the best thing I can do is to put myself in a grateful mood and picture her healthy."

Before we leave, Delight whispers to Mom. Whatever it was, Mom seems less worried. In the car on the way home, I ask, "So, what did she say?"

She smiles. "She told me not to worry. Said she knows for sure she's going to be okay, and I'm almost convinced she's right."

On Sunday afternoon I announce to Mom, who is deep in a book, "I'm going for a walk." When I slip out the front door, she doesn't look up.

Unaccustomed to the bright sunshine, I pull my baseball cap low. I walk down the road past the new grass to the highway and then scramble up and over the railroad tracks, before making my way through the alder trees. Thanks to the snow melting in the mountains, the river level is rising. I love this spot, where Hat Ferry used to take cars from one side of the river to the other. The Indians once crossed on their horses just upstream. I climb onto a bulge of granite at the water's edge and pull off my tennies and socks. A few seconds in the icy water is all my feet can stand. Off in the distance a grouse drums for a mate. For years I thought the sound was a tractor starting up, until Dad told me it was a lovelorn grouse. I'd wondered then about the meaning of the word, lovelorn. But when Dwayne got himself killed, I understood. The warm sun feels like a miracle on my skin. A dragonfly lands on my right thigh. I don't move. It flies up, nabs a bug, and lands on my leg again. My nose itches, and I slowly move my arm and rub my nose. The dragonfly doesn't move. The sun shines through his wings and they glow, like the filament in tiny tube lights. My little visitor flutters downstream, probably looking for more insects.

Dad liked to talk about cables, chains and pulleys, as if he was reading from the Bible. He'd say, "That's engineering . . . makes life easier, like crossing the river on the ferry so we don't have to drive all the way to hell and gone to get home." But for me a ride on the ferry in the wind was asking for trouble. One spring day when I was five, Mom took us across on the ferry. The bridge was built upriver a couple years later, but on that day in 1955 the river was almost at flood stage. The wind rocked and shoved the ferry and kicked waves in the air. Mom liked the wind, so we stood outside the car during the crossing. I wanted to be anywhere but on the ferry. Our car was parked just inches from the front edge of the ferry, and it jerked back and forth as the ferry made its way. Water splashed onto our tires and onto my little black rubber boots. Mom didn't notice. While she held Delight's hand, I stared at the front tires of our car, willing it not to roll off the ferry. When I grabbed Mom's other hand and hid behind her, she said, "Don't be afraid, Echo."

My mind is fuzzed out from lack of sleep and worry about Delight's brain tumor, but I close my eyes and try to picture her healthy, making one of her know-it-all statements. I'd rather have her *that* way, than across the river in the cemetery where Dad is buried. I glance in that direction and say, "Don't worry, Dad. Delight's going to be just fine."

Mom and I drive to Spokane to be with Justin while Delight has her surgery. We wait and wait. Mom reads an entire romance novel. I talk with Justin, mostly about people at the mill, including Nose. But Justin thinks I should get to know him and find out about him myself. I nap on the settee. Finally, when the doctor comes into the waiting room smiling, we know Delight will be all right. The tumor was benign and easy to remove, compared to most brain tumors. He'd siphoned it away and in a few months, when her scar heals and her hair grows back where they had to shave it, she'll be her old self. Can I hope she'll be *better* than normal? Anyway, she'll stay in the hospital a few days and either Justin or I will bring her home.

Tonight, relieved that Delight will be okay, I'm ready to take on another week of graveyard shift.

When I see Janie in the boiler room, she's ready to open the kiln doors. She works while I tell her how much I appreciate her being so kind to me last week, that I'll babysit sometime so she and Danny can have a date, just the two of them. I tell her about Delight's brain tumor and the miracle of having my sister back. She turns sideways and says, "Echo, I'm so glad."

Then I see it. "Janie, my God! What happened to your face?"

She drops the handle of the kiln door, her arms loose like strings, and I realize once again how little she is. "Danny hit me."

"Oh, Janie. You have to get away. Don't you see? He'll just keep doing it."

"Then, when I fell to the floor he kicked me," she says, speaking slowly, calmly, with no emotion. "I'm all bruised up. I taped my ribs, but it hurts to breathe. It hurts every time I move."

I want to ask her what it's gonna take before she leaves him. Does he have to rub shit in her face? But I take a deep breath. "What about the kids?"

"They were asleep. I didn't scream. When I was a kid, I heard my mom sobbing and pleading when my step-dad came home drunk and beat her up. I wanted to spare the kids."

"Mom?" I say into the phone. I know she went to bed about the time I left for work, after our exhausting day in Spokane. Now I'm waking her up.

"What's wrong?" she asks in her husky voice.

"Do you have June's phone number in Portland?"

"Yeah, but it's late. Can't it wait until tomorrow?"

"No, it's Janie here at work. She needs a safe place to go right away with her kids. Her husband beat her up. June knows Janie and the kids. I know she'd let them stay up at her place for a while. Can you call June right away?"

She doesn't say anything. "Mom?"

"All right. I'm still half asleep. Call me back in about twenty minutes."

Later, I tell Janie, "My mom called June in Portland. She wants you to stay at her place up the road from us. She won't be back for a couple weeks, but the utilities are already hooked up."

"I'm not sure I can do it," Janie says, staring at the dials on the outside of the kiln. "It's all so complicated."

"I'll help you move. Justin has a truck. Your kids will be in school." I take her hand. "Look at me, Janie." When she does, it's like her eyes are still studying the dials. "Danny will be at work. We'll just do it."

When Janie nods, she looks like the little doll I left outside on the ground in the rain, when I was eight. Abandoned, sad-faced, limp. The doll was my best friend at the time, and I hated myself for what I'd done.

"Okay, Janie. Now tell me what to do so I can help you here."

With a little coaching, I get the kiln doors open so Janie can check the moisture content of the lumber, and then I hook the dollies to the bobcat and pull them out of the kiln. As soon as I finish helping Janie I hurry off to shovel and sweep, to slop-clean the mill with a quick once-over so I won't get in too much trouble.

By the end of the shift, Janie seems listless. "You just go home and act like you normally would," I tell her. "Get

the kids off to school and Danny off to work. Then you
call me at home. I mean it, Janie. I'll be waiting. If I'm
asleep, Mom will wake me up." What I don't tell Janie is
that Mom will already have her 30-30 oiled and ready.

By the time Danny gets home from work at 4:30, Janie
and the kids are gone. She leaves him a note saying
they're at a safe place, and not to look for them.

"He'll go crazy," Janie sobs when we leave her house
for the last time. While Justin drives off toward June's
with their things in his truck, Janie and I leave in Rooster
to pick the kids up from school. On the way, we pass her
parents' small house in town.

"You and the kids will be safe."

"This is so hard, Echo. You have no idea." She glances
back at her parents' house. "Then there's my mother. I'd
like to help her get away from my step-father. I can't even
take the kids to visit anymore. We meet her for lunch at
The Log Drive."

"After you're away for a while, maybe we can help
your mother," I say. I'll tell Janie anything to get her to
leave Danny.

Mom acts like there's new meaning in her life. When
Janie's kids get off the bus down by the highway and
walk up the road, they stop to have cookies and milk with
Mom. "It gives Janie a little more time to sleep," Mom
says. "And they're such nice children. Besides, I want to
repay the universe for giving Delight back to us."

Oh, no! Now she sounds like Delight.

One afternoon, after I've slept off the graveyard shift, I
wake up early enough to sit at the table and eat oatmeal

cookies with Mom and the kids. When Tiffany lifts a cookie from the plate in the middle of the table she does it slow and dainty. "When I grow up, I want to be Miss America," she announces, taking a tiny bite of cookie.

"You'll be a lovely one, too," Mom says, and I can tell she believes it's possible.

"I miss my dad." Bobby says, his mouth full.

Mom glances at me, takes a sip of coffee and says, "I'm sorry, honey. He loves you all but he has some big problems right now."

The littlest boy stuffs an entire cookie in his mouth, points to the police scanner, and say, "Wassat?"

"Through that little box I can hear the person who talks to every policeman in the whole area," Mom brags. "That way I know what's happening all the time. Sometimes it's better than TV."

"Weally?" he says, wiping crumbs off his face. His eyes are big as he studies Mom with new admiration.

"When you guys are ready," I say, "I'll drive you up the hill. Your mother is probably awake by now, waiting for you."

Mom rides along. We could walk the kids home, but they love to ride in my old car. Rooster's a bit like a carnival ride at the annual logger's celebration. When we pull into June's driveway minutes later, the older boy says, "Will you turn off your car so I can hear the noises?" When I do this, they all laugh as my car wheezes, ticks and bleats.

The littlest boy giggles. "Your car tooted."

Janie stands in the open doorway. She looks tired but laughs with us. It's good to see her more relaxed. The kids run to their mother. When they all turn to watch us

leave, I say my little mantra and turn the key in the ignition. The old boy coughs to life, I give my audience a
thumbs-up, and Mom and I drive the short distance
down the road to our house.

A couple days later, in the half-sleep of a warm afternoon, I dream I'm hearing a siren. It gets louder. Wait, it
*is* a siren. Did someone hit another deer down by the
mailboxes and crash their car? The siren grows louder. I
call out, "Mom? What's happening?" She might know,
thanks to the police scanner. Except for the wailing siren,
and chatter on the scanner, the house is quiet. I did call
out, didn't I? I'm still groggy, still half asleep. "Mom?"
Now I hear a second siren, down by the mailboxes at the
highway. Crap, the sound is coming up the road toward
me.

"Oh, my God!" I jump out of bed and pull on a pair of
jeans. With one leg still not in my pants I hop out to the
living room, and slip my bare feet into my work boots.
"Mom?" No one is in the house or the yard. Out the window I see the sheriff's car roaring up the road, lights
flashing, followed by the ambulance. I stop to tuck my
laces into my boots before running down the steps. The
sheriff's car slows down. The sirens stop. I run in my
loose, sloppy boots, my breasts bumping around inside
my t-shirt, toward a scene I will never forget. My mother,
limping, has her rifle aimed at a young man, walking
ahead of her down the road. This has to be Danny, and
he's stooped over holding his arm. Mom is on a rant.
"You ever touch her again, you little son of a bitch, and I
won't be so careful where I aim next time. I've killed any
number of deer with this gun, even a coyote or two, and

I'm not opposed to puttin' holes in you, as you can see by your arm."

The sheriff jerks open his car door, gun in hand. "I'll take it from here, Mrs. Spangler." He grabs Danny's good arm and waves the ambulance around them, which requires them to drive into the soft ditch and out again to get back on the road. I clomp along behind the ambulance as it swerves up the road, spitting dirt on me. I gotta get to Janie.

When I reach June's doorway, two ambulance drivers are huddled over Janie, who is on the floor on her side, the cordless phone in her hand. I run over to them. "Janie, Sweetie, can you hear me?"

She opens one swollen eye and reaches for me, but one of the men gently places her arms on her stomach before they lift her onto the stretcher. I hold the screen door open, wishing I could do something besides watch, as they carry Janie out to the ambulance.

"Janie," I yell. "I'll see you at the clinic. Don't worry, Mom and I will take care of the kids."

They load her into the ambulance, turn around in the driveway, and head down the road, sirens wailing. I run all the way down the road, stopping once to catch my breath as the ambulance turns onto the highway toward town.

"Mom?" I yell, leaping up the steps to the front door. I'm panting and coughing. She's sitting in her favorite chair at the kitchen table, drinking a beer. A beer? I glance at the kitchen clock. It's noon. The police scanner is turned up. Her rifle leans against the gun cabinet. It's been used. She'll clean it with a rod and a piece of rag

with 3-in-1 oil on it. Then she'll wipe down the outside of
the gun before putting it away empty.

"Kids'll be here in a few minutes," she says. "We'll
want to give them extra cookies today."

"What the hell happened?" She turns down the vol-
ume on the scanner before getting up and limping over to
the cupboard. She pulls out the plastic container filled
with cookies, and sets them on the table. By the way she
lowers herself back onto her chair, I can tell she's tired.

"I was just sitting here reading," she says, looking at
me now. "One of those romance novels I probably
already read. It was starting to seem awfully . . ."

"Mom!"

"I thought I heard a man yelling, then a woman
screaming. It was a ways away, and I wouldn't have
heard anything except the door was open for a little fresh
air. Thought I was hearing things. Then I just knew. I
grabbed my gun and some bullets and headed up the
road as fast as I could walk with my cane in one hand, the
gun in the other, mad at myself for being so slow."

"Why didn't you wake me up?"

"You were sleeping. You've been so tired. Figured I'd
take care of it, or it would take care of me. Felt like it took
hours, but when I got to June's porch, I went up the steps
as quiet as I could. Left my cane outside. When I opened
the screen door . . ." A tear runs down her cheek. "Janie
was laying there on the floor, not moving, and he was
standing over her yelling mean things. He didn't even
know I was there, and when he kicked her I aimed for his
arm and shot. Just to wing him, you know, get his attention.

"I still can't believe you shot Danny."

"It was easy as pie. You should have seen the surprised look on his face, and how he grabbed his arm. I hollered for him to get out the door. He kept staring at the gun." She takes another sip of beer and sets the can down carefully on the table. "And he could tell I would have shot him again." Janie groaned and looked up then, so I told her to call 911. And you know what she said? 'Oh Danny, honey, are you hurt?' I figured, then, that she could probably get to the phone. It was only a few feet away. So out the door we went. I marched him down the road as slow as I could, tryin' to buy a little time. Didn't know if Janie would make the call. 'Course, I left my cane behind so I could hold the gun on him, and I had to go slow anyway. What was I gonna do with him if no one showed up?"

I think about Mom's options and come up empty.

"Guess I'd a marched him on down the highway into town." She wipes her eyes with a handkerchief. "I'm mad as hell for what Janie's going through, and the little ones." She shakes her head. "And I'm sorry I missed hearing about all this on the police scanner."

"Dad would have been real proud of you," I say, leaning over to put an arm around her shoulders.

"You suppose he heard about it on the scanner?"

"You know Dad," I say. "He'd 'a been listening. He wouldn't have missed this for anything."

## CHAPTER 24

Graveyard shift is as quiet as a cemetery.

"The woman who worked this job might come back," I say to the man taking Janie's job at the boiler. "You do know that."

"No one said nothin' to me about it," Dick says.

"We'll see," I say, wondering where they found *this* guy.

"I was on the Extra Board," Dick says, as if reading my mind. "This job is my big break. I already worked a full day shift."

I look at the metal folding chair with the bent leg, wishing Janie was here instead of this goon.

When I stopped at the clinic, I couldn't see her because she was sleeping. According to the head nurse, they had set a dislocated shoulder but she'd suffered no broken bones. I asked the nurse about Danny. She said, "He's patched up, in a room at the other end of the building. He can't get to her." I left a note telling Janie I'd see her soon and that her kids were safe at home, that Mom was spoiling them.

With all the drama lately, the quiet at night in the mill feels good. Also, since none of the equipment has attacked me, my imagination takes a break. But there are new dangers. Park and Bark got together and decided we'd be a *real* twenty-first century sawmill and bought a whole crop of new computers. Now they can keep better track of production. Except Carmel told me Leroy plays a game on his computer, one where you hop a frog across a freeway and try to keep it from getting run over. She said one day he played the frog game all afternoon in his fish tank of an office, while the guys shot angry looks at him from the line.

Shaky Slim takes a break from his security rounds to show me how to play Freecell on Leroy's computer in the planer building. And he tells me that Robo, a big balding man who looks like Brutus, doesn't like Leroy so he writes things about him on the computer for everyone to see: *Dear Leroy. Roses are red, violets are blue, we all think you stink, and yes you do.* Another message says, *Everything you always wanted to know about Leroy, but were too dumb to ask.* You can *click* on these messages and read what Robo has dreamed up about Leroy. But I'm only interested in Freecell. After Slim shows me how it's done, I lose an hour and a half playing the game. Then I have to scramble like hell to get the place clean. End up putting in an hour overtime.

Tonight Lloyd, one of the millwrights, is fixing a piece of equipment. He has those two "l's" in his first name, so he's called LaLoyd. Everyone knows him. When he sees me at the computer in Leroy's office, he saunters over.

"Which one you playing?" Laloyd asks. "Freecell's my favorite."

"Mine, too," I say. I'm still focused on the game, but notice out of the corner of my eye that Laloyd is unbuttoning his shirt.

"What the hell you doing?"

"Echo, check this out." He slips one side of his shirt down over his shoulder.

"Jesus, Laloyd. What happened to you?"

"Last winter I was doing a repair on graveyard shift. Slipped on ice or something going down the steps underneath the debarker. I hung onto the guard rail so tight that when the rest of me went flying down the stairs it about pulled my arm off."

It almost sounds like he's bragging.

"Yeah, they practically had to cut my arm all the way off before reattaching the bone and cartilage and socket. See these staple imprints here? They stapled my arm back on so it could all grow back together."

"I'll bet what you slipped on was hydraulic fluid. But why didn't you let go? I mean, a bruised ass is better than getting your arm ripped half off."

Laloyd slips his shirt back on and buttons it. "Things happen real fast and we have to make hard choices."

"Yeah, I know what you mean," I say, thinking about my mother shooting Danny. "Well, it looks like you're healing up all right."

He nods his head but doesn't move, though, and he looks serious. "I feel lucky. What happened to Weldon over at Eagle Creek could have happened to me. I work inside the hog here, sometimes. I think about him every day."

"I know," I say. "Still can't believe it happened."

Laloyd sighs. "Guess I'll get back to work on the roll case. Takes longer, using only one arm."

"I'll clean elsewhere. Don't worry about me."

Except for the scarf wrapped around Delight's head, she looks just fine when Mom and I pick her up from the hospital in Spokane. The doctor prescribed lots of rest. On the two-hour drive home to Hatfield none of us talk much. When we say anything, we talk softly, as if her brain might be sensitive to sound. Delight keeps her eyes closed, and I drive Rooster with care so he won't backfire. Justin works days, but arranged for a neighbor lady to stay with Delight while he's at work. At least for the next week. And we'll be visiting her, too. By the time we get Delight home and settled, Justin is already at work and the neighbor lady is waiting.

I rush to take Mom home, get dressed for my shift, and stop at the clinic to see Janie on my way to the mill. She manages a weak smile through her bruises and swollen face. She whispers, "Don't make me laugh, Echo."

I'm afraid to touch her, but I want to hold her like a baby so she'll feel safe and loved. Instead I hold the sleeve of her hospital gown. It'll be a while before Janie laughs.

"They won't let Danny see me, Echo. And I know he's in a lot of pain."

"I'm so sorry about all this," I reply. "Sometimes the nicest people have the worst things happen to them. And I'm not talking about Danny."

"He'll be different from now on. He'll straighten out and we'll be a family again."

"Janie. Sweetie. I know you don't want to hear this again, but you've got to get away. He could kill you or hurt the kids. He needs professional help and you can't fix him."

She closes her eyes. Tears trickle down her face. I stay with her a while, feeling like a heel. But I know I'm right and I needed to say it. Finally I whisper, "Janie, I really am sorry."

"Everyone thinks we're such a happy couple." She moans. I can hardly hear her whisper, "And I liked thinking we were, too."

"Honey, people get over things. They get on with their lives." I kiss her on the cheek, tasting the salt of her tears. "And there is some good news, Janie. Delight's going to be fine."

She whispers, "Good."

I've got to go to work now. You rest."

I arrive at work before the swing shift crew takes their last break, intending to visit with Yates. Since I'm early, I decide to do some general cleaning. The equipment goes down for a couple minutes. Robo yells to me, "I can out clean you any time."

"No you can't," I shout, wondering why he has to over-achieve at every job in the mill. This week he's been working the cull chain, showing the guys how to do it better and faster.

"Can too," he says.

"No you can't. You're too lazy." I turn and walk off with my shovel, knowing what I said is ridiculous. A few of the men chuckle.

"Let's trade, then," he yells after me.

"Deal," I holler back.

When the equipment explodes in its usual pounding roar, I work temporarily at Robo's job while he sweeps and shovels sawdust. Even though I'm slow at the cull chain, the other men on the line seem happy to get rid of Robo for a while, and act downright decent toward me.

By the time the buzzer sounds for swing shift's last break, he has the place looking real nice. And here comes

George, who looks at Robo and the clean floor. He puts his fat hands on his hips that look like lower shoulders, and smiles. He probably thinks Robo should do cleanup from now on. But after George leaves for the break room, I tell Robo, "That's a damn good cleanup job." I tell it like it is, even though he really only surface-cleaned, which is all you can do while the machinery is running. Robo struts off toward the break room, practically stepping around his man parts. He catches up with George, probably to do a little more brown-nosing.

With all the equipment shut down for the break, it's payback time. I wave to Yates, who by now knows what's going on, and tighten my dust mask. I climb up on top of the feed table, dragging the air compressor hose with me, and blow that down. I blow off the roll case. I blow off the trim saws, the grading tables, and the cull chain, as fast as I can go. I blow sawdust out of all the crevices and off the motors. As big as you please, I blow sawdust all over Robo's clean floor.

When Robo comes back from his break he says, "God-damn you, Echo. Look what you did to my nice, clean floor!"

"Well, Robo, it looked real good while it lasted."

He's furious. His face is red. When the equipment roars into action I sweep and shovel sawdust, grinning under my dust mask. Yates glances my way a few times, smiling. Too bad George missed all the action.

One evening toward the end of swing shift, I walk into the planer room to clean the pit. I smell smoke. Flames are snaking up from underneath the chip breaker. I swing open the back door of the planer room, yell "fire!"

and slam the door closed. Justin and Nose flip the switch to shut down the planer. When I grab the water hose and spray, the flames leap higher. I put my face mask over my nose, toss the hose to the other side of the pit, run around to pick it up, and single-handedly put out the fire. The hydraulic hose is smoldering, so I spray that down, too. Before anyone can get to the pit, the fire sizzles and dies. When George arrives, I'm shaking as I drop the water hose.

"I'm going outside to have a nervous breakdown."

"Go for it," he says.

I stagger out of the planer building, sag against the wall, and light up. The cigarette calms my nerves, and when it's down to the filter I flip it onto the ground and grind it into the damp sawdust with my boot heel. I light another one. Why not? I just saved the place from going up in smoke and all our paychecks with it. It's a good night so far. I even showed Robo a thing or two.

When I walk back into the planer building, George calls me into his office. He asks, "So, what caused the fire?"

"The chip breaker had a bird nest under it."

George smiles. "What kind of bird?"

"Oh, a big old crow." He's in a smiley-faced mood, but I can see he's getting impatient. "Actually," I say, "it was a friction fire in the shavings."

"You did a good job, Echo. In fact, you did an excellent job."

"Thanks." I study his face and see a look on him that makes me think, *Uh, oh. Here it comes.*

"Rule number one," he states, suddenly serious. "If there's a fire, always leave a door open in the planer room. With all that fine sawdust in the air, if that hydraulic hose had broken, the hydraulic fuel would have exploded and sucked all the oxygen right out of the air."

"Well, that's nerve-wrecking."

"If you think that's bad," he continues, "look what happens when you put a match to fine sawdust. Follow me." Just outside his office, he stoops to grab a handful of fine sawdust with his left hand. He throws it into the air as he flicks his lighter. The sawdust flashes into flames. I duck. He grabs a nearby fire extinguisher and snuffs it out.

On Friday evening I arrive for work early because Safety Dave is hosting a dinner. As promised, he'd ordered in a nice meal to celebrate a month with no accidents. In exchange for listening to his little safety spiel, we get to eat all the fried chicken, mashed potatoes, green beans, and apple pie we want. Yates and I are in the break room, leaning against the wall. She's holding her paper plate, eating. My plate is on the break room table in front of me, and I'm holding a big piece of chicken in both hands, gnawing away. The chicken is so crusty I can't tell what part of the bird I'm eating, and grease is running down both wrists. George comes up to me and says, in his booming fat man's voice, "You know, Echo. We don't want you putting fires out all by yourself in the planer room. We have rules. Call for help. We'll put the fire out safely so no one gets hurt. This goes for everyone."

I drop my piece of chicken onto the plate and fold my arms across my chest, grease and all. Even Safety Dave knows I went into the planer when it wasn't running, that I discovered the fire and put it out quickly. George said I

did a good thing. And now the asshole's using me as a
bad example at the safety dinner.

He continues his rant. "If there's a big fire, there will
be a warning bell and everyone should meet up at the
parking lot. We'll call the fire department. You all know
the drill."

No one mentions that when there *was* a fire, we did
not hear a warning bell.

Next time there's a safety dinner, I'm going to show
up late and eat leftovers, instead of crow.


Mom appears in the door of my bedroom. "Honey?"

She never calls me that. I answer, "Mom?"

"The sheriff is coming to get the kids. He says Janie is
out of the clinic and is well enough to travel. She's getting
help and will be leaving with the kids. To a safe place. He
can't tell me where. Apparently a counselor talked some
sense into her."

"Oh, Mom." I get out of bed to put my arm around
her.

"He'll be here about four. Maybe we can make it special for the kids, going away to be with their mother and
all."

It's Saturday and Mom had asked the kids to play quietly outside while I slept off last night's shift. Now I'm
dressed, and ready for the sheriff. The cookies and milk
are on the table. The sheriff comes in the front door,
takes off his hat, and shakes hands with the boys. Tiffany,
too. This elevates him a notch or two in my book, and
Tiffany is clearly pleased. She gives him her most
charming Little Miss America smile, and the sheriff goes
all soft in his features.

As he talks to the boys about his car, Tiffany and Mom are quiet, studying their cookies. They've become good buddies this past week and a half. She got them on the school bus each morning, and was waiting for them when they came home. She taught them how to play cribbage after dinner, and read their kids' books to them at bedtime. Tiffany had slept with her, the boys on the couch. Now Mom says to her, "I know your mother will be thrilled to see you, Dear."

"And I know I'll see you again, Gram. I just know it."

Mom talks to Tiffany with a softness in her voice she's never used with me. But I don't mind. And when I look at this beautiful little girl, I can see her in the Miss America contest, wearing a gorgeous long dress and a crown, walking down the pageant runway, her eyes sparkling with tears of joy. Mom and I are in the audience, sitting next to Janie.

When the little boys eat cookies, crumbs fly like sawdust. The sheriff talks. He's mature and wise, and knows when to look the other way. People trust him at his job and as a friend, so his second term was an easy win.

The sheriff stands. "Well, time to hit the road. Mrs. Spangler, Echo. Janie asked me to thank you both for all your help. Said she'd call you as soon as she can."

I help the kids out with their little duffel bags. Their clothes are all clean, thanks to Mom. Each child hugs her goodbye, then me, and the sheriff holds the door while the kids climb into the back seat of his car and he makes certain they buckle their seat belts. He gets in and makes a show of buckling his seat belt, too. As he heads down the road, he turns on the flashing lights and the siren for a few seconds. Mom and I stand together waving, both of us blubbering like babies. At the highway the sheriff signals and honks his horn before turning right.

## CHAPTER 25

A sudden screeching of tires on hot pavement followed by a lull, like the silence after a hit and run driver flees an accident. The planer erupts with a violent shriek and giant metal doors slamming shut. I'm never quite prepared for the hideous noise, and this afternoon it's even worse because I've been enjoying the quiet of graveyard shift. But, Riley got himself fired, and the powers-that-be decided not to replace him. The one remaining cleanup person in the planer building—that would be me—now has to work swing shift instead of graveyard. I'd like to say the pay's the same. But it ain't. And it gets worse. George is the boss on swing now.

I start right in honking bark, sawdust, chips and crap onto one of the shaker-conveyors. This is what I do. No big secret. Next thing I know, here comes George, running toward me as fast as his 280 pounds lets him. He flips the switch that turns off the conveyor and yells, "What the hell you doing?" His face is red. He's panting like a big slobbery dog.

I stop and lean on my shovel. I stare at him. "What do you mean, what am I doing?"

"I'm running a load of Beauty Bark up the conveyor into a truck," he says, wiping his forehead with his sleeve.

"I don't see no truck. And what exactly is Beauty Bark?"

"Well," George says, finally catching his breath, "it's just plain bark. But a landscape company's buying it, and they don't want no sawdust or chips in it."

"Oh," I say. "Be nice if someone told me these things."

When Safety Dave happens to be in our neck of the woods, we have a safety meeting. Don't know if he tells Park and Bark when he's coming or if they invite him. Depending on the shift, one or both of them might be here, as well as George. The bosses float around on all shifts, at both the mill and planer. There's no escaping them.

"We'll be working overtime for a while, on all shifts," Park announces at this particular meeting. "I've taken on more orders than usual, and if we all pull together, we can make a real showing for TSI. Besides the overtime, there's the extra bonus on the lumber we turn out. So, the faster we all work as a team, the bigger the bonuses."

Yates and I sit together at the break room table. Our hard hats rest in front of us like upside down orange bowls, next to an overflowing ash tray and empty pop cans. Leroy, stands around with the other bosses, holding his hard hat. He has hat hair, too, but only he has that Clint just-in-from-a-hard-ride Eastwood look. What an asshole. So why do I find myself staring at him so often these days, wondering what he smells like? I'm pathetic.

Park blabs on. He likes to act like he's Superman to the rescue. But his brown eyes never really look at us, just over our heads or at our orange hard hats like he's watching his favorite TV game show. "We're down to one cleanup person and she's working swing," he says. "Justin and Nose have agreed to switch from day shift to swing, since they don't have a family at home waiting for them."

Now it's Howdy Doody time. Safety Dave gets up, takes a deep breath to puff himself up, and starts in. "Your brains are your most important asset," he says, holding up a brand new orange hard hat. "Remember, ignorance is not bliss at this mill. We do not give bonuses to dumb bunnies. If your head is involved in an accident, your hard hat will keep your gray matter from spattering all over the mill."

"Who's he calling a dumb bunny?" Yates whispers.

I don't risk a reply. There's more gray matter in a chicken coop than there is in this place. Why does he waste his time, our time, ranting about something everyone already does? I'll just try to hold up my end of the broom handle, sixty-hour shifts or forty.

"Any questions?" Park asks. It's clear he's hoping for none.

I hesitate, not wanting to call attention to myself. "With all this overtime, will you be hiring a second cleanup person?"

"We're going to take on a second Fifth Person," Park says. "That individual will help with cleanup."

I shake my head. We already have one Fifth Person too many. It's his job to help out wherever he's needed. Since four people work at each station, that must be the reason they give this extra employee that particular name. And what does the guy say when someone asks what he does at the mill? Does he say, "Oh, I'm a Fifth Person?" His job is to help out on the lines, band lumber and do odd jobs, like help with cleanup. Except this guy excels at pacing himself. Now we'll have two of 'em standing around picking their noses and visiting. Hiring a second Fifth Person is like buying fat free half and half.

"Party's over," Park says.

Before Yates goes to her station and I head to my broom, rake and shovel, I tell her, "They just dumb-shit you half to death in there." One thing I appreciate about Yates is that when I say something obvious, she doesn't feel the need to agree. Of course, she agrees.

Narrow, thin boards called stickers separate stacked rows of lumber. When rough-sawn boards are fed into the planer, the stickers automatically drop down into a bin to be returned to the main mill for re-use. But a lot of times the stickers end up in the waste trough, where they tangle up with the edgings and chips and sawdust. That causes wrecks in front of the trim chain, the machine that cuts the boards to exact lengths.

When George helps out on a line, he's one of the worst for throwing busted boards all over—on the catwalk and the floor. Robo, working the cull chain, has the same attitude. They're s'pose to toss the boards onto the conveyor bin. And I know that if I pick up the boards, it'll be just like when you're married. You pick up a pair of his underwear off the floor one time, and it'll be your job for the rest of the marriage. At least that's the way it was for the two weeks I was a little Mrs. I know Robo's still pissed at me for showing him up at the cleaning game. And it is true that if the men don't take time to deal with the junk boards, they're able to work faster. But it's not fair. I find Leroy and complain. He stares at me like I'm a bug on his windshield and says, "You don't expect the boys to do your work for you, do you?"

As much as I want a good housekeeping award, I guess I'll have to settle for doing my best.

One evening, after bending over to pick up another junk board, I notice something strange going on at the cull chain. "You guys are pulling an awful lot of good wood and putting it on the economy carts," I yell, leaning on my broom. "There's not a defect on them. No saddles. No knots. These beauties are trim boards."

"Robo told us to do it this way."

"Why?"

"Ask him."

So I find Robo, now working the automatic stacker, and yell, "Robo, what're you doing? They're pulling all good boards at the cull chain."

"Well, I'm buying a couple units off the back porch. Might need two or three units."

"Oh, okay," I say. Does the man think I was born yesterday? It's true. We can buy units of economy grade lumber for our own use at a good price. But we're not s'posed to stack our own units of perfect lumber—trim boards—and then pay the economy price. I walk over to see Alex on the trim saws. "How's the wood running, Alex?"

"Seems pretty good," he says. "Got a lot of good boards this time."

"Well," I say. "I'll tell you what. This is shit wood compared to what they're pulling on the economy line."

"What?"

"I said, this is shit wood compared to what they're pulling on the economy line."

"Oh, yeah?"

Turns out Alex has a bone to pick with Robo. Almost everyone does. The next evening, with Robo working the automatic stacker and Alex on the trim saws, I clean house near Alex just before break, hoping for new info.

"I wrote a letter about what's going on," he yells in my direction. I move closer so I can hear him better, and lean on my shovel handle. He says, "Drove it to Spokane this morning and delivered it to The Big Boys in person. Don't trust Park and Bark." Alex keeps working, lining boards up using a red laser light as a guide. "It all hit the fan. Turns out Robo had a little business. He'd been telling Sharlene a friend was picking up a few units of economy lumber for him. He was paying $137 for each unit, then selling it for $250 since it was better quality wood."

"And I'll bet he's still working here, huh, Alex?"

"They gave him a warning, told him he couldn't buy any more wood. He probably knew if he got caught it'd be no big deal."

From the catwalk above the cull chain, I can see the men throwing junk boards onto the floor. It's Thursday night at the end of swing shift, and it's their last chance to make things right by stacking the junk boards onto wheeled carts. But they don't do it, so I stay an hour late. Since we're working overtime these days, this means I work a 12-hour shift instead of an 11-hour shift. I stack all the boards off the floor right on top of the cull chain table. About half a unit. Then I prop a sticker up in the middle of it with a big flag of toilet paper taped to it. Maybe that'll get their attention. In the morning when the shift starts, the cull chain crew will have to scramble like hell to grab boards and sort them onto carts before new boards start coming down the line. My hope is that the day shift crew will get mad at the swing shift crew, and from now on my work will be a little easier.

The next afternoon when I arrive at work, there's a note from Carmel on my locker door. She wants to meet me Saturday afternoon at The Log Drive Cafe. It's been a while. I've been wondering how she's doing.

On Saturday I wake up about ten o'clock to the gobbling noises of a flock of wild turkeys, harvesting grasshoppers in the field near the house. I peek out my bedroom window at them. The little tags that grow on their throats always make me smile. Looks like you could pull a tag and unzip the turkey. Lots of chicks with the hens this year. Coyote food. Hope there'll be a few of these birds left in November, so Mom can shoot one again for Thanksgiving. We'll have dinner at Delight's place as usual, overlooking the river. Mom and I will do all the cooking. Probably a whole different tone to the event, which makes me wonder what she'll say for grace this year. Her hair's growing out a little freaky, but she wears colorful scarves like a gypsy fortune teller. She's even seeing clients again. Mom keeps threatening to do a past-life regression with her. Lord help us.

At The Log Drive, Carmel and I slide into a booth and order a piece of apple pie with ice cream. I wave at the table of geezers. I swear, they live here and at the Calf-A.

"All the men were talking about the boards you stacked on the cull chain table Thursday night," Carmel says. "It was so great. When the machinery started up the men pulled boards like crazy, sorting them onto the carts." She leans toward me across the table. "There was a lot of cussing and yelling."

"Good. I was surprised when no one ragged on me about it yesterday, but I'm sure I'll get an earful on Monday. I'm probably in big trouble and I don't even care."

Carmel shakes her head and smiles. "I don't think you are," she says. "I heard George tripped on a pile of cull boards the men hadn't picked up, and sprained his ankle. That happened just before you pulled your little trick. The toilet paper was a nice touch."

"Good timing, too," I say. "All the overtime and stress and meanness is getting to me. I needed something good to happen."

"Speaking of stress and meanness, did you hear about the woman sawmill worker in Coeur d'Alene who committed suicide last week?" Carmel asks, reaching into her shirt pocket. "Here's the obituary from the newspaper."

"Oh, God, no. How awful." I take the piece of paper and read a little. "Her name was Linda. Divorced. No kids. I think I'll order flowers for the service. Want to chip in? I'll ask Yates, too. The flowers can be from the women at TSI in Hatfield."

"Good idea," Carmel says, rummaging in her purse. "Here's $10.00."

"We can't know for sure what happened, but I'll bet the men were mean to her. All I know is that forty hours a week is bad enough. Being the only cleanup person with all this overtime is killing me. I think they're trying to bulldoze me out."

"You're good at your job and you're a hard worker," she reminds me. "You can't take this personally."

"I know, but I don't pee standing up. Anyway, let's not talk about work anymore. You're looking good, Carmel. How are things with Melvin and the kids?"

She leans forward again, and whispers, "A couple of weeks ago I saw a flock of Canada geese rise up and form a V, like they do when they're flying south, you know. Right then I decided to leave Mel and move back to Texas with the kids. When I told him, we had a big blowup and I didn't back down. He begged me not to leave, promised to be a better husband. He's been nicer ever since."

"You really would have left him?"

"Yes, again. Thanks to working at the mill, I'm a lot stronger, more determined, or something. I think he sees it. Anyway, he's looking for a job. It's a start."

"Way to go, Carmel. I'm happy for you."

"It's only been two weeks, but I'm more hopeful about us."

## CHAPTER 26

George, still limping from his tripping accident with the cull boards, meets me at the time clock on Monday afternoon. "You'll stand in for Yates. She fell asleep while riding home on her motorcycle last night. Bruised up but no broken bones. Back to work in a day or two."

Yates was fine when I talked to her on the phone about sending flowers for the woman sawmill worker in Coeur d'Alene. She said she was tired, but must have gone out for a spin on her bike after we talked. Probably to The Tool Shed. I'm starting to think Yates is accident prone.

The pace of production is berserk. Both the equipment and the employees are working at breakneck speed. It's a wonder sparks from the equipment don't start fires. The second Fifth Person is actually doing cleanup while I stand in for Yates at the automatic stacker. I gloat a while about not getting in trouble for stacking the cull boards on the chain. George's sprained ankle probably helped my cause. He reminded the crew that all cull boards on the floor had to be taken care of by the end of the shift.

Yates' job at the automatic stacker is easy, compared to her old job with the cants and log edgings over at the mill. I don't mind doing her job while she's gone, because all I have to do is place stickers between every layer of lumber. I'm wearing my favorite navy turtleneck, which is soft and comfortable to work in. The fabric's not thin, but then it's not real thick, either. Just right for cool, early summer evenings. Not only do I refuse to wear a reflective vest, I also don't wear a bra. I have two moles on my back right where the bra straps go, so wearing a bra irritates those moles and makes them itch. Drives me half crazy.

Working away, I don't notice when the rough edge of a sticker snags the front of my turtleneck and tears it. When I happen to look down, I see one of my nipples poking out through a hole in my turtleneck. Whoops! The puppy's nose is showing. I quickly rearrange my shirt and keep working. At break time I put on a second thin shirt over my turtleneck. The next afternoon a note at the time clock asks me to report to the office before I do anything else.

"You know, Echo," Sharlene says. "This is really George's job, to talk to you about this, but he asked me to remind you that we do have a dress code. You really should wear a bra. If you don't, you need to wear something that doesn't show your nipples. A shirt with an abstract pattern will do. No one would notice your nipples, even if you ripped it. The one you have on today is fine."

"How embarrassing," I say. I tell Sharlene why I don't wear a bra. We joke about it a while, agreeing that George lacks the balls necessary to talk directly with me about this matter. I promise to be more careful with my fashion statements, at least on the job.

Back at the planer, George asks, "Well, did she have a talk with you?"

"Yeah," I say. "She also said it was your job to talk with me, but we agreed you were too much of a chicken shit to do it. But it won't be a problem again." Instead of giving him a chance to say anything else, I stroll off toward a pile of sawdust.

"Your hearing is important," Safety Dave yells at yet another safety meeting. "Your ears are not mere appendages."

At the mention of ears, I take the opportunity to look at Nose, to see if he still has the tufts of ear fur. He does. I realize how disappointed I'd be if he shaved his ears. Maybe someday I'll touch his ear fur.

"And don't make a spectacle out of yourself by not wearing safety glasses," Mr. Safety continues. "Protect your eyesight. You want to see a board if it flies toward you through the dust because, folks, it *can* happen." He repeats his previous rants, lifting a new orange hard hat up like a torch. "Remember, kids. Your hard hat is the only thing between your brains and those snoose can lids that whiz around the mill when the planer goes down. We know who throws them, don't think we don't."

When a player nails a hard hat with a snoose can lid, he gets a point. For once, Robo isn't winning. Justin is the current champion.

Leroy pipes in. "We're doing well so far with both production and safety. It looks like this week's bonus will be even bigger than last week's. Your average for the month is gonna be sky high."

But why doesn't Leroy mention the elephant in the break room? Several of the men got together and decided that Alex, who knows the ropes, would write a letter to The Big Boys saying we're being worked to death with no end in sight. Alex delivered the letter to Spokane.

Park gets a call from Spokane, of course, and orders us all to this safety meeting.

Bullfrog speaks up. "We need to talk about when this overtime will end. We can't keep doing this much longer. A person wants to have sex with his wife *once* in a while, instead of being too damn tired all the time."

"What's the matter, Jerry," Leroy says, "Can't you find *anything* in the dark?"

Is Leroy referring to Bullfrog's inability to run me down with his fork lift? At the same time, I'm smiling because Leroy said something so clever. And I like to look at him. After all his meanness and unfairness, how stupid is that? Besides, he's married. Probably a Republican. This new interest of mine is so crazy I don't think I'll tell anyone, not even Yates.

Bullfrog sputters and turns bright red. Everyone laughs. No one mentions Viagra. Personally, I can't imagine anyone having sex with Bullfrog. Then I glance at Nose again, who catches me looking at him. My face is hot. I study my boots. Jesus, it's like I'm a teenager again. For a minute or two, I even forget I'm at a safety meeting.

"Another couple weeks," Park assures us. "We'll get back to normal then. That's the goal."

Normal? I guess he means returning to a forty-hour work week. Justin stands next to me against the wall, his arm touching mine, giving me strength. Yates, recovered from her spill off the motorcycle, is on my other side. Standing here between these two is what normal feels like.

At the end of the meeting I ask Justin, "How're you holding up?"

"Eat, sleep, work," he replies. "I'll be glad when we're back to a forty-hour week. You know, Auntie, the word is 'get the boards out.' There's a lot of pressure to keep the machinery running, no matter what. Then, too, there's all that bonus money at the end of the month if we don't screw up."

"Justin, you have to take care of yourself. That's the most important thing."

"Yeah, Auntie. But you know it yourself. You smell a new truck. I smell a new truck. Half the guys here have new trucks on their brains underneath those hard hats. It's not all about sex."

The phone rings at home so seldom that it scares us when it does. Delight might call to check up on Mom, or once in a while TSI will call asking me to come to the mill early or to work late. Occasionally a solicitor makes the mistake of dialing our number. If that happens Mom says, "Can you hold just a moment?" She sets the receiver down and goes back to reading her book. Five minutes or a chapter later, she reaches over and hangs up the phone. They don't usually call back.

So on Saturday afternoon when the phone rings, Mom lays her book in her lap and picks up the phone. "Hello?" Her face lights up in the biggest smile I've ever seen. "Janie!"

I run into my bedroom, pick up the second phone and say, "Janie!"

She tells us she's in Portland staying with June's daughter and her family. They have a big, old five-bedroom house. The boys share a room, and she and Tiffany share another room. June has decided to stay there this summer to help take care of the kids while she attends truck-driving school.

"Truck driving school," I say. "You're kidding. You don't even have a driver's license."

"I do now," Janie laughs. "I love driving those big rigs. 'Course I'm so short I have to sit on a booster seat, but I can still reach the pedals and shift the gears."

"How long does the school last?" Mom asks.

"You can finish in a month if you're a fast learner, and I am. Turns out I'm a real good driver. After getting certified I can drive anywhere, making pickups and deliveries. They don't let you drive alone at first. I'll drive with a trainer for a few months."

"Oh, Janie," Mom says. "I'm so proud of you."

"Thank you, Mabel," Janie says. "And thank you for being so wonderful with the kids. They still talk about your cookies." Janie pauses. "Echo?"

"Right here, Sweetie."

"You don't know how much you helped me. You were so right about leaving. A volunteer with the women's shelter came to the hospital and talked to me, told me the same thing you did. Her first husband had been abusive. But I have to tell you, leaving Danny behind was the hardest thing I've ever done. I still miss him. You know, he moved to Spokane and started counseling. He calls the kids every Sunday, and sends money for them. We'll see what happens."

"You sound good," I say. "I'm real happy for you. But when will we see you again?"

"Soon, I hope. One of these days you'll hear a great big horn honking right there in your driveway. That'll be me." Janie says. "Just a second. Tiffany wants to say hi."

"Mrs. Spangler?" Tiffany's butterfly-wing voice says.

"Yes, Dear. How are you?"

"I love you," Tiffany says.

"Oh, Honey. I love you, too," Mom says. Her voice cracks. The old girl is softening up, thanks to recent events.

"Know what?"

"What?"

"When I'm big I'm going to drive a truck, just like my mom, that is when I'm not being Miss America."

## CHAPTER 27

"Need you to babysit the new hog," George tells me at the start of swing shift. "You can do cleanup later."

I flash him my *all-right-if-you-insist* look. He knows I don't approve of the new chipper. This piece of shit is smaller than the hog over at the mill. If this one gets a scrap of wood longer than four feet, the throat plugs up. And besides, there's too much cleanup to do. With the planer working full tilt to meet the mill's overblown production targets, sawdust and cull boards stack up real fast. George leaves and I stand around with my thumb up my butt, making sure the chipper keeps chomping and grinning.

About fifteen minutes into the shift, a squeal splits the air. Boards can twist and curl at any time during their trip through the planer building. They can almost tie themselves in knots, either because they dry funny or the tree grew crooked. If a board like that doesn't jam in the planer equipment first, it can erupt and fly through the air like a spear. With the whole place in such a frenzy to get the boards out, Justin or maybe Nose is probably in the planer room unjamming the equipment.

A man screams, "Shit!" The word bounces off the walls, over the freight train noise of the machinery.

A sudden chill sweeps over me. It's Justin. A louder yell comes next. "George!" His name echoes all around the building. A hard object slams against the floor, or a wall, or what?

Without thinking, I take off running. My boots clomp along the catwalk, down the stairs, and across the next catwalk toward the planer and Justin. All the equipment shuts down. I hear a second pair of boots. George is running, too, now, charging over the top of the trim saw, tromping along the boards on the chain. Still limping, he swings his bulk over the roll case and up onto the feed table. George and I reach Justin's station at exactly the same time. There at the end of a catwalk, lying on the floor, is Justin's orange hard hat, smeared with blood.

I scream, "Oh, Jesus, no!"

The break room! I run ahead of George and there sits Justin, on a chair next to the table. His face is the color of chalk, but at least it's all there. His eyes are closed. His hand, still wearing his glove, is wrapped in a bloody mass of paper towels.

"Justin!"

He opens his eyes a little. His voice, weak and hoarse, says, "It's my hand, Auntie. What's left of it."

"Oh, my God! Oh, my God! What can I do?" I try to recall my nurse's aide training. I yell, "Where's the ambulance, for Christ sake?"

George, still panting from his dash across the equipment and over the boards, says, "I just called. It's on the way, Echo. Calm down."

"Justin, Sweetie," I say. "Please. Let me help you." My heart is breaking at the sight of my beautiful, hurt nephew.

Nose puts his hand on my shoulder and leaves it there, and I relax a little. He says to Justin, "We'll take care of you, Buddy. You sure whacked your hard hat a good one. It bounced off the planer wall. Cracked like a nut."

A new guy shows up. "I'm a paramedic. Work up in the log yard." He assesses the situation. "You need to take that glove off."

"Bullshit!" Justin groans.

The log yard know-it-all says, "You're in no condition to say what should happen here, kid."

"You want to make a bet?" I say. "I'm his aunt and I'll back him up every inch of the way."

"Why in the world would you want your glove left on?" he asks.

Bullfrog, standing around gawking, says, "You'd better take it off."

"Oh, shut up!" I yell at Bullfrog. "The air is filled with fine sawdust. We don't want to contaminate that hand any more than it is. The glove stays on." Blood is oozing onto Justin's sleeve. I can see he's in shock. "Don't touch him," I growl. The men stand back.

"Where's the damn ambulance?" George asks. "Christ, we could have driven him to the clinic twice already."

At last we hear the siren, coming across the bridge toward us. A few minutes later the attendants come running into the building. They immediately cut off a sleeve of Justin's jacket and inject a shot of pain killer in his arm. Justin groans, "Not my jacket."

"Justin, I'll keep it for you," I say. He earned the jacket with his name and Esterbrook, Inc. embroidered on it while he was still in high school and an intern at the sawmill. It can't be replaced.

The attendants place Justin on the stretcher, and I call Mom from the pay phone near the break room to give her the bad news. Then I call Delight. "You need to get to the clinic. Justin hurt his hand and needs you." When Delight begins to howl, I interrupt her. "He's going to be all right, Delight. Just meet me at the clinic. Don't drive too fast, but do it."

I race to my car and drive like a bat to catch up with the ambulance, expecting to hear a siren and see flashing lights. But there are no lights. The ambulance pulls into the emergency entrance of the clinic at the same time George and I arrive. Ignoring him, I leap out of my car and run into the waiting room. "I want to see my nephew. He was in the ambulance," I say to the receptionist.

She replies, calmly, "The doctor will let you know when you can see him. Please have a seat."

When I'm this upset, there's no sitting down. I need to pace. They must know this, because one end of the small room is free of furniture. I walk back and forth, back and forth, past George who sits leafing through a *Sports Illustrated*. My worry wants an outlet and there isn't one. Delight rushes into the room, out of breath, wearing a big paisley scarf around her head. "Where is he?"

I take both of her hands and we sit down together. "The doctor will be out soon."

"I'm trying to picture Justin laughing and throwing a Frisbee," she says, then sobs. "Oh, hell. How bad is it?"

"His glove is soaked with blood. That's all I know. They'll take good care of him here." It's true. The clinic has seen worse mill accidents. Still, there's no way to know how much of Justin's hand is left. Holding Delight's hands, I study my own rough, capable hands, calloused in spite of always wearing gloves at work. My veins are prominent. Hers are barely visible. And unlike mine, her hands are smooth and soft, with manicured nails.

When the doctor working the emergency room appears, we stand up. Before George or Delight can speak, the doctor says, "We need to get him to Spokane. A doc there specializes in hands. I'll call and arrange for him to meet the ambulance." He pauses. "But he'll probably lose at least part of a few fingers."

Delight sags against me. I hold her up as we follow the doctor into the emergency room to see Justin. A nurse warns us to stay back. Bright lights shine on his bare hand, held up in the air by a supporting device. I can see through the remaining flesh to the inside of his little fingernail, and blood is still trickling out. Three fingers are mostly gone, and he's lost the tip of his index finger. I brace myself as a wave of nausea sweeps over me.

Delight begins to howl and sob again, "Oh, God!" I grab her as she collapses.

Justin was so beautiful, so perfect, so whole. Now part of him is missing. I want to smash something. But I have to be calm for Justin and Delight.

He opens his eyes, "Hi, Mom." Then he looks at me, "Auntie."

No one's been paying attention to George. Justin nods toward him and shakes his head. "Sorry," Justin says, his voice weak and defeated. George says nothing, just nods his head.

Safety Dave pushes his way into the room and talks to the doctor in low tones. The doctor shakes his head, and says, "You want us to take a urine sample? This man's already been given morphine. We're trying to keep him from going into shock, and all you care about is a urine sample? Excuse me. I've got work to do. All of you, please, go out to the waiting room so we can stabilize his hand for the run down to Spokane."

Leroy is now in the waiting room, along with George. He would have come from his home. Justin is . . . was . . . their golden boy. Always so fast at his job. I introduce Delight to George and Leroy. They act like they're glad to meet her. Then the ambulance driver walks in, opens the doors and says, "We put in a new battery. Should have lights and a siren now. We're ready to roll."

They lift the gurney with Justin on it and slide it into the ambulance. Leroy says he'll cover for George at the planer, and leaves, so I guess we're stuck with George for the next few hours. Delight and I climb into Delight's newer, more reliable, car for the two-hour trip to Spokane. Safety Dave and George follow along behind us, a caravan on the way to bigger medicine. Half way to Spokane, the flashing lights and siren quit on the ambulance again. Now they can't go as fast through the traffic. If minutes count, Justin is screwed. At least it's summer and there's no snow on the roads.

Delight is crying. It's a good thing I'm driving.

"Delight, Justin will be fine. He's strong. We need to be calm for him."

"I'm sick to death of being calm!" she sobs. "I used up all my calm for that fucking brain tumor."

This isn't like her. "Delight?" I steer with my left hand and take one of her hands. "I'm picturing Justin healthy and laughing, and I want you to close your eyes and do it, too."

"Don't you close your eyes," she barks, a smile in her voice.

"Don't worry. I can picture Justin with my eyes open."

At the hospital, Justin is taken into the emergency room and we wait. A few minutes later a tall gray-haired man, wearing a white coat and a concerned expression on his tanned face, comes out to the waiting room. Delight and I both start to ask him questions.

Safety Dave interrupts. "I'm the safety officer for Tri State, where the man with the missing fingers works. I need a urine sample to test for drugs."

Without saying a word, the doctor turns and re-enters the emergency room. Seconds later he hands Safety Dave a plastic bag. It's Justin's bloody glove. "Take this and do the tests, if it's that important. You've got more than enough blood to test for anything."

When Safety Dave leaves, Delight and I step forward. She says, "I'm his mother. Can you build up the pieces of fingers he has left?" She's pleading. "Build something there? Use plastic? At least save two fingers?"

"I'm sorry, but they're too badly mangled," the doctor says. "There's not enough bone to do much with. But I'll save what I can. That's my job and I'm good at it."

"Thank you, Doctor." Delight seems resigned to the new state of affairs, not that there's much choice.

We leaf through old magazines, the void between us too big a distance to cross.

"Let's go see the babies," she says, dropping her magazine onto the low table in front of us.

Several hallways and an elevator ride later we stand at the glass window, looking into the brightly lit room where three newborns rest in tiny bassinets. Delight sighs. "I remember when Justin was born, how tiny and helpless and beautiful he was." Her voice sounds dreamy. "Ten little fingers. Ten little toes. He grew up to be so big and strong and good." She sighs. "And now his hand." A tear rolls down her cheek.

"I know," I say. "We don't think about our hands or what they do for us, until we can't use them. But I know Justin. He'll be fine."

Delight nods, "Of course he will."

"Just imagine, Delight. We were babies together at the clinic nursery, almost fifty years ago."

We look at each other as if for the first time, and both smile. She doesn't look away and neither do I.

"Echo, I've wanted to say some things to you for a long time now. So just listen." She turns away and stares at the babies. "I've always envied how strong and capable you are. I'm so weak, compared to you. I think that's why I turned inward, to the mind, and worked at developing other powers."

"Delight, I . . ."

"Let me finish." Her eyes are still focused on the babies. She doesn't even blink. "I also know about you and Dwayne, from the way his death hit you so hard. I could tell. I know you loved him first—and last. I never loved him like that. And after thinking about it for a long time, I've decided it's all right that he was seeing you. He was a weak man. I went after him and he married me, even though he always loved you best. Somehow just knowing that, I lost respect for him, and myself as well." She turns to me, as old and tired-looking as I've ever seen.

I stare at the babies again but don't see them. And I realize how desperately I need Delight to be upbeat, to

make one of her hopeful, ridiculously positive statements. It's like we're counter-weights, or something. And
now she says she envies *me* and forgives *me* for being
with her husband? No words come to me.

"I really am sorry, Echo. For everything."

I put my arm around her, as much for support as
anything. I'm shaking as if I'm cold. A nurse walks past,
studying us—two women with identical facial features, so
different in every other way, both of us sad, wearing
drastically different clothing while not actually watching
the newborn babies.

"I don't know what to say, Delight. I guess now I'll
have to forgive you and him, even myself. It's just plain
stupid, I know, but being pissed about it all has become,
well, a habit. Loving Justin helps. Seeing him grow up,
being his aunt, was and is amazing. You know I'm crazy
about him, that I'd do anything for him."

Delight rests her head on my shoulder.

Yes, Justin. One of the things Delight and I have in
common—Justin, Dwayne, our mother. And Mitch, although she doesn't know that.

"Oh my God! I'd better call Mom, let her know what's
happening," I say. "She's probably worried half to death."

"I'll bring her with me tomorrow to see Justin,"
Delight says, taking my hand. "Think about what I said,
Echo. Please. Just promise me that."

"Let's take care of Justin first," I say, still holding her
hand.

By the time we get back to the waiting room, Justin is
in a semi-private room. He's on his back with his
bandaged hand elevated. His eyes are half closed and

he's clearly under sedation. George is already in his room.

Dave says to Justin, "You're lucky. When that planer blade caught your glove it could have sucked in your whole arm."

"Well, I know one thing," Justin says, slowly, just above a whisper. "You're gonna chew my ass for getting hurt, so you might's well get it over with."

"That's not fair," George says." You're medicated, and right now you don't give a shit."

"You got that right," Justin says, managing a smile.

We all laugh, except not one thing is funny. And the beautiful young man I love like a son will never be the same. I'll get 'em all for this.

## CHAPTER 28

When an employee gets hurt, the bosses at the mill want to blame someone, anyone but themselves. Safety Dave knows my name and he knows I do cleanup. He also knows I'm Justin's aunt. He was at the clinic with us yesterday. But the day after the accident, Mr. Safety calls a meeting at the beginning of the shift.

"Where the hell was the cleanup person yesterday?" Dave asks, eyes fastened on George. "It's her job to keep the planer room clean. When the jam-up happened, it was a mess in there. From what I can tell, boards on the floor contributed to Justin's accident. What's the word on that, George?"

"We're short on people," George announces. "The cleanup person was working elsewhere at the time."

Yeah, right, you dumb ass. Instead of cleaning up the mess in the planer room like I normally would at the beginning of the shift, you told me to babysit that worthless new chipper. But . . . yeah, I'm the cleanup person, so I *do* feel some responsibility.

Yates stands next to me, leaning against the wall, holding her hard hat over her stomach like an alien orange pregnancy. She does this, she says, to help keep the safety meetings in proper perspective. She moves her arm to touch mine and leaves it there, reminding me I'm not alone.

"Okay, kids. Listen up," Safety Dave yells. "Justin could have been pulled into the planer blades. He could have lost his whole arm. We simply cannot have people injured on the job."

Yeah, especially your best workers, like Justin. Why not that asshole, Bullfrog? I taste metal. My anger toward the mill bosses is like a fuse that's been lit. Their amped up schedule to get more boards out is unreasonable. And now Delight has gone and *apologized* to me. Like I should just up and forgive her for stealing Dwayne, for being the pretty one, for being weak and selfish. For everything.

Mr. I-need-a-urine-sample blabs on. "We're adding new safety features, and you *will* be required to follow them, to the letter. From now on you *will* shut down the equipment and lock out before attempting to remove a board that's hung up."

Listen to him, I mumble to myself. He's practically spelling out each word as if he invented safety. It's just like with driving. There has to be an accident before the powers that be will install a stop sign or a light or a guard rail. At the time of Justin's accident, management *said* you should turn off the equipment before you unjammed a wreck, but the unspoken rule was to fix a problem *without* stopping the machinery, *without* slowing production. This was against existing regs, including OSHA.

"You all know how to lock out," Dave says. "To remind you, each piece of equipment has its own control panel. You just pull down the control handle to the OFF position and put a padlock on it." Dave moves his right hand as if he's locking out. "You'll each have a flat washer with your name engraved on it." He holds up a flat washer. "They're being made as we speak. When you do a lock-out, you'll put the washer on with the padlock so the rest of us will know, then you put the key in your pocket." He put his hand in his pocket with the pretend key, like we're in a special needs group. "You're the only one with the key," he adds. "So no one can start up that piece of equipment until you unlock it. Another thing, courtesy of headquarters," Dave announces, "There will now be a suggestion box placed near the break rooms here at the planer and over at the mill. We care about what you think."

Yes, well, aren't we the best little take-good-care-of-our-workers twenty-first century sawmill? I for one will be telling 'em a thing or two. They'll need a suggestion box the size of a chip truck.

When the meeting is over, Yates and I leave the break room together. I plod along, head down, putting one foot in front of the other. Yates says, "Echo, it wasn't your fault. I'm not going to say things will be wonderful here at work, but things will be different. We'll make sure of that. You and me." She walks close to me, her head down, too. "Echo, Justin is young and tough and has a strong spirit, like you. He'll do all right."

When I lift my head to look at Yates, her eyes are shiny. I don't say anything, but I remember the parrot incident. Yates does seem to have special talents. Okay, she's better with parrots and owls than with men, but still, maybe she's right about Justin.

Groping my way out of bed, I do a rest-home shuffle, running my hand along the thin wood paneling on the wall for support. In the kitchen I pour a cup of coffee. Mom sits at the table looking out the window, so still she appears to be comatose.

"Mom?" I stop pouring my coffee.

"I don't know how they knew," she says, staring at the tall pine tree at the edge of the field, "but when we got home from Spokane with Justin yesterday afternoon, old Pete called us from The Log Drive. You know, he's even older than I am."

"Sure. Pete must be eighty-five by now."

"Eighty-six," Mom says. "Look at that squirrel, running down the tree with a pinecone nearly as big as he is."

"What about Pete?"

"Well, anyway, he said to bring Justin down to The Log Drive. He said he knew Justin would probably want to stay home, but it was important, that he had a surprise for him. Wouldn't take no for an answer. Then he said, 'Help him walk if you have to, but drag his butt down here.'"

I sit at the table across from her. Out the window, the big pine tree comes into focus through the steam from my coffee. The squirrel is running back up the trunk. Beyond the tree is the edge of the woods, still scorched from the fire Dad started a few years ago one spring while burning grass. The volunteer fire department drove across the field and put out the fire. Luckily, things were still green enough that the fire didn't take off and burn all the way to Canada. Dad never burned dead grass off the field again. I guess that's why I think about it now, about how fast everything can change.

"Anyone home in there?" Mom says.

"I was thinking about the fire," I say. "So, did you take Justin to The Log Drive?"

"Poor Justin. He was in no shape to go anywhere, but he said, 'I'll go. Pete was Grandpa's good friend.'" Her eyes tear up.

I look back out to the tree. The squirrel is way at the top now, balancing on a branch near a pine cone. I recall my own adventure twenty feet up in the cold and ice last January on my first day at the mill, hanging on for dear life, trying to kick loose frozen strips of cedar bark.

Mom continues, "There must have been a dozen guys at The Log Drive who'd lost body parts in the woods or at the mill. When we got there, Pete walked up to us, all bent over, leaning on his cane. He held out his arm, the one with no hand on it, and said, 'See son, we want you to know you're not alone.' One guy took off his artificial arm and laid it on the table, others pulled up their pant legs to show their plastic legs. 'Course, some of them don't even have artificial anything. They just pin up their empty sleeves or pant legs. Others have steel hooks where hands should be. One guy named Bullfrog, of all things, put his glass eye on a saucer. Gus knew all of these men. Justin was so touched. Everyone was wiping their eyes with sleeves or hankies. Justin shook hands and arms, even hooks, using his left hand, thanking each one of them. A couple old guys, I forget their names, told me they still miss Gus."

Bullfrog has a glass eye in addition to his cataracts? And he cares enough about Justin to be there for him at The Log Drive after work? The squirrel runs back down the tree with another pinecone. A fat tear runs down my face and drips into my coffee.

With all the scraps of lumber around, I expect a wood suggestion box. But, no. What shows up is a white plastic five-gallon bucket with a slot in the lid. They even leave a pencil on a string and several half sheets of paper right there, inviting us to make comments. I can't believe my luck. The top is clamped and locked, complete with a washer, maybe to show us a good example of a proper lockout. When no one is near the box, I cut the string, take the pencil and a piece of paper, and head for the bench in the corner of the machine shop. It's not even break time, but this is official business.

Later on I return with the pencil and drop my suggestion into the box. *We need a side-headed chipper like the main mill has. The new chipper we have gets clogged up. With our new safety law, we'll have to stop the conveyors, lock out, open the door of the chipper, and try to get it unplugged. A new side-headed chipper wouldn't plug up so often, allowing us to get more work done without interruption. Yours truly, Anonymous.* Written with my left hand and unsigned, I want them to think a man thought it up, that it came from a source of *intelligence*. Besides, I want to fool George.

The second night, I send another comment down the slot. *I'd like to see all the bosses, including Leroy, roll up their sleeves and take turns doing cleanup for one week. This would be especially helpful now that we have only one cleanup person. Sincerely, Echo Spangler.*

Having only one cleanup person doesn't make sense. To do cleanup with this amped up production schedule, it would take an eleven-hour shift, six days a week. Now that Justin is gone for a few months, one of the more experienced workers will replace him. The second Fifth

Person will stand in for that guy. I know they're keeping Justin on the payroll while he heals. To my way of thinking, they need to replace the lazy ones with a few more good women. 'Course, they can't fire anyone except for drugs or alcohol, thanks to that three-year moratorium on firing workers who were with the mill when TSI bought it. The men know this.

On Friday evening a little while into the shift I stop sweeping and look around at the mess the men have already made. At the trim chain, Chuck says to me, "Now that you're here, I don't have to pick anything up."

"Why the hell not?" I ask.

"Because you can do it."

Cull lumber comes off the feed table onto the trim chain. These unplaned boards aren't real pretty. They end up being cut with a chop saw into big 2 x 4 stickers to lay between units. Other cull material gets stacked outdoors on carts and priced at $40 a stack. Farmer lumber. People drive up to the mill and buy the stuff to make pallets or rabbit hutches or whatever. People even build shacks to live in out of cull lumber. But the men working the trim chain don't want to be bothered to stack this material in units, so they throw it on the floor and the stuff just tepees all over the place. You can't even walk through the place without tripping over a board. With any luck, George will sprain his ankle again.

It's comment time. *Chuck needs an easy chair while working the trim chain. We don't want him to get a sliver in his ass while napping. Let's make him feel more secure and comfortable. Also, Echo should be able to pick up more edgings and stickers off the floor. Chuck shouldn't have to do any of it. He needs his beauty rest. Signed, Anonymous.*

I like to think that when management reads my comment, Chuck will get written up for dozing on the job, as well as for not picking up the wood scraps he keeps throwing on the floor. I know that nothing's likely to change because of my comments, but by venting my feelings I hope to cut down on the number of Rolaids I chew to settle my stomach.

As if the cull board problem isn't bad enough, one of the Daves at the trim chain chews tobacco and spits so much that he put a five-gallon bucket between him a guy named Bill, who also chews. Come to think of it, where'd Dave spit before? Never wondered, and now I don't want to know. A couple weeks ago, the bucket started out with some sawdust in the bottom. Every now and then one of them tosses in a handful of sawdust to absorb the spit.

"Getting time for you to take that bucket out to the Dumpster, don't you think?" I ask Dave one evening.

"Hah!" Dave says. "They tell me that's your job."

"Bio hazard," I say, leaning on my broom, wondering who told him it was my job. "Chewy category. I'm not touching it. No way in hell."

"That's what *you* think," Dave says, lining boards up with the red laser light.

Here comes George. "Echo, I want you to pick up all those boards over by the cull chain and the trim chain, all of them, gone by the end of your shift tonight."

So I pick up all those damn boards and stickers. Off and on while I work, I wonder why no one has mentioned the spit bucket. I end up working fourteen hours and make a full unit of farmer lumber out of that mess, enough lumber for a few dozen rabbit hutches.

On Monday I arrive a little early with half a pound of venison burger from the road kill Mom and I drug up to the house a few months ago. For three days the meat's been in a sealed plastic container under the sink at home, and thanks to warmer summer temperatures, it stinks like a dead cow alongside the road in mid-summer. The universe had provided, now I'll share the wealth. No one's around yet so I hurry over to the spit bucket. Plugging my nose, I open the plastic container, dump the rotten meat into the bucket, and sprinkle sawdust over the top to hide the evidence. I can't help but smile. On my way to clock in for the shift I hum the song "Stand By Your Man," only I change the word *Man* to *Spit*.

As soon as George spots me he jumps all over me. "You can only put in ten, maybe twelve hours a shift, not fourteen," he says. His face is red and his hands are resting on his hips.

"Well," I say. "You told me to pick up all the boards."

"Sure, but you don't have permission to work that much overtime. The place doesn't have to look like Martha Stewart's living room."

For the rest of the shift I practice slop-cleaning. I only surface-clean. I don't blow down the machines, or the motors, or the chains. If George only wants me to work ten hours, this is what he gets. Anyway, working a fourteen-hour shift could start to wear on me, give me an attitude problem.

I tell George, "I can come in Sunday to finish up, if you want."

He says, "Yeah, if you'll clean the place for a change."

"Now what do you mean?"

"Well, the place is nothing but a pig sty. Just look at this mess," he says. "The place is filthy."

I'm on a roll and I feel bitchy. Next I test the new lockout rule. Not much of a test, really, since the rest of the shift workers are already gone. But you never know. A mill-wright could start up a piece of equipment while I'm cleaning under it. And I do want to practice safety. So I lock out the feed table, put my name tag washer on the padlock, and place the key in my pocket. Then I thoroughly clean the machine.

Home in bed, Tummy and I are sawing logs when the phone rings. The clock says 5:00 a.m.

"Echo, I hope I woke you up," Leroy growls. "You know good and well the day shift can't start working with the feed table locked out. I'm writing you up and docking your pay for every minute the planer is down this morning."

"Oh, shit," I say, and hang up the phone on Leroy. I pull on a pair of jeans and a big shirt. At the front door, I grab the lockout key out of my filthy work pants, slip on my sandals and run down the steps to the car. "Oh, God, please start right away." It is summer, but the air is cool in the mornings, and my car starts best if the temperature is around seventy degrees. When it starts after a few tries, I gun the engine and roar down the dirt road, raising a low cloud of blue smoke and dust. At the highway, I glance left. Good, no one's coming. I tromp on the accelerator and lay rubber pulling out onto the highway, then break speed limits on the way to the mill. I roar into the parking lot and slam on the brakes. Shit. I still have to make the five-acre dash to the planer building. Usually I allow extra time to walk the distance. At exactly 5:24 a.m., panting like a dog, I hand Leroy the key.

All he says is, "What the hell happened to your hair?"

I forgot about my hair. Last night I showered, washed my hair, and blew it dry before crawling into bed. Before leaving the house, I hadn't given it a thought. He's only seen my hair pinned carefully in place, out of sight under my hard hat, or mashed against my head from wearing the thing. Oh well. I might get written up for taking the key home with me, but at least my pay won't be docked, that is if he'll stop gawking at my hair and start the equipment.

"Bye, Leroy," I say, on my way to the EXIT sign. He's still staring at me—probably in love with my hairdo. "Sorry about the key. Won't happen again."

When I get back home, Mom is sitting at the dining room table, drinking coffee. After explaining my trip into town, I decide to stay awake, to eat breakfast and then take Mom over to Delight's to see Justin. Yesterday she baked a batch of homemade bread. We'll take a loaf with us.

On our way, we stop off at the mall so I can buy Justin one of those floppy little bean-bag teddy bears, like the one I bought for Carmel when she was sick.

Delight meets us at the door. Justin is resting on the couch watching a movie, his hand wrapped like a white basketball, his arm held at about ninety degrees in a sling that looks like a dish towel. He greets us with a lethargic, mischievous grin, but he doesn't get up. He clicks the remote to kill the movie. Mom walks over to him and holds his head against her chest. No one says a thing.

When it's my turn, I sit down next to Justin and hand him the teddy bear.

"You are *not* too old for this bear."

Justin takes the stuffed creature, holds it up to eye level, smiles, and says to the bear, "Is your name Dave, too? Well, Dave, looks like I'll have to pick my nose with my left hand from now on."

We all laugh. Yates is right. Justin will be okay.

Delight shakes her head, now wrapped in a blue bandanna, but doesn't scold Justin for being vulgar. Instead, she holds the loaf of bread we brought her and offers us coffee. I help Justin into the dining room, not that he needs help. It's a chance for me to touch him, to show him a little tenderness, to do *something*.

"TSI called yesterday," Delight says. "Their insurance company will pay Justin about $25,000 for his lost fingers when the doctor releases him from his care. They were nice about it, said they always feel terrible when one of their employees gets injured, said he has a job when he's ready to go back to work."

"Hard way to get a new truck," Justin says, sadly.

"At least there are lots of different jobs you can do," I say, knowing how hollow it sounds.

"But nothing can bring back my fingers."

Mom takes Justin's good hand in hers, Delight stares into her coffee cup, and I say, "I know, Sweetie. And I know it's too little, too late, but the mill has started enforcing the lockout rules. 'Course, I already drove home with a key and got called on it. Oh, and now we have a suggestion box. I've been giving them a piece of my mind."

At work I keep writing suggestions, for stress relief and entertainment. Besides my gnawing anger about Justin's accident, I'm thoroughly pissed at George for being so nasty and unreasonable about the cull boards.

*Caught: George walking behind a forklift while the forklift driver is putting a unit on the in-feed chain to the feed table (without letting the driver know he's there.) He could get hurt. Also caught, George and Sparks going between the units and the in-feed table while the feed table and the planer were both running. Kind of risky, don't you think? Especially if someone decides to move the units forward? Caught, the whole works, but only men, including the bosses, throwing busted boards on the planer room floor, on the cat walks, in front of doorways, and in front of the trim saw stairs. Those are tripping hazards. Besides, shouldn't bosses set a good example for the rest of us? Sincerely, Anonymous.*

George comes up to me after the first break. "You been using the suggestion box?"

"Well, I did once. A good suggestion, too. I signed and dated it. You found it, didn't you?"

Before the end of the shift he makes the rounds, saying, "No more comments in the box on my watch!"

Yates and I ignore him, of course. I don't know what Yates says in her comments, and I don't know if the men use the suggestion box at all, but I hope that by putting in my two cent's worth, improvements will be made at the planer. And I'm making comments for all the amputees at The Log Drive. I change my writing a lot, depending on what I want to say, and I don't usually sign or date my suggestions. I've seen Leroy's and George's writing.

Sometimes I make my letters real tall, like Leroy's string bean body type, or round and fat to imitate George's body type. Or I change the slant and cross my t's way at the top, or in the middle. I make my e's funny, too. My sneaky writing skills would drive a handwriting analyst crazy. Since the box still sits in its place, the next night I write another suggestion.

*We're sick to death of breathing fine sawdust. We need a decent ventilation system instead of the dust bowl effect caused by the fan at the trim saws blowing the sawdust over to the feed chain, and the fan there blowing it back toward the trim saws. Sets up a god-damn dust cyclone. I'm sure OSHA would agree with me that this is unhealthy. We're getting nose bleeds, and when we aren't blowing blood we're blowing black junk out our noses. The rest of it settles in our lungs. Respectfully yours, anonymous.*

*P.S. Before winter, we need heat on the floor. This is our third winter without heat.*

I lay off putting suggestions in the box at the planer for a few days. Instead I drop one in the box at the main mill.

*It sure is strange that the swing crew can no longer put suggestions in the box at the planer. Now we have to use the suggestion box at the mill to let the bosses know what's going on. Love, Anonymous.*

## CHAPTER 29

Toward the end of the shift, I check the time again. Good, only another half an hour to go. I resume shoveling sawdust onto a conveyor bin. But something's wrong. I grip my shovel handle. I wait, and listen. At first I'm not sure I hear it over the usual din. But there it is—the roaring-train hum of millions of bees, a noise that always means trouble. Every damn time. And it's getting louder. A loud smack, like a gunshot, interrupts the roar. This could mean a 2 x 4 in the air, a heat-seeking spear of wood, or, just a big wreck on one of the lines.

All the machinery shuts down, and the buzzer that usually announces the end of our breaks blares *Ahooga, Ahooga.* I close my eyes and wait. A couple minutes go by. In the distance I hear a familiar sound. A siren. Pain grips my chest. The last time I heard a siren . . . I consider the worst that could have happened and instinctively, I walk toward the grading table. Yates was learning a new job, one where she got to sit in an elevated chair for a good view of the boards. As I get closer, George yells, "Don't yank on her, goddamn it!" Maybe after a lifetime of *worst* I expect more of the same, but I stop walking. If it's bad, just maybe I can delay knowing for a little while longer.

Nose walks toward me. He's panting from running. His face is white. I stare at him as his arms unfold and reach toward me. I ask, "Is she going to be all right?" He holds me against his chest. Bits of sawdust grate on my face, but I keep my eyes wide open to avoid drowning. I hold my breath, waiting for him to answer. His silence changes everything.

Later, sitting with Nose in his truck, I stare out the open window, seeing nothing, my eyelids heavy in the summer darkness. Then I notice the nearly full moon and the flying bugs in the halo of the yard light.

"I didn't see it," Nose says. "One of the Daves working near her said 'No one saw it coming. A 2 x 4 hit the bang boards, shot back and hit her . . .'" Nose stops.

In slow motion, I turn to him. My voice is flat. "Tell me. I need to hear it."

"Dave said it was the strangest thing, said the board seemed to . . . uh, it was almost like it was meant for her. When it hit her in the side of the head right below her hard hat, she flew sideways off the chair and fell to the floor like a rag doll. The amazing thing is, she got up in slow motion, bent over, picked up the two by four and set it on the line."

"She picked the sonofabitch up and set it on the line?"

He nods. "That's what he said. But then she slumped back onto the floor. When she tried to sit up again, she collapsed. She just let go. He said it happened fast. I'm so sorry, Echo. I know you two were good friends."

When Nose puts his hand on my arm, panic surges in my chest. I want his hand there, his hand that's attached to strength, to an energy source, a lifeline. But at the same time I want to shrink away from it. And instead of staring at nothing, I want to stare at his hand, or his face, or think about yesterday when Yates sat next to me on the bench in the machine shop, blowing smoke, telling me she trained the parrot to say, "I think I love you," but that she had to *ask* him to say it. She said she was gonna train him to say it all by himself, just out of the blue, so she wouldn't know when to expect it.

"We were sisters," I say. I can barely hear my own words. All I can feel is his hand gently rubbing my arm. "We were more than sisters." Even I don't know what I mean for sure, except that it has to do with the parrot and Willie Nelson and not being that close to my real sister. I whisper, "I can't believe it."

"About ten years ago," Nose starts, clears his throat and continues, "I lost my little brother in a hunting accident in Montana. That's where I'm from. He was walking down an old logging road in the woods, wearing an orange vest. Some fool, a local, thought he was an elk. It took me months to accept that it had happened, that he was gone. Then I moved here. It's called shock, and I know for a fact how real it is and how bad you feel."

We sit in his truck without talking, and I become aware of the strong smell of sawdust and pitch, as if I've never noticed it before. I'm connected to the strength of one friend; numb with the loss of another. Finally I'm steady enough to move. When I slide off the seat and both my boots hit the ground, my knees give way and I catch myself on the door frame. Nose comes around the front of his truck and walks me to my car, his arm around my waist. He opens my car door. I cling to him for a minute. "Thanks. Your kindness . . ." I drop onto the seat. When I turn my key in the ignition, Rooster starts. With a death grip on the steering wheel, I drive slowly home. I am the center of all sadness.

I stay away from the mill the next day and the day after that, and then the weekend comes. I'm AWOL and I don't care. They can call it sick leave or whatever they want. They can even fire me. Mom feeds me graveyard stew. I force myself to eat. Nose calls every day to see how I'm doing. I can hardly talk. I walk in the field, stepping over coyote shit and dried-out corpses of weeds. Grasshoppers leap up around me. I find myself walking up the road to June's empty house, where I sit on the porch thinking about losing Dwayne, first to Delight and then to the logging truck accident. I think about Weldon, about my Dad, about Justin's hand. Then I focus on Janie and her kids, and how Mom came to her rescue with a gun. Maybe I'll borrow her 30-30, go berserk, and shoot up the machinery at the mill.

When the weekly issue of *The Hatfield Gazette* arrives in our mailbox, Mom reads the obituary for Yates. The part that I will wonder about for the rest of my life is this: *She is survived by her husband, Toby Greenaway, and a daughter, Nicole, 16, of San Diego, California.* That is where the service will be held. I order flowers. Yates would have got a kick out of a bouquet of pine branches with empty beer cans tied in them, but instead I settle on Scotch pine branches with the brightest, most exotic and colorful flowers available, along with one large white chrysanthemum. I also drive to Yates' trailer house to pick up the parrot, Mousse, and bring him home. I call the pet store to tell the owner what has happened and they work out a payment schedule with me, which is how I learn that Mousse costs as much as a good used car.

When Mom and I play cribbage, we don't talk much—not about my former temp jobs, not about Rush

Limbaugh, not about President Clinton's sex life, and not about Yates. Mousse sits in his cage on top of the chest of drawers in the living room, where we usually put our little Christmas tree during the holidays. Mom says, "I guess we'll decorate the birdcage instead."

The parrot squawks, "You are very beautiful. . . *squawk*. . .yes you are, oh, yes you are." Mousse even imitates the call for the spotted owl, at least the first part, *Who . . .who . . . yeeyowhhhhhh. . .* followed by another *squawk*.

On Sunday afternoon I sit at the table and look out at the pine tree. When clouds overtake the blue sky, the long shadow thrown by the tree recedes back into itself. When it begins to thunder and lightning and rain, I walk down the road, cross the highway, and sit on the big rock by the river. Rain and tears drip down my face. My T-shirt and jeans are soaked. I think about the phrase *there are no accidents,* and how little I understand about anything.

I walk a few hundred feet downriver to stand in the rain on the inside curve of land. Even though the river is down, the water continues to eat away at the outside bend, like my job at the mill eats away at my life and the people I care about. Except for Nose. He's good. Maybe too good. What does he see in me, anyway? If he likes me because I'm tough and capable, he'll soon find out how weak I am.

With my eyes closed tight, I stand still and listen to the quiet power of the river flowing past. The river always reaches its destination. Part of me wants to tie rocks to my ankles and wade in, put myself out of my misery. But what about Mom? Sure, she has the parrot for company.

And she could always go live with Delight in her big house, but Delight refuses to play cribbage, thinks of it as a big waste of time. Mom would hate that. I turn and walk toward home.

When I open the screen door, Mom is reading in her recliner by the window. She looks up. "Leroy called," she says, letting her book fall to her lap. "I told him you'd call back."

"I think I'll go for a drive first."

I throw on some dry clothes and head out the door. Rooster starts right up. I sit for a minute, staring through the wet, bug-spattered, cracked windshield at nothing. The rain has stopped. In slow motion I shift into D and drive slowly down the dirt road. The yellow heads of tansy alongside the road are now almost at eye level as I pass by. I inhale the smell of weeds. When I reach the highway I don't know which way to turn. I light a cigarette. Maybe I'll turn left and drive up to the Old Plantation Tree Farm, where I first met Yates, but then I find myself turning right, as if pulled by a magnet, as if there could be no stopping me even if I chose to do the right thing.

I drive past the turnoff for the mill and see the tops of the buildings, even the debarker ramp where I hung from the beam stabbing at frozen cedar bark on the first day of my sawmill career. I think about Leroy, and wonder what he's doing right now. He's probably calling me again, to tell me I'm fired. Nose wouldn't be there yet, not until swing shift. I smile, thinking of his ear fur, his warmth, his kindness.

Rooster slows as we gain elevation. I mash my foot down harder. We both know what to do and where we're going. I pat the dash. "Come on, boy. You can make it." By the time we reach the top of the pass, the accelerator has been floored for several minutes and we're only keeping pace with the semi-trucks. At the top I pull over, just like we always did, all those other times. I turn off the ignition and listen to Rooster's familiar ticking, gurgling, sighing and popping noises, hoping he'll start again. It's still spring up here and the air is cool. The only trees this high are alpine firs, too stunted to ever be threatened by a chain saw. In a patch of green meadow near the turnout, glacier lilies glow yellow, too cheerful for my mood.

If Rooster won't start I'll flag down the first semi-truck. The driver will look like Nose, and soon we'll be on our way to Colorado. He'll drop me off and I'll change my name, start a new life, one that's safe and quiet. I leave all my sadness behind. But Rooster starts, and now I worry about getting down the other side of the mountain without burning up the brakes and going a hundred miles an hour. And we make it, passing all the semi-trucks, passing nearly everyone.

The casino parking lot is almost full, as usual, like the parking lot on Saturday afternoons at the Northtown Mall in Spokane. I shouldn't go in. I should turn around and drive back up the pass, sail down the other side, go home and pretend nothing happened. After all, I was just going for a drive. But, what the hell? The words *should* and *shouldn't* don't have much to do with my life right now. I'm here and you never know, I might get lucky.

Inside the door the scene is familiar. It's dark and smoke-filled and noisy and colorful. I sit down on one of my favorite stools in front of a Keno machine. I'll stay a few minutes. I insert a five dollar bill and pull down the handle, trying for as many cherries as I can score. No luck. Again and again. Time means nothing here. I've noticed that before. It's as if you open the door and enter the twilight zone. Scientists should study casinos about that time thing. When I do finally check my watch it's 7:48 p.m. and I'm a little drunk. Pulling the handle makes me thirsty, and waitresses keep coming around to ask me what I want to drink. I'm also suddenly hungry, but if I leave my machine someone else might sit down, insert a dollar, and win all the money I've invested into it. I pull the handle again. Sixteen dollars spills out into the tray. A puny return. I can do better.

A quick hamburger in the restaurant, a stop at the restroom, and a visit to one of several ATM machines to clean out the balance of my checking account. Back to another game of Keno at a different station. I should head home. I look at my watch. It's 2:12 a.m. Jesus, I can't drive home in the middle of the night. What if Rooster breaks down? At least I don't feel tired, thanks to time spent working graveyard shift. Hah! Maybe I can at least win back what I've lost. I've done it before. This is a game of chance, pure and simple, with no skill involved. But I don't have much luck at being lucky. And I've often wondered if the machines aren't rigged so you lose.

My arm freezes. I could swear I was just kicked in the chest. Shit! Am I having a heart attack? Tears flood my face and drop into the mug of beer in my left hand, but I keep pulling the handle down, over and over, with my right hand, even though my chest aches. I can't believe my stupidity at being back here in the casino. Sobbing now, I think about the meanness at the mill, about

Justin's missing fingers, and Delight's brain tumor. I howl for Janie, for Carmel, but especially for Yates. I miss her so much. While I'm at it I cry because Dwayne got killed and before that Delight robbed him from me, and now *she* forgives *me* and I'm gonna just to forgive *her*? Feeling sorry for myself feels good, and I keep groaning and sobbing, and feeding more coins into the machine. Seven cherries line up. Yes! Finally, I earn $160 dollars back of the $710 I've spent.

By dawn I've won back only $286. I'm ready to leave. One last stop at the restroom, where I splash cold water on my face. Rooster starts on the second try, and we stop for gas near the casino, then aim east, with the morning sun in my face. At the turnout on top of the pass I pull over, lock the doors, leave the windows down a crack, lie down on the front seat and sleep for a couple hours. I wake up to an odd recollection about Dwayne, probably because of the greasy hamburger I ate at the casino. He'd loved his mother, but she was a terrible cook. She burned everything, even toast. So he learned to love burned toast. He complained about modern toasters and how you couldn't burn a piece of toast if you wanted to—and he did. And when his mother cooked meat, she always left the fat on it. The kids weren't allowed to scrape the fat off when they ate, so he grew up with a coating of tallow on the roof of his mouth. He said once in a while it got scraped off by something she burned, like toast. And now the surprising thing about this memory is that it feels like he's here with me. I hug myself and head down the mountain.

Just before noon, I reach the sawmill. Time to talk to

Leroy and face the music. First I enter the planer building, and there he is near the time clock. The equipment is running full tilt—slamming, roaring, clanging.

The instant he sees me he yells, "You're fired. Just get your things and go."

I walk up to him and stop about a foot away. He backs up a little, and continues to yell above the noise of the mill. "Where the hell have you been? I've called your house several times. Your mother doesn't even know where you are. We needed you here. The mill is filthy."

He's so serious-looking, in his hard hat, as if the workings of the mill are all that important. Feeling sorry for him, I move in closer. I put my hand on his arm and lean toward him. He doesn't move. Slowly, ever so slowly, I plant a gentle kiss on his cheek, quite close to his mouth.

"That's for Yates," I say so quietly that I don't know if he hears me. He stares at me, his eyes unblinking as if startled. I back away.

Leroy continues to study me. He loosens up a little. Color returns to his face. He says, "I'm really sorry about Yates."

I nod my head and bite my lip as I back toward the EXIT. My voice cracks a bit as I yell over the noise in my head and the mill, "I'll be back to work tomorrow afternoon." Without giving him a chance to say a thing, I open the door and head toward Rooster.

## CHAPTER 30

The next day when I clock in for swing shift George acts as if nothing out of the ordinary has happened. Just as I expected. And Leroy was right. The place is a pig sty. While I was AWOL, the millwrights installed one more device to deflect boards before they can sail out and smack someone in the head. The second Fifth Person is standing in for Yates. Or maybe he's replacing her.

No one pays any attention to me as I slop-clean around the equipment, thinking off and on about the kindness of Leroy's words about Yates, and kissing his cheek. Then half an hour before the end of the shift, the buzzer rings, *Ahooga, Ahooga.* Before we can wonder if there's been another accident, George's voice booms over the intercom, "Everyone to the break room, now."

Two nurses stand near the restroom. This can mean only one thing: A surprise piss test. The mill hasn't done this in a while, but maybe they're actually getting serious about safety, trying to catch employees who work while under the influence. Not that a flying 2 x 4 could have been any one's fault. We line up and take turns going into the restroom with a specimen bottle. The nurses are sneaky. First of all, they use a heat sensor to make sure the pee is warm, that we aren't giving them a family member's "safe" pee. I've heard that a few guys keep jars of drug-free pee in their lockers for just such an occasion. And between bathroom users, a nurse pours blue liquid into the toilet so you can't take water out of it to put in your specimen bottle.

Now it's past time to go home and Stan is the only one still sitting on a chair near the nurse's station, gulping a big glass of water. His job is to babysit the band saw, the razor-sharp S.O.B. that threatened to chase us all around the mill a few months ago. Maybe Stan really was asleep at the switch when it happened.

"Why are you still here?" I ask.

"My urine came out cold."

While it's true he's always bundled up, even in summer, I wasn't born yesterday. He probably gave the nurse someone else's pee he had stashed in his locker. I say, "Boy, you really *are* cold blooded."

"I guess so. Can't leave 'til I produce another specimen. 'Bout ready to drown from all the water and coffee they're making me drink."

"At least you're getting paid overtime for it."

A nurse offers him a specimen bottle. "You gotta go yet?"

"I'll try," he says.

The next day Stan is gone. Fired. He didn't pass the piss test. Probably *maryjowanna*, as the smart-alecks call it. I might smoke, drink and gamble away my grocery money, but, hey! At least I don't do drugs.

Tonight I'm sweeping in the area of the cull chain. To my surprise the men have been picking up most of the cull boards. Maybe George decided they could do this, versus my working a 14-hour shift. Or maybe he doesn't like tripping on the boards and spraining his ankle. Or, do you suppose the men feel bad for me because I lost my best friend? On the three work days I was AWOL, they probably had to pick up the boards all by themselves.

"Echo!" Dave yells.

"Yeah?"

"Did you let a fart? Smells like something died over here."

I carry my broom over next to Dave on the trim chain line. He's right. I make a face and say, "Could be your spit bucket. I told you it was time to haul it out to the Dumpster. I'm not allowed to touch bio-waste."

"Told ya so," he says, in a whiny voice. "No sirree, ma'am, it's *your* job to keep this place clean. It's women's work." To make his point he spits a big wad of chew on the floor. "You can clean that up, too, bitch."

I swing on him before either of us sees it coming. My leather glove smacks him alongside the head and for a second he loses his balance. "Don't you ever talk to me like that again!" I snarl. "And if you have a problem with that, you talk to George about it."

Shaking and mad as hell, I stomp off and don't look back, but I do wonder what the hell's gotten into me. First the trip to the casino, then I kiss Leroy on the cheek, now I smack one of the Daves alongside the head.

After break I see George heading toward the trim chain. I follow along at a discreet distance so I can hear what happens. Lord knows what Dave will tell him, but I don't care.

"Good God, what the hell died over here?" he says, holding his nose. "Jesus, you guys. I let you have a spit bucket, but you gotta take care of it. You can just live with this smell the rest of the shift. Then you damn well better haul that bucket out to the dumpster. I don't want to have to tell you again."

If only I could tell Yates about my big success with the rotten venison in the spit bucket. She'd say something like, "It's about time you grew a pair of ovaries and took charge!" God, I miss her.

Friday at our last break, George hands out written work performance reviews. When I tear open the envelope, I feel a kick in the stomach. My review is not good. I won't be getting a raise.

Before the shift ends I ask the fat man why he gave me a bad review.

"Don't worry. Leroy won't fire you. He says he won't fire anybody who's doing their job."

"But if I'm doing my job, and I'm the only cleanup person to boot, why did I get a bad review?"

"I call it as I see it," he says, big frown, hands on hips. "You've been written up for locking out and taking the key home, you flaunted safety precautions on several occasions, and you've been gone a lot. Take your recent disappearance of several days. You use foul language, and you're nasty to the men." His eyes are bulged out, like he's ready to snort and paw the ground.

Lips tight, my arms crossed in their defensive posture, I feel like I've been run over by a forklift. I'm going to throw up or cry, but no way in hell will George see me do either one. Uncrossing my arms, I turn and walk slowly toward the time clock with my head held high. I bite my lip, and taste blood.

## CHAPTER 31

Tonight while I sit alone on the bench in the machine shop, I say out loud, "I still wanna know what you said to the parrot." I imagine Yates sitting next to me, kicking her leg up and down, listening, making me feel all heard and understood. "I mean, after you talked to him at the mall that day he acted like he was on Valium. Now he mostly ignores me, although he has quite a crush on Mom. Says to her, out of the blue, 'I think I love you' and he tells her she's beautiful. Now she's teaching him the ten-codes from the police scanner. Maybe if you'd told George what you told Mousse, he'd be acting more like a human being, too."

God, I miss talking to Yates. She listened to me like she might hear a spotted owl answer her call, if she'd just pay close enough attention. Suddenly an idea pops into my head. It has to do with being smarter than the parrot, and it's brilliant. I'll write a letter to The Big Boys.

On Saturday morning I call Carmel, who says, "I got a bad review, too. Leroy says I'm slow and I miss too much work. And now I can't get a raise, either."

"What do you think of us writing a letter to The Big Boys so they'll know we got unfair reviews. While we're at it, we can tell 'em first hand how most of the men treat women at this mill, and how we aren't s'posed to put suggestions in the comment box anymore."

"Good idea," she says. "I'll help."

"And," I say, "we'll ask if there aren't other safety features they might add before another person . . . dies." My voice cracks.

"I don't know about you," Carmel says, "but I'm not the best letter-writer in the world."

"Can you meet me at The Log Drive this afternoon? We'll write *something*. I'll call Janie." Then it occurs to me. "June! She can edit our letter. She was a teacher, and Janie's there so she can put in her two cent's worth."

"June might want to add a few lines about safety," she says, "Especially since she knows how little has changed in sawmills since Weldon died."

So we meet at The Log Drive and work on our letter. Carmel writes out her complaints, in her own words. We both state how long we've worked at TSI. We write about our bad reviews, how we believe we received them only because we're women, and that now we won't get raises. I write about being the only cleanup person at the planer, when the planer has always had two people. I blab everything I can think of. I list my more hazardous jobs, and how a male forklift driver tried to run me down, more than once. And how one guy turned the roll case on when I was still on it. I mention a few of the inappropriate comments made by the men, even my supervisors. I pride myself on not once using the word *asshole*.

Carmel chips in about how the men she works with try to smash her hands with 2 x 4s, that they tell her women don't belong in the mill. She adds that they try to "bury her" on the line. We both write about Yates' death, saying she was our good friend. We ask why the second bang board hadn't already been installed. There's more. We don't hold back.

I call June in Portland. "Yes," June says, "Janie told me about the conditions for women at the mill. Weldon would have wanted me to help with the letter. He never mistreated women employees, I'm sure." She suggests we fax her the letter, says she'll work on it right away. She gives me the phone number of a print shop in Portland where she can pick up our fax. We fax our draft to her from the service counter at the IGA.

On Friday morning, June calls. She and Janie worked on the letter together and it's a full five pages, single spaced. At ten in the morning I pick up the revised fax at the IGA and sit in my car to read it. Janie has added that one reason she took the boiler attendant job on grave-yard shift was to get away from the men. She added that OSHA regulations aren't always followed, nor have all necessary features been installed to help prevent other fatal accidents. They add this: *We are aware of Equal Employment Opportunity laws and would like to re-solve these workplace issues without aid of an attorney.* June made the letter so *professional.* The letter ends: Respectfully yours, The Women Employees at TSI. All of our names and complaints are right there in the body of the letter, including Janie's.

As if Yates is sitting on the passenger seat of my car, I say, "Feels like I'm about to leap off a cliff."

I turn onto the highway heading south, praying I'll make it all the way to Spokane without breaking down. If all goes well, I'll have just enough time to deliver the let-ter to headquarters and get back for my shift.

Today the temperature hovers around eighty degrees, and Rooster's windows are wide open. My bird nest hair is blowing all over hell and I'm smiling, knowing I look like a wild woman. I sing what I can remember of my favorite song. *Blue skies, smiling at me, nothing but blue skies, do I see.* By the time I reach the end of the song, I'm bawling so hard I can't see to drive. I pull to the side of the road, turn off the engine and sob, hoping no one stops to see what's wrong. A few minutes later I blow my nose and say out loud, "Goddamn it! If you want blue skies, Echo, picture blue skies."

Ready to go, I turn the key in the ignition. *Click. Click.* "Come ON!" I scream. *Click. Click. Click.* I leap out of my car, slam the door hard, and jerk up the hood. Where is the fucking stick to hold up the hood? What do I think I'm trying to prove anyway? I don't know how to fix anything in this mess of oily, sooty junk. So I hold the hood up with one hand, jiggle on wires with the other, and yell "Shit! Shit! Shit!"

A car pulls up behind me. A kid about twelve years old with purple hair, a ring in one eyebrow and another one in a nostril, strolls over to me. The crotch of his pants droops down to his knees.

Oh great, now I'm in for it. People will see my picture on a TV show about missing persons.

He says, "You need some help, lady?"

Maybe this kid is okay after all. "I turned off the engine for a few minutes and now my car won't start."

"I could try my new jumper cables," he offers. "Can't hurt anything."

Next thing you know, he's parked his silver Honda Civic in front of my car. He connects the jumper cables. "Now try it."

My car starts. I'm happier than I've been for a long time.

"Thank you so much. You must be an angel."

"No. Just a freshman at Gonzaga University," he says, unhooking the cables and closing the hood of his car. "You need to keep your car running. Don't turn it off. Well, I mean don't turn it off anytime soon."

And I don't, either. When I stop at a light I rev the engine, just to be safe. At headquarters I pull into the paved parking lot, park in the handicapped zone and leave the engine running. At the office I ask for a stapler and a red pen. I staple the five pages at the corner so they won't get separated, and print URGENT! at the top of page. After I turn in the letter, I use their bathroom before hopping in Rooster and heading north toward the mill. I fly along at top speed, meaning I don't exceed the speed limit by more than ten miles an hour. Two hours later when I pull into the parking lot at TSI, I tame my hair with bottled water, dash across the yard and stand, panting, at the time clock with exactly one minute to spare. Mission accomplished. Now I'll do my job and wait for the shit to hit the fan. While hiding behind my safety glasses and hard hat, I act as innocent as I can, checking often for signs that George has received a call from The Big Boys.

But the shift comes and goes with no sign that our letter has stirred the sawdust in either Spokane or Hatfield.

On Monday afternoon when I report in for swing shift, a hand-lettered announcement is posted on the bulletin board near the break room. SAFETY MTG RITE AFTER LUNCH BRAKE. MUST ATEND.

Because of the butterflies in my chest and stomach, I can hardly concentrate on using my broom and shovel.

God, I'm glad my job doesn't include any math. I pop Rolaids. I do what damage I can to the various piles of cull boards and sawdust. George is mysteriously absent and since he's such a bother, it's like half the shift crew is missing. With him gone, I'm almost enjoying my work. But where is he?

Maybe our letter is what you'd call "whistle blowing," and when I think about it that doesn't sound so good. Then I remember Justin's missing fingers and the aching loss I feel for Yates. Still, I'm worried about the backlash and what might happen at the safety meeting. But there's nothing to do but think my nagging thoughts sweeping and shoveling, picking up busted boards, and acting busy.

Park and Bark are both at the safety meeting. George shows up and sits near the front, spilling over the seat of a metal folding chair, looking subdued. Not one of them makes a joke. Safety Dave isn't even here, which is odd since it is, supposedly, a safety meeting. The tone is serious. The other employees probably expect a layoff, or news that the mill will change the way they do business, as a result of Yates' death.

Instead of George saying his usual thing, "I suppose you're all wondering why we've called you together like this," Park centers himself in front of all fifteen of us, including the millwrights, and clears his throat. He holds our letter in both hands like a prayer book. Shit. I stare down at my boots, and reach into my pocket for another Rolaid. If he starts to read that letter out loud, I'll leave the room.

Park begins: "We met with the day shift earlier to make this important announcement." He looks around the room, clears his throat, and continues. "Some employees, whose names will not be mentioned, have written a letter to The Big Boys charging that certain behaviors taking place here at the mill and the planer are not appropriate, and that, in fact, dis-crim-in-a-tion (he emphasizes each syllable) has been occurring."

Leaning against the wall as usual, I suck on my Rolaid. Several of the men are staring at me, but I calmly watch Park, as if I'm only mildly interested in what he might say next.

"The Big Boys are taking this letter very seriously. They've reminded us of the laws in place forbidding the behaviors that are outlined in this letter. In so many words, we've been instructed to clean up our act. I wasn't even aware these problems existed, so I want you all to know I feel not only blind-sided but extremely disappointed."

Try oblivious. He definitely knew about my run-ins with Bullfrog on his forklift. And why doesn't he mention the safety problems?

"I believe that Leroy and George are both strong leaders," Park continues. "I know they don't want trouble on their shifts. To help us get to the bottom of this, two psychologists hired by The Big Boys will visit the mill in the next week or two. We'll all be interviewed at least once—on company time, of course—and I ask that each of you be totally honest when answering their questions. This is also a good time to talk about feelings related to the recent unfortunate death. After the interviews, the psychologists will prepare a report and make recommendations to headquarters. These interviews are critical. That's all I have to say." He pauses and makes eye contact with several of us, including me. I swallow hard and glance away, toward Nose.

"Leroy?" Park says. "Do you have anything to add?"

"You've all been working hard, doing a good job," Leroy says. "As far as the visitors coming to the mill to interview us, let's all treat them with respect, as if they're guests in your own home." He nods to the group and moves to the side.

George struggles to an upright position. "I second what Leroy said. I see these interviews as a good chance to make working conditions better for all of us. Now let's get to work. Let's get some boards out."

With Coach George's words, we all head to our work stations. The word *unfortunate* sticks in my craw. Unfortunate is when a coyote gets one of your chickens. Would it kill them to say *tragedy* or *devastating loss*? How dare they call what happened to Yates *unfortunate*!

The following Monday Park greets each of us as we clock in. He tells us two psychologists, a man and a woman, will conduct their interviews at the mill first, then at the planer. All employees will be interviewed separately by each psychologist.

I hear they're staying at the nicest motel in town, and it sounds as if they're here for the long haul.

By Wednesday, the psychologists still haven't interviewed anyone in the planer building. What can be taking them so long at the mill? Carmel is the only woman working in that building on either day shift or swing. Maybe the men are giving them an earful about how working so much overtime is wrecking their sex lives. Anyway, since Park's announcement, all the men are being *oh so polite.*

The woman psychologist is young, about thirty-five, with straight dark hair cut all one length, just below her ears. She's tall and matchstick thin, wears a dark suit and, of all things, high heels. This might be the first time high heels have ever walked these floors. I imagine the dust particles zooming toward her dark suit as if the cloth is magnetized. She obviously has a college education, and probably enjoys what Delight would call *breeding,* or maybe class. She reminds me of an exotic bird that has dropped down out of the sky into unknown territory. Can I be comfortable in the presence of a woman dressed so nicely, when my own clothes are already filthy, my face dusty, my hair so . . . difficult?

The man is more sensibly dressed, wearing Dockers pants and a sport jacket, but no tie. Older, maybe in his mid-forties, he's short with sandy hair, a round face, and a kindly expression, friendly blue eyes. He sets up shop in the break room, and conducts interviews in between breaks. The woman is in George's office, in a corner of the planer building. Each employee is scheduled for a thirty-minute interview, although we're told we can sign up to visit with one or both of the psychologists for longer periods for free, after the first series of interviews.

When each man goes for his interview, either George or I stand in for him. The second Fifth Person is actually helping out, doing a little slop-cleaning. When someone returns to the line from an interview, there are no comments. What we tell the psychologists is confidential. God, I certainly hope so, because suddenly it's my turn.

When I enter the break room gripping my hard hat, the man stands and extends his hand. I'm filthy from head to toe. I remove my glove and see that my bare hand is too dirty to touch another human being, especially one wearing clean clothes. "Uh, I'd shake your hand but I'm dirty right now."

"That's okay," he says, dropping his hand. "Please, have a seat." He indicates a chair kitty-corner to his seat at the head of the break table. "You're Echo Spangler?"

"Yes, sir,"

"And you're one of the women who wrote the letter to TSI in Spokane. Is that right?"

"Yes, sir."

"Well, I've read that letter several times, of course. I have it right here." He reaches into his brief case and pulls out the letter. "Looks like you've worked here about six months."

"Closer to seven," I say, to let him know I'm paying attention."

"Well, I'm going to ask you a few questions, even though you may have already stated the answer in the letter. This way you can take longer to say things. If we don't get through my list of questions, I'll want you to come back another time to finish. You ready?"

*Has another employee ever told you that you don't belong here?*

I hesitate. Gripping my hard hat on my lap, I start. "They usually don't actually *say* it, although one of the men who throws cull boards all over hell, oh, excuse me for cussing, has told me picking up the boards is women's work. Then there's the spitting on boards and on the ground when they see me coming to clean, and calling me a bitch."

*Has another employee ever done something on purpose to put you at risk of injury?*

"Oh, boy," I say. "This could take all day. There's Kurt at the edger, when I stand in for anyone at that station. He tries to pinch my fingers between the boards and once he turned the roll case on before I could get off of it. Oh, and Bullfrog tried to run me over with his forklift several times. When I told Leroy, he and George demanded that I wear a reflective vest, which I refused to do because I would have been an easier target for Bullfrog. I'm not that stupid. Did you read the letter I wrote to Park about that?"

"Well, no. That's all very interesting."

Then he says, *I know there are inherent dangers associated with work in a sawmill, but there are also OSHA regulations regarding employee safety. Has management ever had you do a job without regard to safety regulations?*

I start again. "My first job at the mill last January was to hang from an icy steel beam twenty feet up in the air to untangle frozen cedar bark. Seems like a harness should be provided for that job. Another thing I should tell you is that if you do have an accident, even one that's not your fault, and you fill out an accident report, you lose your bonus. There's a lot of big talk about safety but until recently we were expected to cut corners and not do anything to slow production. That's how my nephew, Justin, lost his fingers about a month ago." My eyes well up. I bite my lip.

When the man stands, I know my time is up. "I do have more questions for you."

"And I have more answers," I say. This time when he extends his hand, I smile and shake it, grateful that I can leave, that I managed to keep control of myself, that we didn't talk about Yates.

## CHAPTER 32

"I hope you gave that guy an earful," Janie says on the phone, after I told her the questions the male psychologist asked me.

"Too much to tell 'em and too little time," I say, "but I get another chance next week."

"Good." Janie sounds happy. She tells me, "I finish truck-driving school on Friday. Can you believe it? Me driving a great big semi-truck? But I love driving, and I'm good at backing into tight spaces. I'm even good at reading maps, so I can find the destinations."

"Excellent," I say. "We don't want you driving around out there lost."

"Echo, guess what my *handle* on the radio is. I use TALLANDFREEANDME, as if it's all one word. Say *that* real fast. The tall part's a lie, but who cares and it will fool all the other truckers. They don't have to know I use a booster seat. On Monday I leave for Kansas to make my first delivery and pickup. Of course I'll be driving with a trainer for a while. The company knows a little of my history, so when I asked to work with a woman, they assigned me to Sherry. She's an instructor part-time. We get along great."

"Can you get up here on your way back?" I ask. "We'd love to see you. I'm sure your mother would, too."

"Well, since you mention it. Looks like the turnaround will be fast, with two of us driving. So on the return, I'm planning to drive west on I-90, detach and park the trailer in Spokane, and drive up to Hatfield in the truck. It'll be the weekend after next, so Sherry will be able to take a day off and guard the goods. This means she'll hang out at a nice motel near where the container and trailer are parked."

"Janie, that's the weekend of the loggers' celebration. Sue must have told you."

"She did say that. Mom and I always liked the parade. I've been in it a lot. I love all the noise and excitement." Janie's quiet on the phone for a few seconds. "Echo?"

"I'm here."

"Sherry knows about my mother's abuse. She also knows that I'm planning to rescue her that weekend."

"Oh, my goodness," I say. "Janie!"

"There's plenty of room in the truck for her to go back to Portland with us. We aren't supposed to take on passengers, but Sherry considers this a special situation. Mom can't tell Dad she's leaving him, otherwise he'll beat her up. I'm timing my arrival so I pick her up about eleven o'clock on Saturday. Echo?" she says again.

"Janie?"

"Will you be my backup?"

I think about the term *backup*, and what it means on the TV cop shows. While one cop kicks down a door, two or three other cops are right behind him, all of them with guns. Several more are outside, hiding in the bushes, and there's usually lots of shooting. "Well . . . yes. But what exactly do you want me to do?"

"Just be there. Just park down the street a little ways. I need you there for moral support."

"I'll bring Mom and her 30-30 along, just in case," I joke.

"Echo! I don't want my step-dad shot," Janie says, groaning like she's been wounded. "I just want him to leave my mother alone, to let her go."

"Oh, sweetie," I say. "I'm sorry. I was joking."

"It's okay," she says, sniffling. "It's just that so much has happened so quickly and I'm a nervous wreck about it all. My mother is finally ready to let go of him and start a new life, and now I can help her do that."

At my next interview with the male psychologist, he says, *I know that a sawmill is noisy, and you have dust and sawdust to deal with. Are there things management could do to improve working conditions?*

"There was a suggestion box for a while after Justin's accident. I put in lots of suggestions, including a request for a ventilation system. Right now it's not healthy, and with all the dust blowing around, you can hardly see so it isn't safe, either. In the winter, we don't have floor heaters. It's miserable. But I guess they didn't like our suggestions, because nothing changed and then they removed the suggestion boxes. If they'd install safety features before accidents happen, that would be . . . uh . . ." My throat is closing in on my words and I close my eyes to fight the tears.

"I'm sorry for your losses," he says. "It's perfectly all right to show emotion. I see a lot of tears."

"Don't say that," I groan, "If I start crying I might never stop."

"What you say and do in these interviews stays here," he says, leaning toward me, "but I can tell you this. The accidents at this mill have come up in every single interview. You should know that your letter will do some good. Now, I do need to ask you another question or two from this form."

*Do you ever feel like management is trying to get rid of you by making your working conditions intolerable? If so, how have you handled that?*

"Well, it seems that way. But I need this job, so I try to do what they tell me, unless there's a bio-hazard, then I won't touch it."

*What do you mean?*

"Well," I say, aware that I've started every answer the same way. "Once I refused to pick up toilet paper off the ground out back behind the planer. Oh, and George let a couple of the men have a spit bucket at their station. They chew and spit, you know. Then they wouldn't dump the bucket in the dumpster, said it was my job, women's work." I don't mention that I smacked Dave alongside the head when he called me a bitch, but I do tell him about the rotten venison I put in the bucket and covered with sawdust, which more or less took care of the problem.

The man's face lights up with a big ear-to-ear smile. He shakes his head. "I thought I'd heard just about everything," he says, looking at me with what seems like admiration. "But that one takes the prize."

"Oh, well, huh," I say, "I could tell you a few other things I've done to make a point. The bosses sure aren't any help."

"We'll see what we can do about that, too," he says, standing up, extending his hand. This time I'd washed my hands just before coming in for my interview, and I shake his hand without hesitation. "Echo Spangler," he says, "You're all right. You just hang in there."

I smile through tears at this nice man who thinks I'm "all right."

On Saturday I call Carmel. She says, "Did you notice how the woman, what's her name, Loretta, asks the same questions the man does but changes them to ask about your *feelings*? That threw me for a loop."

"Yeah. I don't know what to say. You can't say, 'Well, Jesus Christ, that makes me feel like shit" to a young woman wearing a dark suit and heels who's so clean you could eat off her!"

We both laugh and snort at the idea of eating off the woman psychologist, and then we both start to cry.

"I had a hard time talking about my feelings," Carmel admitted, sniffling. "Trying to tell her how I *felt* made me feel bad, made me cry. Then I worried that I wouldn't be able to stop."

"I know," I say, wiping my eyes and reaching for my hanky. "I know."

"Then she said, 'When do you allow yourself to feel?' When I got home I cried for over two hours; thought I'd never stop. Melvin wondered what was wrong and tried real hard to comfort me. But I couldn't tell him, really. It's just that life is so difficult all the time. He's done his share to contribute to the trouble, of course. But I didn't *say* that."

"He still being nice?" I ask.

"Yeah," she smiles, blushing a little. "We're doing lots better."

"I'm glad," I say. "But I feel like I've been run over by a truck. And since the woman counselor is coming to

Hatfield once a week, and we can each talk to her five times for free, I'm gonna do it."

"Me, too," Carmel says. "And I think things will get better at the mill."

"I think so, too," I say. At least it sounds good to say so.

It's true that following the interviews by the two psychologists, everyone acts as nice as pie to each other. Even George acts like a human being.

Nose calls me at home late one morning. "I can't say anything specific that went on in the interviews, but I want you to know you're not alone. I put in a good word for you and the other women working in the mill."

"Thanks, Nose. I put in a good word for you, too. I wanted them to know that good guys work at the mill, too."

"Thanks, Echo. All the men have complaints about safety and management. We're glad to tell someone a thing or two. There's even talk about forming a union. 'Course, no way is TSI interested in that happening."

It seems like forever, but after only a week Park and Bark call a safety meeting. George does his usual Buddha imitation on a metal folding chair. Come to think of it, he's probably the one who sat on the chair in the boiler room and bent the leg all to hell.

"You know why we're here," Park says. "The interviews were a success and recommendations have been made to headquarters. A team of mill safety specialists will be coming in to do an analysis and we'll be making changes to improve safety." He pauses and looks around the break room. "There will also be new rules regarding respect. It doesn't matter what the shape or color of a person's skin is, heads will roll if we hear of any more harassment. There are laws forbidding disrespectful behavior, and we will all follow them. Sharlene will show a video to make sure everyone understands exactly what these laws mean and how we're to behave from now on."

Park pauses again to look around the room at each one of us. "As of this coming Monday, you'll each receive a five per cent raise. On Friday, a brochure outlining our behavior policy will be included with your paycheck. You must read the brochure. Our mill is going strong when others are closing, and we want to keep it that way. You're all good workers. Now let's get some boards out."

## CHAPTER 33

"Wish you'd a let me put bullets in this thing," Mom says, patting the butt end of her 30-30. The business end of her gun points towards the floor on her side of the car.

We're parked kitty-corner and down the street from Janie's mother's house, with our windows rolled down. Waiting. Like in those cop shows on TV. Last night Janie called Mom to make sure we'd still serve as backup when she rescues her mother, and to confirm her plan.

"Now, Mom," I say. "You *know* how you can be with a gun."

"Puts meat on the table," she says, patting her gun like the head of a favorite dog.

"And husbands in the hospital," I remind her.

"He had it coming. The little S.O.B. I let him off easy."

I puff on a cigarette, blowing smoke out my window. "Where *is* Janie, anyway?"

"Said she'd get here about eleven."

"Then what?" I ask. "Remind me."

"Like I told you, she'll park her truck in front of the neighbor's house."

"Which one?"

"The blue one, next door."

"Okay. And then?"

"The plan is that Sue will be watching out a side window, and when she sees Janie she'll grab her two packed suitcases and leave the house. She'll send her husband out to the store for something about 10:45, so he won't be home. That's the plan, anyway."

Except Mom can get details wrong. And was Sue able to get her no-count husband out of the house? Sounds pretty much like he does what he wants, when he wants. Which is why we're here, acting as backup. "Any other details, Mom?"

"Only that if she pulls up in the truck and goes into the house, we need to listen for yelling or other loud noises. If that happens, our job is to drive up in front of the house, walk up to the door and . . . "

"Do what?"

"That part wasn't clear," she says, patting her gun. "But she said not to call the sheriff."

"Where is she?" I say, tossing my cigarette butt out onto the street. I answer my own question. "She probably got hung up in the parade traffic downtown," I say. "It's about time for the parade to start."

The loggers' celebration is always chaos. The organizers don't learn from year to year how to manage people and traffic. Mom and I usually park as far away from downtown as possible and walk to see the parade.

"Strange timing for a rescue," Mom says, just as the cab of Janie's beautiful shiny semi-truck rolls along Alder Street, toward the house she grew up in. The truck looks new, a deep dark shimmering blue, with a sleeping cab— probably where one driver sleeps while the other one drives. Thankfully, she's not pulling the trailer.

I want to honk and wave, but I know better. When she spots us, she holds up her left arm and pretends to pull the air horn a couple times. I smile flutter my fingers so I won't attract attention from the house.

Her truck purrs along like a giant kitten, compared to my car's snorting and popping sounds. She stops softly, quietly, in front of the house next door, the blue one. Mom and I stare at the front door of Sue's house. Nothing happens. Two or three minutes go by. Feels like an hour. Where *is* Janie's mom?

God, this is nerve-wrecking. I reach for a Rolaid. Janie opens the door of her truck and leaps down onto the street. She glances our way, a worried look on her face, and walks slowly toward the house. She opens the screen door, then the door.

A man yells. A woman screams.

"Go!" Mom yells.

I say my mantra and turn the key in the ignition. *Click.* Again. *Click.* A third time. *Click.* "Start, damn it!" I try again, and Rooster's fan belt squeals. I slam the gearshift into drive and lay rubber as I pull into place in front of the house and stomp hard on the brake. Before the engine settles down, we throw open our doors. I reach the front door first. Mom comes up behind me, breathing hard from hurrying, gripping her gun.

The screen door opens into the living room. Janie's step-dad has a grip on Sue's hair. "You're not running out on me, you good-for-nothing little bitch!"

"Let go of me," Sue screams.

He yells at Janie, "I suppose you're behind this, you and your big ideas." He lets go of Sue's hair and lunges toward Janie.

"No!" Sue yells. "Enough!" She swings an old hard-sided suitcase against his legs.

He roars, loses his balance, and falls to the floor. When he rises onto an elbow, one knee up, his face is bright red and his glasses are crooked on his nose.

"Let me at him," Mom growls, bumping me aside. She aims her rifle at him. "Don't even think about it, buster."

He must have heard the story about who shot Danny, and when. He freezes, staring into the barrel of the gun aimed at his chest. He holds himself so still that he doesn't appear to be breathing.

Sue is sobbing now.

"Come on, Mother," Janie croons.

But Sue is frozen in place, too. "Oh, Janie, maybe I shouldn't go."

"Yes, Mother," Janie says calmly. "You have to. You can always come back."

"Like hell," Sue's husband growls.

"Oh, shut up," Mom snarls. I've never heard my mother's voice sound like that. I hope he's smart enough to keep his yap shut.

Janie says to Sue, "Mother, the kids are waiting to see you."

"Get out, then, bitch," the man says, staring at the floor.

Mom pulls back the hammer on the gun.

"Jesus, Mom!"

Sue looks at the door. Janie tries to take a suitcase from Sue's hand, but she has a grip on it, so Janie picks up the other suitcase. Holding her mother's arm, she leads her out of the house. While Mom holds the gun on the perp, I watch out the door as Janie hurries Sue down the sidewalk to the truck, and boosts her and the suitcase up into the cab. She runs around to the driver's side with the second suitcase, and climbs into the driver's seat. The truck's been sitting there waiting, engine idling, and now Janie pulls away down the street as if we have all day.

I don't know what to do next. Mom can't hold the gun on this goon forever. I take a light hold of one of her arms and slowly walk her backwards out the door, while she aims the gun at the man. This gets awkward real fast, so I grab my hefty mother around the middle from behind and tell her exactly when to step down. Mom's no lightweight, but I lift her down the last step. Once we're on the sidewalk, I keep walking her backward along the sidewalk while she keeps a bead on the front door with her gun. I'm none too sure the gun is empty, and lucky for all of us, the man is smart enough not to appear in the doorway. When we reach the car, I put Mom in the front seat and run around the other side, leap in, and turn the key.

But will he start?

I turn the key. *Click.* Again. Rooster, my hero, starts. Mom leans back in the seat, patting the butt end of her 30-30.

"You all right, Mom?"

"That S.O.B.," she says, still the menace in her voice. "Now tromp on it."

So, I do, exceeding the speed limit before catching up with Janie and her mother in the big blue semi-truck. We follow close behind her.

A few blocks later Mom and I ask at exactly the same time, "Where are we going?"

We drive toward what looks like the entire population of Hatfield, lined up to watch the Loggers' parade. As the big blue semi-truck and my old red car inch forward, sirens wail in the distance over the marching band music. When Janie blows her air horn, people move aside and cheer her on. A load of enormous logs appears to float above the heads of the onlookers. A fake owl sits on top of the logs. The hairs on my neck prickle at the sight of the owl as I remember Yates puffing herself up to make the call for the spotted owl. She would have loved all this excitement. My heart is thumping against my ribs and I'm happy, sad, and excited all at once.

"Oh my God!" Mom yells. "She's leading us into the parade."

Sure enough, Janie is creeping up behind the logging truck, and Mom and I follow just inches behind her like a faded red pull-toy. The crowd erupts as Janie honks the air horn several more times. Now even more people notice who she is. They may have matched her up with the story in *The Hatfield Gazette—Janie, the darling cheerleader from high school days who fled her abusive husband, the former star quarterback, after a neighbor woman (whose name was withheld) shoots the husband.* They cheer, especially the women, maybe because of the bold, black windshield decal TALLANDFREEANDME.

What they don't know is that Janie has just rescued her mother, a story that probably won't make it into the newspaper.

Mom sees people she knows and waves to them.

"Don't start waving your gun, Mom."

"Give me some credit," she says. Then she makes a snarling noise, and I hope she's being playful.

When I glance in the rearview mirror to make sure Janie's step-dad's not chasing us, I see a string of classic cars in mint condition. Right behind us is a yellow

DeSoto, chrome flashing in the bright sunlight, bearing a license plate that reads LEMON PIE. And here we are in Rooster, old, dull, and dented from bouncing off snow banks. We're leading all these beautiful vintage cars in a parade. How embarrassing.

Rooster struts along the parade route, behaving himself.

"There's Justin," Mom yells.

Nose stands next to him, wearing a cowboy hat. I rev my engine. Rooster pops and farts blue smoke. Nose grins hugely, showing his nice white teeth. I smile and wave like crazy. This might not be bliss, but it's about the most fun I've had since forever. Speaking of *bliss*, where is Delight at a time like this?

Janie gets the most attention. Leroy, here with his wife and kids, runs out to her truck and climbs up onto the running board. I tear up at the sight. The man is human after all. When Leroy rejoins his family, a clown jumps on Janie's running board and, at the exact moment he pretends to kiss her, she blows her air horn. The crowd cheers again. But I wonder how Janie's mother is doing during all of this. She waves every now and then out the passenger window, but not with much enthusiasm.

There's Carmel, standing in the crowd along with her three kids and a bald man her same height. Is that Melvin? He's wearing sunglasses, and while I can't get a good look at him, he appears to be rather ordinary looking, in his shorts and T-shirt. I wave and yell, "Hey, Carmel!" She looks happy and so does Melvin. The kids are having a good time, too.

The parade route stops at the junction with the high-way heading south, toward Spokane and the rest of the United States. In the other direction, the highway leads to Canada. A sheriff's deputy has stopped traffic for the parade to pass. Then he stops the parade for a few minutes so the traffic can go on its way. At this end of the parade, there's not much chaos. While we wait behind Janie's truck, I spot a float with several young women sitting on stumps holding broadaxes. They must be contestants in the lumberjack contests. The front of their t-shirts say CHESTY CHOPPERS. Some of the women are sitting with their backs to us, and I strain a little to read the slogan on the back of their shirts. "Hey," I yell to Mom. "Get a load of that: *We break apart more than just hearts.*"

The deputy waves Janie and us off to the side near the truck stop. The sheriff's car pulls up behind us, lights flashing.

"Oh, no," I groan. "Here comes trouble."

The sheriff gets out of his car and nods to Janie. No handcuffs in sight. So far so good. Janie's step-dad probably called 911 to report a kidnapping and assault with a deadly weapon. I'm prepared to take the blame. I won't let Mom spend her final years in prison. The sheriff and Janie talk a few minutes. Looks friendly enough. He's probably asking about her kids. Then he climbs up onto the running board. He shakes Janie's hand. After stepping down he walks around to the other side of the truck, steps up onto the running board, and talks to Janie's mother. Oh. Now he's heading in our direction.

"Hello, Sheriff," I say. "We in trouble?"

He smiles. "I'm going to let it go this time." He leans down and looks over at Mom, who sits smiling, looking like an innocent old lady. "Mrs. Spangler?"

"Sheriff?" Mom nods in greeting.

"You don't have any bullets in that gun, now, do you?"

"No, sir," she says.

"That's good," the sheriff says. "You've been a busy woman. You ever want a job on the force, you just let me know."

"I'll keep that in mind," Mom says, patting her gun. "Hate to sit still too long at this age. Somebody might throw dirt over me."

When the sheriff laughs out loud, I hardly recognize him. He's usually so serious. "Guess I'll be on my way," he says, still chuckling. "You two take care now."

After the sheriff kills his flashing lights and leaves the scene, Janie climbs down out of her truck and walks around to get her mother. Mom and I open our doors and meet Janie and Sue for hugs all around.

"Good to stand up again, after all that excitement," I say.

"For sure," Janie says. "But my legs are still shaking."

"I confess I got a fright when I saw the sheriff's car," I say.

"He did get a call from my step-dad," Janie says. "But the sheriff had been to the house before, when the neighbors called on him. No worries there."

"Echo," Sue says. Her voice is weak and her eyes are red. "Thanks for being so brave for Janie and me. And Mabel. You're my hero." She hugs us both.

"I just want you all to know," Mom says, "there weren't any bullets in my gun this time."

"Mrs. Spangler, you're too much." Janie grabs Mom's hand.

"We need to get out of Dodge," Janie says. "I'll be in touch. Echo, let me know what happens at work."

"I'll do that."

And then they leave. All at the same time, I feel relieved, happy, sad and left behind.

Mom says, "I need a beer."

# CHAPTER 34

At work the men no longer complain about being too tired to have sex. I guess Park and Bark took the psychologists' recommendations to heart, because Park stopped trying to prove that we're the little sawmill that could. At the safety meeting, when Leroy tells the employees that Justin is coming back to work, the room erupts into a low roar of happy grunts, howls, and whistles.

"I want to reassure each of you that no one will lose his easy job to him."

There really aren't any easy jobs at the mill or the planer, but some jobs are easier to do if you have only one good hand. One of the forklift drivers, Rich, not Bullfrog, says, "Well, hell. I'll trade with him. He can drive my forklift. He can have my job any time." One of the grader guys pipes up, "He can have my job, or we can take turns. He doesn't have to do only hard stuff. Let's give him a little break when he comes back."

Three months after Justin's accident, he'd hounded his doctor into signing a full release so he could come back to work. Justin showed me the note the doctor wrote for him to give to the mill. *Do not strain the hand. Do only what you can do comfortably.* With this release, Justin received his "finger money," close to $25,000. He drove to Spokane to kick a few tires on new trucks, but he didn't buy one.

Justin wears a specially sewn leather glove to fit his remodeled hand, with extra leather protecting the tender stubs of his fingers. At first he runs the automatic stacker. The job is easy. I've done it. All he has to do is place stickers between layers of lumber. The automatic stacker has its own bander, too, but it goes haywire. So Justin tries to work the banding with his bad hand while doing something else with his good hand. Of course, the banding slips and bumps hard into his sore hand. I see him double over, holding his hand down by his stomach. I cringe. Everyone who sees it happen hurts with him. You can see it on their faces.

Later I see him walk over to the feed table. Nose is working with a new guy, but lets Justin take his place feeding boards into the planer machine. And just like that, Justin is doing his old job. I sneak over to where he's working, stand as near as I dare, and holler, "Justin! George is going to wring your neck!"

"This is better," Justin yells, flipping boards, sending them on their way. "I know what I'm doing."

But George catches him and hollers, "Justin, get away from that feed table." So Justin has to leave the job he loves.

A job comes along that he can do. He'll plant saplings in the city park to replace the giant cottonwood trees that had to be cut down. As a community service and for good public relations, TSI offered to plant new trees. So George takes Justin over to the park and tells him, "One hand, one shovel, look busy. Talk nice to people who come by to ask what you're doing. Tamp the dirt down with your feet and move a branch or two once in a while with your good hand."

Justin shines at this little job, but it doesn't last long.

We're all surprised when Justin reclaims his old job next to Nose at the feed table. On Saturday afternoon he stopped by to see me and Mom. He tells us how he did it. "I walked into George's office and announced, 'I want my old job back.' George said, 'Your hand's not healed up enough. It's gonna take more time. You gotta realize that.' So with my bad hand I pounded as hard as I could on his desk and said, 'See. My hand doesn't hurt.' You should have seen George's mouth drop open. Then he said, 'How did you heal up so fast? When I lost my little finger, it took forever for it to quit hurting.'"

I ask, "You mean to say it didn't hurt you to pound on the desk?"

"Oh, God," Justin groans, closing his eyes. "It hurt so bad I almost passed out. Hurts just thinking about it."

Late in October, Park and Bark and Safety Dave take turns going to a leadership training course in Spokane. George gets a new assignment as the shipping clerk, which is an important job, mind you, but he doesn't supervise anyone. Sharlene is now his boss. Standing in for George is a special boss from headquarters. He travels around to TSI's different mills to work as a supervisor when there's been trouble. His name, no surprise, is Dave, and he's nothing at all like George or any other Dave working at TSI. These changes were proposed by the two psychologists who interviewed us. The employees joke about the leadership training for the bosses, and call it Charm School. Better late than never, as they say. Even the men seem grateful.

One result of Park's trip to Charm School is that he offers a bonus lunch if you break the record at your station. Thanks to that crop of new computers, management can keep track of production at each station. Even though the reward is puny, Justin about kills himself trying to break the record. During his third week back at the feed table, he and Nose break the old record, and then go on to break their new record. Production at the mill goes up again.

But Justin and Nose stop breaking the record when they discover they can only earn one bonus lunch a week. "Hell," Justin says to me one day. "We were breaking the record for nothing, and it wasn't doing my hand any good. Now that we know we can break the record whenever we want, we don't have to prove it anymore."

"Yeah," I say. "I overheard a couple guys down the line yell, 'Wish they'd slow it down a bit, I'm getting wore out trying to keep up.'"

On one of my sweeping and shoveling forays in the area of the feed table, Nose throws a knot at my hard hat. This time I break the rules and stand near him for a few minutes while he flips boards. I don't say a thing. Too much noise, anyway. I notice again how good it feels to be near him. He saw me following Janie in the parade. Justin probably filled him in on our little rescue adventure. While I stand next to Nose, he and Justin show off a little, each turning boards at lightning speed. Before I leave the planer room, I touch Nose's arm and give him a thumbs-up signal and my biggest smile. He nods and smiles back. Good eye contact. Yates would have taken a different approach to letting a man know she's open to taking things up a notch. But I'm more subtle, at least when it comes to romance.

Justin told me that on the day of the rescue and parade, a man standing next to him and Nose asked if I'd be interested in selling my classic car. Justin played hard to get for me. He told the guy I might have plans for the car, that I'm attached to its clean lines, that it's been a real good car, and added that I'd already refused other offers. Justin gave the guy my name and phone number, "Just in case you can talk her out of it."

And what do you know? The man calls a few days after the parade. Mom yells in the background of our phone conversation, "But I love that car. I don't *want* you to sell him." This doesn't hurt the negotiations. I tell the man, "I don't know. The car's like one of the family. I'll have to call you back."

Mom and I have a little talk. I tell her I'll ask twice the amount Justin says it's worth, and remind her how nice it will be for us to have reliable transportation. She sighs. I add that I'd put a gun rack in it for her rifle. Finally, she agrees. That's how I sell my car for an astronomical price. But, hey, it is my fiftieth birthday. It's what I deserve. When I ask Justin to drive to Spokane with me and his grandmother to buy a new Toyota pickup, he claims to be busy. He says Nose is available and would be an excellent escort. And when Nose calls me the next day—what a coincidence—I invite him and ask if he'll drive us there. At the agreed upon time, Nose arrives in his old yellow International pickup truck, and the three of us head to Spokane.

Mom sits between us. To my embarrassment, she begins to ask Nose one question after another, like a talk show host. "So," she says, "where you from, young man?"

Nose leans forward a little, glances my way and smiles. "Well, Mrs. Spangler, I grew up on a ranch in southwest Montana."

"Really? And how long you been in these parts?"

"About ten years."

"I know your nickname is Nose," she says, "but I'm not sure I want to call you that. What's your real name, son?"

"Conrad Pelligrini."

"Conrad?" I say. "No kidding."

"Yep. My father is Italian and my mother is Polish. You can call my Con, if you like, Mrs. Spangler, just not Connie."

"I'm thinking of changing my name, too. But for now you can call me Mabel, if you don't mind."

"All right, Mabel."

"So why'd you leave Montana, Con?"

"Oh, several reasons, but for one thing I always preferred my horses under the hood of a good truck." He pauses to pat the dash, which, unlike Rooster's dash, is clean. "My mother is the rancher in the family. She's a strong woman, besides being practical and fair, and she out-ranched all of us, even my dad. Frankly, I don't care for how the chores don't stop when the snow falls or the temperature drops below zero. Maybe I'd like ranching better in Hawaii."

I'm dying to ask if he's ever been married, but I'm too chicken.

Mom asks, "You got any kids?"

"I have two grown sons who help my folks on the ranch. They're both married to local girls and live nearby. My wife died about twelve years ago from cancer."

"Well, I'm sorry to hear that. Bad stuff happens to us. Tangled with cancer myself, and feel grateful to be alive sitting here today with you and one of my girls. How many women get to have identical twins?" Mom pats my hand.

Nose leans forward again to look at me. "You and your sister are twins?"

"You mean to say she didn't tell you?" Mom says. "Well, those two are as different as night and day, each one perfect in her own way."

I want to blurt, I didn't know you felt that way. I was sure you liked *her* best. But I just smile to myself.

"Can't wait to meet her," Nose says.

All I can think in response is, If Delight steals this guy from me, too, I'm gonna take her and Mom's 30-30 for a walk in the woods. I'll make good on that Old West saying, *Shoot, Shovel, and Shut up*!

At the Toyota dealership, Mom and I kick a few tires. "Ow!" we both say.

"Why kick tires if you're buying a brand new truck," Mom says. "They'll think we're from the sticks."

Nose smiles and gives us this advice, "Pay no more than $2,000 less than the asking price, even less if you can." And when he sees that we're ready to make a deal, he says goodbye. I hug him before he leaves. In turn, he hugs Mom.

It just so happens the dealership is having a White Sale, so Mom and I drive home in a shiny new silver and white Toyota pickup with an extra-cab. I buy a two-wheel drive truck, since the four-wheel drive units sit too high off the ground for Mom to get in and out of without help.

On our way out of Spokane, as we come to the North-town Mall, I pull into the parking lot that's nearly as big as the entire town of Hatfield.

"Why we stopping here?" Mom says.

"Gonna buy me some big-girl panties. Silky pastel ones with lots of lace," I say. "You want some? I'm buying."

"After this year, I'd say we earned 'em. Let's do it."

"And Mom, I'll still get you a gun rack for the new truck."

She shakes her head. "I don't want to clutter up this beauty with a piece of junk in the back window. But I do still miss Rooster."

"He'll be in the parade next year," I say. "Maybe we can ride along? You can ride shotgun."

"Maybe Con will ride with us," Mom says, studying me.

"Now, Mom," I say. "You've been reading too many romance novels. Let's go buy us some frilly underwear."

Occasionally, Nose takes a break with me up in the corner of the machine shop, at which times I practice calling him Con. He tells me he doesn't drink much because he saw what happened when his father got drunk. He also tells me that he dated a woman in Montana quite a while, and that her daughter is now married to one of his sons. "She was nice enough, but she drank too much for my taste."

Whoops. Guess I'll be slowing down on my alcohol intake.

I learn more about why he admires his mother, who keeps things together at the ranch. Which is probably why he's more evolved than lots of other men, when it comes to women.

He's easy to talk to, and I find myself blabbing on about how Delight stole my boyfriend and married him, about my two-week marriage, and how I formerly gambled and drank too much. I leave out a few details, like Mitch, but I expect I'll tell him everything, eventually. It would be dishonest not to.

Mostly I sit in the machine shop alone. On occasion I picture Yates sitting next to me, her foot flying up and down, exhaling a cloud of smoke. I believe she'd say something like, "It's kinda dead around here now, with everyone being so damn nice."

And I'd say, "Yeah, but I've stopped gobbling Rolaids."

On an afternoon when the yellow larch needles are falling on the hillsides and a few flakes of snow drift down on the log yard, Leroy walks from the mill over to the planer to find me. When I see him walking toward me, I don't cringe. He stops a couple feet away from me and yells over the roaring and clanging noise, "Janie will be here for a pickup around the time of first break. Thought you'd want to know."

After stopping what I'm doing a dozen times to check my watch, the buzzer finally sounds, *Ahooga, Ahooga,* and I hurry to find Janie's truck.

"Janie!" I yell. She's standing next to her semi-truck cab, hands on her hips, one foot perched on the high running board. Another woman comes around the truck toward me. "Sue!"

"Mother went to truck driving school, too," Janie says. "We drive as a team now."

"Congratulations," I say, hugging her, then Janie. Both Janie and her mother look beautiful and happy.

"I love it," Sue says. "Sure see a lot of country. Just last week we were stopped by a cattle drive over in Montana and saw cowboys in tight jeans herding cattle. We sometimes open our windows to smell the sage brush and pine trees. At night we hear coyotes."

"Wow," I say. "Almost makes me want to go to truck driving school."

"You'd probably like it," Janie says. "You go all over. This load's destined for a Home Depot in Michigan."

"It's so good to see you two," I say. "How're the kids?"

"The boys are doing well in school," Janie says, "and they have lots of friends in the neighborhood. Tiffany is working with a top-notch trainer. She's a former Little Miss America herself, who went on to be a Miss America Runner-Up a few years back."

"And June?"

"She's decided to stay in Portland as long as she's needed," Janie says. "She loves the kids. Oh, and Danny's still going to counseling. He hopes we can all be together again. I told him I'm filing for a divorce, but that he can live in Portland and see the kids."

Sue pipes in, "We're on the road so much that it's hard for an ex-husband to find either one of us. It's like a mobile witness relocation program."

*Ahooga, Ahooga.*

"I know what that means," Janie says. "But, Echo, I want to tell you a secret. And you can only tell your mom, okay?"

"What? You know I can do that?"

"Leroy's wife works with abused women. After she talked to Leroy about my mother, he sold his boat to pay for her to go to truck driving school."

I'm stunned. "Looks like I'll have to kiss that man on the cheek again."

And then they climb up into their truck, wave good-bye, and toot the air horn.


"Echo, how are you today?" New boss Dave says to me one December afternoon.

"Well, gee, I'm fine, thank you. Even my feet are warm, thanks to the new heaters."

"Good. I wonder if you might switch to day shift for a couple days at the mill, to help us get ready for a big inspection. Their cleanup person is off hunting, and we could really use your help."

"I'd be happy to," I say, feeling charmed. "When should I start?"

"Tomorrow, if you can do it on such short notice," he says. "You can leave early to get your rest. I'll have the second Fifth Person help you."

"I'll be here."

"Thanks, Echo."

The change will be good. I'll be able to see what's happening in that building, and visit with Carmel on breaks. Now that no one is trying to run over me or pinch my fingers or trip me up somehow, work's a lot less stressful. The men are even picking up their cull boards and dumping their spit bucket. All this politeness takes a little getting used to. Not that I'm complaining.

Shortly after I show up for day shift at the mill, one of my "other duties as assigned" is to take over on a line when someone has to go to the toilet. Standing in for the men at times like this gives me a feeling of power. I know from my last stint on day shift exactly when I'll need to stand in for the men. Everyone knows. Leroy relieves a guy named Sam on the tail saw at 6:45 a.m., but I take care of Mumbles at exactly 6:17 a.m., and then there's my good buddy, Spit Bucket Dave, on the trim chain. He goes at exactly 7:23 a.m. Cliff used to go right on the dot at 7:00 a.m., but now he's up at the log yard. I play hard to get. I pretend not to hear the men yelling for me to relieve them. They wave their arms and yell my name. When I finally look up, I wave back and then resume shoveling or sweeping. They yell some more to get my attention.

I holler back. "What do you want?"

They shout, "I have to go to the toilet." Or just plain, "Echo, get your butt over here." They have to yell. The mill's a noisy place.

Spit Bucket Dave on the trim chain has been real polite to me since I smacked him alongside the head. But now he pretend-growls, "You know what I want. Don't make me tell the whole world I have to take a shit!"

"Oh, okay," I say, putting down my broom and strolling over to take his place. One morning I say to him, "You can go to the powder room when I *say* you can go."

"Echo!"

"Just kidding around."

Late morning on the third day, three men wearing silver hard hats, representing The Big Boys, walk around in the building with Leroy. They take lots of notes, and as usual, Leroy kisses up to them.

On one of the last days of 1999, while the rest of the world worries about Y2K and anticipates the end of civilization, I await the results of the big inspection. When the report shows up on the bulletin board by the break room, I flip through the pages. A list of additional safety features are scheduled to be added, including a harness to be worn when cedar bark is untangled from the ramp above the debarker. Later in the report I find exactly what I'm looking for and I have to smile. The inspectors have written, *Housekeeping is excellent, as always.*

## THE END

# ABOUT THE AUTHOR

Rae Ellen Lee grew up on a stump ranch in northern Idaho. She worked for the U.S. State Dept. in Washington, D.C., Switzerland, and (then) Yugoslavia before attending the Univ. of Idaho, where she earned a degree in Landscape Architecture. Employment with the U.S. Forest Service in Idaho and Montana followed, until 1997, when she resigned and moved to the sailboat, *The Shoe,* with her new husband, Tom. She wrote about that experience, in *I Only Cuss When I'm Sailing* (first published as *If* The Shoe *Fits).*

A second memoir, *My Next Husband Will Be Normal – A St. John Adventure,* reveals the risks and funny side of life in paradise after Rae Ellen and Tom move to the U. S. Virgin Islands and Tom realizes *he* is really a *she.*

In addition to the two memoirs and two novels, she has also published *Powder Monkey Tales – A Portrait in Stories,* by Wesley Moore alias Posthole Augerson, a geezer of some renown in northern Idaho. A farm boy from Illinois who headed west in 1941, Wes became a woods worker and powder monkey, who used dynamite to help build roads for the logging industry in the 1940s and 1950s. This booklet captures the history and humor of her father, in his own words. Watch for her illustrated humor book, *A Field Guide to Geezers,* forthcoming in spring 2013.

Rae Ellen now lives, writes, hikes and sketches in the Western U.S. Feel free to email: rae@raeellenlee.com. For additional information and updates, visit her website **www.raeellenlee.com**.

Following is an EXCERPT from my previous novel, set in an old mining camp brothel in Montana that I once lived in and renovated.

*THE BLUEBIRD HOUSE*
*A Madam. A Diary. A Murder.*

## CHAPTER 1

Two weeks after my accident, I am released. Even with good insurance, the hospital has its limits. A steady stream of patients had arrived with various illnesses, not one of them as bizarre as my reason for being hospitalized.

Alone now in our cavernous house with my pets, I move slowly, and only when I must. My body's bruised condition and the stiffness in my joints regulate my movements. I rest. I read. I watch *Days of Our Lives*. At other times I stare out the picture window in the living room over the Prickly Pear Valley. I sit silently, watching the afternoon light change on the Big Belt Mountains. When the moon rises you cannot see it move unless you look away and then look back again. That's the way the light changes on the mountains, except, when the cloud shadows gallop soundlessly across the rock on their ghost legs. When the cloud shadows race along the face of the steep mountains I always think of immense dark leaves let loose, fleeing ahead of a storm—until they reach an unseen line of fences and the outer limits of their freedom.

I study the horizon to the north, with its odd, shallow dip like an antique wash basin. The Missouri River once passed through that basin, until the mountains lifted and the river took an elbow turn to the east toward the Great Plains. When the uplift occurred, I suppose that, too, was nearly imperceptible.

I've read there are no accidents in life, that things happen for a reason. My accident must mean something, and that is what I ponder while I rest and stare out the window. Maybe I'm being reminded that *I* have never been the dominant creature, not once, not in any situation. A heavy, oddly-centered anger sometimes seethes and roils in my chest underneath the faded purple hoof print, and it isn't anger at the animal. Instead I've been thinking about love, about how I don't really love Bradley, and how by staying with him all these years I haven't loved myself. Like some slow geologic event, I had barely noticed it happening.

I can recall no joy in our marriage that was unbearably good, the way I've heard other women, like Myra, talk about their relationships. Years ago I read *Total Woman*. Other women were reading it, too, but we never talked about what the book did or didn't do for us. I even wore *Wind Song* perfume for a while, but nothing I tried seemed to make me more of a woman, or Bradley more of a man, or our marriage any more like the song of the wind.

We've been married twenty-six years. I remember the night I met him at a dance at the University of Montana, where he was taking business management and I was studying biology. I loved to dance. He knew the steps and danced smoothly, confidently. But we only danced one other time after that—at our wedding reception. Mom and Dwight were pleased that I'd done so well at college, landing a man with a secure future in business. Boy, was I surprised that first year of marriage, and bewildered, too, at how little there actually *was* to being married. But then my two beautiful boys came along and kept me busy. When they went off to grade school I got a job as a biological technician at the state water quality lab and found that my college studies were good for something besides landing a husband.

When Bradley's in town and at home in the evenings, he reads war stories, works on the computer, talks on the phone or plays golf with his associates. I've heard his subtle reprimands about my cooking and housekeeping so often I no longer listen. He says, "Molly, if you'd get rid of the dog and cat the house wouldn't need to be cleaned so often." But the house is never what I'd call dirty, even though I no longer spend all my free time cleaning. I do love my pets. He's probably jealous. I find it curious how pets can take the place of one's significant other, especially when he proves to be other than significant.

Years ago I began to notice that after Bradley was home a few days from his business trips I'd develop flu-like symptoms. When he'd leave again I'd recover. In case my symptoms meant something besides an allergy to Bradley, I went to my doctor. After several tests he found nothing wrong with me physically. Then he asked if I'd ever considered counseling. Later that week I arranged free sessions with a counselor through the employee assistance program at work. It didn't take the counselor long to tell me, rather bluntly, "You're a caretaker and it's making you sick." She didn't say I should leave my husband, but I figured that's what she meant. The weird part was, I couldn't do it. Bradley needed me. He still needs me.

But how important will the words loyalty and faithfulness be when I'm in a rest home someday? I don't think they'll matter much. What I'll want when I'm old is a deep well of memories to drink from. Yet who am I without Bradley?

And then, without bidding, I relive the details of my afternoon in the woods, and once again I hear the sound of my bones snapping like twigs under the weight of the wild animal. He was the dominant creature, in control and forceful. I was his prey. After he charged, after time had stopped, I was left behind, abandoned to my silence and pain. My helplessness swims over me, pulling me under.

## CHAPTER 2

What can it hurt if I rob the food chain of a few stems and shoots? Pushing my way through willows and alders, I take care to step over the occasional mound of frozen moose droppings. Chickadees flit from branch to branch, chittering like Gregorian crickets, as my boots chuff along the frosty ground. *Chick-a-dee-dee-dee.* Occasionally I hear a bird's faraway clear whistle—*fee-bee.* It's a perfect Montana spring day—just right for hunting and gathering—and I'm determined to take a little wilderness home with me to our modern, oversized house in Helena, the house that Bradley built.

A clump of red-osier dogwood bushes stops me. A

long wine-colored branch, straight and round as a fishing pole, will give me two or three pieces for the face of my window shutters. The frames are built. Now is the best time to gather the stems, before the bushes sprout leaves. At midday, the air is chilly in the shade of the firs and pines where the dogwood branches grow long and straight. The pruning shears snap cleanly through a stem, and I add it to the growing bundle on the ground near my feet, pleased that soon I'll be able to replace one boring set of beige, pleated drapes with a bit of color from the wild. Cascading all around me is the chatter of birds, like the sound of a stream filled with miniature waterfalls. At home, when I look at my finished shutters, I'll think of today and of chickadees.

I wipe my wet, cold nose on a sleeve then reach up for a perfect branch. Suddenly the woods fall silent. A slight breeze stirs the tips of fir branches, otherwise no bird sounds, no movement. Nothing. Curious about this strange hush, I turn my head.

At first only a puff of breath, behind me and off to my right. Then a small cloud, like steam from a radiator and a loud snort, an announcement. I hold my breath, my heartbeat. When I turn my head further, I see a looming dark form, too close and slightly out of focus. Where did he come from? Another grunt, this one louder, angrier. A hoof strikes frozen snow. I must keep calm. I've seen bigger. I will put something between myself and the beast. The bush in front of me doesn't offer much of a barrier, but moose don't see well. If I move slowly, he might not notice me. I step sideways with the right foot, and gradually bring the left foot along. I do this again, and then sink down, moving under the branches, around to the other side. Maybe the moose will get confused and think he's seeing things. I take another slow step. I'm almost there. The bush is now between me and the moose.

I don't know if I hear a pause before the moose lunges, or how I know he's coming at me through the bushes. Dropping to my knees with a lurch, my glasses fly off my face and catch in a low, red stem—a stem just right for twig shutters. Now crouching to shelter my internal organs, I clasp my hands over the back of my neck to protect my spinal cord. Or is this what you're supposed to do when you meet a grizzly? Oh, God. Please help me.

It happens so quickly, so inevitably—the furious snorting, the pawing, the crashing of brush over my head and the one step, heavy as a logging truck, onto my back, crushing me into the ground. I hear bones break with a dull, muffled snap, and my ears are filled with the thundering vibration of hooves pounding frozen ground. In the seconds before I pass out, I smell the musty, acrid exhaust of the large, unwashed animal.

When I come to, the pain in my back bites like the jagged, rusty teeth of an old crosscut saw. I must cough, but when I do the pain surges. The ground spins me around. Bushes blur. I wipe my mouth and see blood on a sleeve, a sleeve on an arm that I am barely able to move.

My car is somewhere out near the gravel road. But which way is it to the road? I pass out again. The cold wakes me up. The road. I must reach the road. I can hear Bradley, if I live to hear him again, saying, "What in the world were you doing out in the woods alone?"

As I drag myself onto all fours, a few broken branches fall away from me while others cling to my clothing like claws, or fish hooks. The relentless pain in my back and chest sears like hot coals, and I am dizzy again. Not far away, the creek trickles past between ice-bound banks. If I listen carefully maybe I can hear the direction the creek is moving. The loudest trickles should come from downstream, not upstream, and the creek flows downstream toward the road. But the slope of the ground appears level, except for patches of snow, broken branches, and the mounds of frozen moose shit I now see everywhere.

Groaning, I drag my pain, as if it is contained in a basket, forward on arms so weak they feel as if they belong to a stranger in a dream. Pieces of branches, now like broken wings, dangle from my jacket. Other branches hide the creek from me, but I believe I'm crawling toward the road. Every time I move the pain strikes, hot and forked as a lightning bolt. My legs trail along behind me. Moving ahead is too painful. Oh God, please don't let me die out here. Cold and numb, I inch my way forward, my hands freezing.

Wait . . . a sound . . . a car on the road. Without my glasses, I reach toward the invisible noise, toward a blur of brush. Moving forward again, slow as a glacier, I realize it will take hours, days, for me to reach the road. I will die from my wounds. I'll freeze to death tonight a short distance from help. Using my elbows I crawl toward a slant of afternoon sunlight in a clearing. Finally, finally, I flop a leaden arm over a bank of snow. But is it the edge of the road?

"Wake up, wake up," a man yells. "Jesus, what happened to you?"

I open my eyes to a gray wool hat and a face so near

that I can see individual wiry hairs in his brushy, walrus mustache. I close my eyes and groan. My teeth rattle against each other. "Moose . . . help."

"Hold on. I never found a half-dead person before. Gotta get you into the truck."

With more gratitude than I have ever known, I give in again and let the darkness reclaim me.

Curled in the fetal position on the seat of an old pickup truck, I am wrapped in a dirty blue blanket smelling of stale beer. The pain, like knives, stabs at me, over and over and over. My head rests against the man's thigh that smells of oil and sawdust. My feet bump against the door handle. During the few moments I am conscious, the truck rattles and shakes and hammers the bumpy, icy road. I doze and, moaning, wake up to the engine roaring in my ears. Soon, white snowy silence. Then I hear a growling rumble as the man shifts down, and the jarring clatter of loose tools and beer cans on the floor. *Am I worse off now than when I lay in the woods?* But I don't care. All I want is to stay alive, to sit on a mountaintop one more time with the sun on my face, to hear birds singing. Drifting off again, I dream that Bradley cannot find me, that this strange mountain man takes me to a deserted old building in a long-ago place in another century, and hides me there.

Please see www.tinyurl.com/7yansvo for the Kindle edition and Amazon.com for the trade paperback. Thanks for your interest.

Printed in the USA
CPSIA information can be obtained
at www.ICGtesting.com
LVHW050119301123
765222LV00003B/42